RESURRECTION

Agustin Rios

Dedicated to the Brave and Valiant People of the Republic of Panama

"... Yo he puesto la mano osada,
de horror y jubilo yerta,
sobre la estrella apagada
que cayo frente a mi puerta.

Oculto en mi pecho bravo
la pena que me lo hiere:
el hijo de un pueblo esclavo
vive por el, calle y muere.

Todo es hermoso y constante,
todo es musica y razon,
y todo, como el diamante,
antes que luz es carbon ..."

Jose Marti

"... And I have placed my daring hand,
stiff from horror and from joy,
on the burned out star
that fell at my doorstep.

Hidden in my angry chest,
a sorrow that goes on hurting,
the son of an enslaved people
lives for his people, grows quiet,
and dies.

All is beautiful and eternal,
all is music and reason,
and all, like the diamond,
before light ... must be coal."

Library of Congress Catalog Card Number: 88–80848

ISBN 0–8403–4734–0

Printed in the United States of America
10 9 8 7 6 5 4 3 2 1

RESURRECTION

Agustin Rios

In late April, 1987, the High Command of brutal Central American military dictatorship met for a spiritual seance at the private residence of Number One. Shortly after midnight in the heavily guarded mansion, an important, high ranking officer invoked the name of a prominent Catholic priest from the country's colonial past. Fearful of growing political unrest and severe economic hard times, the officer asked for guidance in this most troubled moment of the military's questionable tenure. He begged for the long dead clergyman to give them some sign or omen with a prediction of events to come. In the darkness, the assembled men and accompanying women waited for the sign to appear. They were not disappointed.

A clear voice spoke from somewhere near them, but from nowhere they could pinpoint exactly. With a profound Castilian accent they had not heard before, and using occasional words almost forgotten in their modern dialect, the voice addressed them each by their Christian name, then gave them their message.

Sometime soon, the voice said, they could expect a promising solution to the nation's problems. Word would arrive from the western provinces of the possibility of great personal gain, and an unusual turn of events would result from a daring plan. But best of all, the voice explained, each and every one of the assembled company could expect their just reward, some more deservingly so than others. Divine intervention was not entirely out of the question.

With that the voice chuckled and the room went cold. The officers and their ladies looked around and listened for some further explanation.

One was forthcoming. . . .

PANAMA

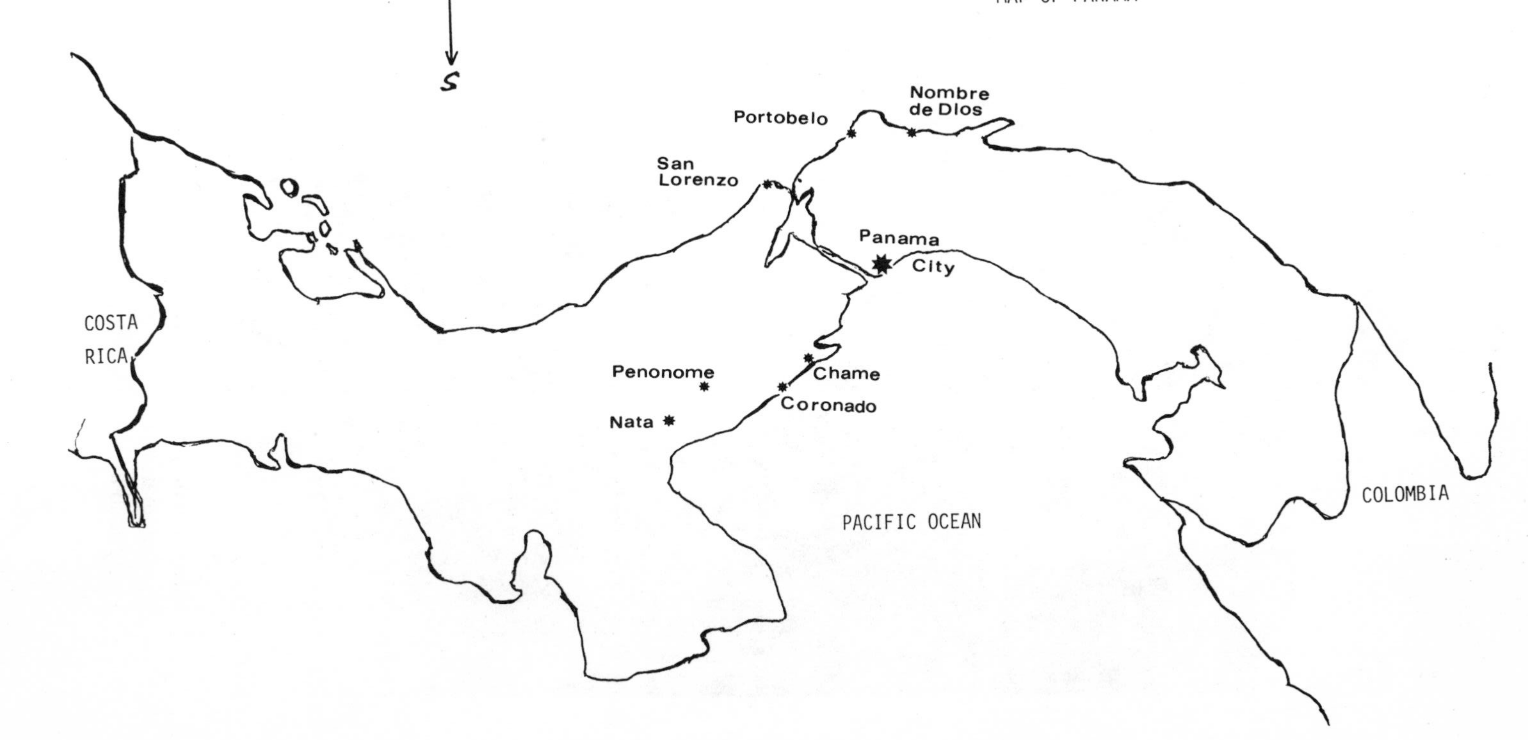
N
S
W
E
ATLANTIC OCEAN
MAP OF PANAMA
Nombre de Dios
Portobelo
San Lorenzo
Panama City
Penonome
Chame
Coronado
Nata
COSTA RICA
PACIFIC OCEAN
COLOMBIA

RESURRECTION

Dramatis Personae

Eva Icaza: Unemployed social worker, 23 years old, of an old, wealthy Panamanian family recently fallen on ruinous hard times.

Roberto: Eva's love, a 24 year old unemployed engineer turned radical socialist. Also of an old, wealthy Panamanian family; now disowned by the same.

Bob Friedan: Middle aged American State Department official assigned to Panama, a career diplomat and a widower.

Phil Travis: Bob's protege, a young man starting out in the State Department.

The Military

—The Quevedo Faction

Colonel Anastasio Quevedo: Long time second ranking officer in the national military, now in disfavor among the members of the high command.

Major Villalobos: Colonel Quevedo's assistant.

Lieutenant Roma: In charge of Colonel Quevedo's field batallion, a loyal Quevedo follower.

—The Arias Faction

Captain Gustavo Arias: Rebellious young officer technically under Quevedo's command. Heavily involved in Panamanian G-2 Intelligence operations. An exceedingly ambitious, ruthless, and greedy man.

Lieutenant Cruz: Captain Arias' field commander. An uneducated, vicious Arias' devotee.

Mr. Santos: A civilian G-2 intelligence officer assigned to the Arias batallion. A notorious criminal.

—The High Command

General Caron de Piña: Number one in charge of the Panamanian armed forces.

Mr. Matos: The "Tropical Man", General de Piña's right-hand man and chief of G-2 Intelligence operations.

Captain Angel Mendez: West Point graduate, technically the Chief Administrative Officer of the Panamanian Military under the direct command of Colonel Quevedo. Of an old and wealthy Panamanian family, a childhood friend of Eva Icaza and Roberto. Special assignment officer for General de Piña.

Lucia Prados: Military campfollower and socialite.

An American Congressman: A leading House Democrat encharged with foreign affairs on a fact-finding mission to Panama.

The Clergy: The Caravacan brotherhood, 1125–1987 A.D.

Father Rodriguez and Friar Gomez, Caravaca de la Cruz, 1543

Father Silvera, Nombre de Dios (1498–1582)

Bishop Fernando Patria Leal (Sandoval), Panama, 17th century

Father Sandoval, Nata de los Caballeros

Father Miguel, Nata de los Caballeros

Corsairs and Associates, Colonial Administrators

Sir Francis Drake (1545–1596), loyal subject of Elizabeth I

Sir Henry Morgan (1635–1688), wealthy Jamaican landowner

Armando Benitez (1646–1710), Panamanian Patriot turned corsair

Don Francisco Luna (1613–1694), official in the service of the Spanish Royal Crown (Philip the Fourth and Charles the Second), former Corregidor of the Panamanian port Portobelo, former Oidor, Governor, magristrate, etc.

Don Juan Perez de Guzman (c. 1625–1689), President of the Audiencia de Panama.

Don Francisco de Haro (c. 1619–1671), 'Alferez Real' (military commander) of the Audiencia de Panama

Aurora Alvarado de Drake (1649–1710), betrothed to Armando Benitez, great granddaughter of Francis Drake.

Mr. Vazquez, died, 1987, former notary Public of the city of Penonome, Panama.

The good and valiant people of the Republic of Panama

RESURRECTION

"I can't quite remember you . . . like I'd like to. It's been so long. You know it's been eleven years . . . to the day. Eleven. Eleven years. I was thirty nine. Pretty young."

Across the hillside the winds blew out over the tropical grasses and shrubs. They blew against a backdrop of gray, heavy clouded sky and rolling mists. Now and again fat drops of rain raced by to herald the coming of a late afternoon storm. A man sat quietly beside a simple but well-attended grave at the crest of a mountain slope. He looked out on the wild, densely forested valley before him and placed a hand on the tombstone. In the passing of a cooling gust he closed his eyes and smiled.

"Same me," he whispered.

Away in the distance a squall line was already sweeping over the valley. Dark, hanging clouds with even darker tails floated through the low wooded areas on their way to where the man was resting. With his fingers he made out the inscription on the tombstone and opened his eyes again to watch the approaching storm.

"I guess it isn't really news, but it makes me proud to tell you that your son is a big-shot lawyer back in Washington. Corporate, that's all he'll even touch. Sets his own hours, deals with who he feels like. Kid's got it made. You always said he'd be some thing to see. Well now he is. God I'm proud of him. And your girl, you wouldn't believe it. She's some kind of assistant editor at the Times." The man looked down at the earth and changed his expression slightly. Some thought had tugged at his mind momentarily. He shook his head slowly and gazed out again at the valley.

"She's . . . a winner too. That's probably a surprise. But we've been through that before."

For a brief instant the rain began to fall in earnest, then stopped. The clouds were boiling over adjacent hillsides and the man caught a glimpse of something he especially liked. From where he sat he could actually make out the fury of rain and winds whirling through lush green woodlands below. He was on top of the storm.

"Guess we're running out of time."

Behind him his car sat on a small lane that dead-ended only a few more yards up the line. One door of the white, old foreign make stood partially open. Some odds and ends were strewn around on the roof and hood. It gave the impression of being the car of a man in a hurry, or a man not particularly interested in a neat, clean car. There were signs of abundant rust on the vehicle and it looked as if it had gone through the usual wars of a lifetime on the crowded, fast streets of the tropical capital city. Still high above the tempest at the peak of Cerro Azul, it stood waiting for the escape that would by necessity occur shortly, when for an instant it became the focal point of a stray and fleeting ray of sunshine. The car's owner looked at it, saw the sunlight fade, and frowned.

"I have this bad feeling, darling," he said, eyes on the car, "that I'm at the end of the world, you wouldn't believe the damn things that are going on. How in the hell did it come to this." He rubbed his forehead with the palm of his hand and leaned against the tombstone. In a minute he looked back at the storm below and caressed his wife's name. "I'm in pretty deep. You know I drink a lot now, and I take a lot of pills, and I've got a hundred bad things going out there, every one of them's getting ready to collapse down on my head. There's nowhere to go. This looks like it. Doesn't seem to be working out . . . yeah, I know, you told me not to get into it, I remember. You knew these people real well . . . I was still learning. . . ."

He smiled and watched as a small animal scurried for cover in the brush a ways below him. His eyes wandered off to a rough shelter-like structure not too far away. It was constructed of wooden poles and a gray canvas canopy. More drops of rain were falling and he felt two or three splash off his neck.

"I was pretty sharp in uniform, wasn't I?"

Reaching into his breast pocket, he produced an old photograph and examined it closely. The winds were coming up briskly and his stretch of land would see the storm momentarily.

"Time to go now," he said, returning the picture to his pocket. "I'll be back soon, I think I still have some time left. A lot depends on things I can't control too well anymore, you understand. Hell, I. . . ."

The man stopped talking suddenly. His last words were forced and broken. Gazing out for a last look at the valley and its treasures of wind and green, he set his jaw firmly and rose to one knee.

"I've got you to come back to and that's all there is, but that's fine, that's all I need. You sit tight. I love you. Always will." With that the man rose quickly and walked back up to his car. The deluge arrived just as he was swinging in through the driver's door. It wasn't until he had the door shut that he saw the flowers on the seat. He cursed softly, eyed the downpour streaming off his windshield, and picked them up. After a moment of gathered determination he wrenched down the door handle and leaped out of the car. The man sprinted off through the rain at a fiftyish pace bounding stray rocks and clumps of grass until he was back before the tombstone. Now soaked from stem to stern, he bent down in a slow and stately way to lay the flowers on the grave. Straightening up, he stood there for a long moment, then walked away back up to the car.

Elena Mia, 18 de Mayo, 1976
Descansa en Paz
Querida

Caravaca de la Cruz
Imperial Spain
August 29, 1543

1

"This . . . is a mistake. It was a mistake from the beginning, it will go on being a mistake for God knows how long. Eons, I suspect."

The old priest looked up at a high chapel window from his chair and watched the morning sunlight filter in. In his hands he held a large object wrapped in rough, white cloth. It rested on a wooden table before him. A young, bearded man sat across the table looking on.

"Such a terrible mistake," the old priest sighed, now turning his eyes to the cloth wrapped object.

The young man stroked his beard.

Faint sounds of sheep and sheep bells made their way to the dark inner chamber from somewhere outside, somewhere fairly close. The chapel stone seemed to make the sounds linger and fade on into each other in the quiet of the room. But neither man was listening. The priest appeared to be lost in thought, the bearded man apprehensive. With difficulty, the priest moved the object toward the younger man by pushing its base across the table. When he reached the midpoint he stopped and grimaced. Whatever it was, it was heavy. The old man sighed again. Then he spoke.

"Sadly, I must tell you about this . . . thing. Soon you will be its guardian. I have not slept for almost two nights now, and I am tired. So I will be brief. Listen well."

He paused, examined the object for the last time, and resumed his speech.

"As you leave for the New World, you will have in your possession a holy relic for the brotherhood in the Audiencia of Panama. You and you alone will know of this relic from this moment until it is delivered. You must hide it well and guard it with your life. You have been chosen to deliver it because of the great trust you have earned among the brothers of our order. Remember that when you board your ship in Cadiz, you will be on your own . . . with no one to help you. And you will be surrounded by scoundrels of the worst type. Tell me if you wish to back out. You may do so, at this very moment, if you so desire."

The young man looked at the priest intently, then slowly shook his head.

"No, my Grace," he replied softly, "I do not wish to back out."

The old man closed his eyes and nodded.

"So be it," he said.

For a moment the chapel grew even dimmer as a cloud passed overhead, blocking the sunlight from the windows above. The young man shifted position slightly in his chair and continued to stare at the priest and the object. Presently the priest began to remove the cloth cover to reveal what was underneath. The weight of what he held prevented him from unwrapping it quickly.

"This is the product of a vow," he said, tugging at a tightly bound cord, "a solemn promise made at the request of a dying man. We were obliged to honor our indiscretion."

With the cord now sufficiently loose, the priest pulled off the cloth and let it fall on the table. When the uncovered object came into full view, the young man's eyes grew wide. There, before him, stood a solid gold Caravacan Cross nearly two feet tall. Studded with emeralds and reflecting the soft light of the chapel, it was easily the most beautiful creation he had ever seen. The priest was now struggling to hold it up.

"Allow me," the young man said, rising out of his chair to steady the cross with an outstretched hand.

There was an instant of indecision as the old priest relinquished his grasp during which the cross almost fell, but the young man seized it firmly and held it up. The old priest, seeing that it was now secure, sat back into his chair and rested. He breathed deeply and looked up into the young man's eyes.

"Now it is yours to protect and deliver." he said. "Incan gold sent here by Diego de Almagro from the Indian kingdoms of Peru, brought to us by a Caravacan brother, his confessor. Diego received his blessing here before sailing off to the conquest. He swore he would carry the faith of Caravaca to the New World as gratitude for the favors bestowed upon him by the Virgin. It was his wish that the gold he won from the Incas be fashioned by the brotherhood into a cross to adorn an altar of the Spanish Americas. Brother Juan Alonso gave his word to Almagro that his wish would be granted . . . shortly before Almagro died. And we are men of honor. You have the cross we made for him from his gold. As you can see, it is exquisitely well done."

The young man gazed at the splendid work and studied its form. A true Caravacan Cross, a crucifix with the Christ figure suspended over two horizontal bars. The emeralds were embedded in the vertical staff and at the ends of the horizontal bars. There was an indescribable sadness in the countenance of the Christ.

"Did Almagro say which church would receive this crucifix?" the young man asked.

"He did not," the old priest answered sharply, "but we have taken the liberty of deciding for him. The cross shall go to Nombre de Dios in the

Audiencia de Panama, Viceroyalty of Peru. We do not wish it to grace the altars of an island church, and we do not wish upon you the hardship of an overland trip to the City of Mexico in New Spain. You will go directly to the port of Nombre de Dios where you will turn it over to Brother Andres Silvera. Then your mission will be over. You will return to us on the next available ship. I understand that Nombre de Dios is a terrible place to live. It is hot beyond all belief."

The young, bearded man ran his fingers across the surface of the crucifix and eased the weight of the heavy thing off onto a forearm.

"You said . . .," he began before pausing.

The old priest looked away, then back at the man before him.

"Yes?"

"You said," the young man continued, "that I would be in possession of a relic, and that I alone would know of it. What is the relic, and is it true that no one else knows. . .?"

The old priest closed his eyes and covered them with his hand.

"The gold of the Christ is mixed with gold from a fragment of St. Isidore's ring. It is meant to purify the crucifix from the sins of Almagro's greed. The cross must be destined to atone for our crimes against the people of the New World. It is our hope that through this relic we will convert the Indians to our Holy Catholic faith. Do you understand?"

The young man stood silent and nodded. The old priest cleared his throat and brought his instructions to an end. He opened his eyes and looked up at the young man.

"The brotherhood knows, of course. But all are sworn to secrecy. If they are asked, they will deny all knowledge of this . . . thing. This is to protect you and the crucifix during your voyage and later, when men would do anything to you or anyone else to get their hands on it. Wrap it carefully before you leave, and there is one more thing. Take this, too."

From a drawer in the table he produced a large scroll wrapped in red velvet and tied with a black cord. He laid it on the table beside the cross.

"These are instructions for Brother Silvera in Nombre de Dios. You may not read them, as they do not affect you. See to it that they, too, are guarded with the utmost discretion. Now prepare this thing and go."

The young man leaned forward and supported the golden cross with his shoulder while he picked up the white cloth it had been wrapped in. With great care and attention he wrapped it, bound it, and lifted it over to a table by the entrance of the chapel. There he knelt before the chapel crucifix and prayed. The old priest watched him until he had finished, then rose slowly, crossed himself, and made the sign of the cross in the direction of the young man, now returning for the scroll. When he arrived at the table, the young man looked at the priest and then at the scroll.

"I will go to the sacristy tomorrow at dawn for my blessing. I will leave immediately after that for Cadiz. I will go alone."

He looked up at the priest one final time.

"This thing you have given me to do, I do gladly. But I, like you, have deep concerns. I have had dreams, and I have prayed for answers. God has not spoken to me about them. God willing, St. Isidore of Seville goes with me. God forbid that I carry the blood of the Inca."

With that he picked up the scroll, crossed himself, and began a slow walk over toward the wrapped cross by the entrance. The old priest watched him hoist it to his shoulder and struggle out the door.

Panama City, Panama
May 26, 1987

2

"That same guy is back, Sir, he insists on seeing the General. He refuses to leave."

"Then throw him out the door! See to it that he breaks an arm or a leg! Stop bothering me with this nonsense, this is not a home for disturbed boys! Enough!"

The Colonel was furious. He had wheeled around in his chair to confront the Sergeant who had brought him the news and he continued staring in the man's direction even after the Sergeant had beat a hasty, saluting retreat.

"Imbecile!" he muttered as an aide closed the door.

Outside in the great room foyer there were shouts of protest and sounds of a scuffle. Soon they died down and equilibrium was restored. The Colonel turned back in his chair to face the others sitting in his office. He wet his lips and calmly reached out to pick up a glass of water. The room was quiet save for the constant whirring of a large air conditioner.

"You were saying, Captain," the Colonel said after taking a drink of water.

"I was saying that it's getting harder and harder for me to make my contacts. It's bad enough that the bastards can't be trusted in the first place, but now you add to that a feeling that seems to grow stronger every day . . . that our protection isn't what it used to be, that we aren't willing to take any risks. They think we're fat cats sitting on big bucks . . . and who knows . . . maybe some of us are."

The Colonel, a melancholy man with troubled, faded eyes, sat studying the Captain with an impassive expression.

"Just who might you be referring to," he asked quietly.

"No one in particular," the Captain replied, looking away. Like the Colonel, he had an ample midsection. Though easily ten years younger than his superior, he shared the same frog-like look that seemed to come with rank and better tailored uniforms, two stick legs and a puffy body rising straight up out of the waist. A major by the window cleared his throat and spoke.

"I for one am not rich, Captain, I hope you were not referring to me."

The Captain smiled.

"Then you must tell me your definition of poor, Sir, so that I may emulate your failure."

"Why have you come here today, Captain," the Colonel interrupted, sitting forward in his chair. "If you have something to tell us, by all means, come to the point."

The Captain looked at two lesser officers seated beside him, then back at the Colonel.

"We have come here to ask for your permission to begin operations on our own, my Colonel. We are also here to ask that you allow us to use muscle where muscle is needed. We need to make believers of our . . . associates. It is a small request."

"Permission denied," the Colonel snapped, regaining his hostile edge. "You'll do as you are told, when you are told to do it. There is ample reward in this for everyone."

"There will be nothing for anyone!" the Captain shouted suddenly, leaning out toward the Colonel. "They are already sidestepping us, they have already found mules and established routes that leave us completely out of their operations! They cannot depend on us anymore! The General has grown satisfied and complacent! He spends his days playing with. . . ."

"Silence!!" the Colonel screamed, standing straight up, hands and face quivering. "You will show a measure of respect for this organization, there will be discipline!! Another accusation of that type and I will have you behind bars, is that clear?!?"

The Captain stared at the Colonel for a moment, eyes still full of anger. Then he eased back into his chair and slowly nodded his head.

"Yes," he said after a long pause, "yes that is clear, quite clear, my Colonel."

The Colonel pulled a handkerchief out of his pants pocket and wiped it across his mouth. He was still trembling.

"You may leave now," he said, "and I will forget you came here. But I swear to you, if you ever bring this up again, I will take whatever steps are necessary to bring this talk of mutiny to an end. Now go."

A smile had returned to the Captain's lips, and before he got up he looked at his junior officers. Giving them an amused wink, he looked over at the Major by the window.

"Yes, I will resume my vows of poverty," he chuckled, now slowly getting up from his chair. The junior officers rose with him. "But Colonel," he said, straightening his tie, "life is change . . . you of all people should know that."

"Get out!" the Colonel said abruptly.

"Good afternoon," the Captain replied.

Quietly, the Captain's party filed out the door and donned their caps as they left. The Colonel took another drink of water and sat down at his desk. The Major stood up at the window and walked over to where the Captain had been sitting. As the Colonel picked up the telephone, the Major sat down.

"This is Colonel Quevedo, get me the General right away. . . .

". . . Hello, my General? Yes, this is Colonel Quevedo. Yes, my General. Listen, Captain Arias was just here with his friends. This is getting serious. We must have a meeting, the sooner the better . . . what? no, I . . . who? . . . but General Piña, they are . . . yes, yes, of course, but I don't . . . yes . . . yes . . . yes . . . of course, General, but you . . . I. . . . Yes, Sir. Right away, Sir, but I'm warning you. . . . Yes, Sir, of course, right away, Sir. . . ."

He heard laughter from somewhere outside of his office, and somewhere in the building they were hammering on something. The Colonel buried his face in his hands and leaned back in his chair. He could smell the Major smoking a cigar and he imagined the smoke curling up and dissipating in the breeze of the air conditioner. He felt sticky and unclean.

"Major," he said softly.

"Yes Sir?"

"Major, go to Parque LeFevre to the retreat. Meet a courier there. Bring me the package. It is important."

"Yes, Sir."

"And Major. . . ."

"Sir?"

" . . . Instruct my adjutant to change my personal bodyguard again. Make sure the replacements are also boys from . . . the province . . . hometown boys. . . ."

"They will be changed before sunset, Sir."

"Thank you, Major. Bring back a bottle of brandy, too. The cheap kind . . . the stuff we used to drink. . . ."

3

At two o'clock the slow, clouded rollers of a dull Pacific reached their usual northern destination on the quiet midtown beaches of Panama City. On that particular afternoon they did little more than rise high in the shallows and die, sandy froth bowing to the oceans' end. Two middle-aged lovers sat holding hands on a bench under some palms not far from the stagnant surf, and an old man walked calmly along the waters' high point, bending down occasionally to examine what the tides had left. Just a few yards beyond cars sped by on a principal city artery where birds perched on the great Balboa's mighty head and shoulders, greening him with each hour of the passing legend. From a high rise a short distance away a young man focused his binoculars on a steamer on the horizon. It was hull down and heading away.

"The problem is," he mumbled, adjusting the focus, "the problem is that I can't understand how things like that can just go on. There's your normal ship doing normal ship's things, heading someplace normal ships go. Probably has a normal cargo. I'd bet on it."

He lowered the binoculars for a moment and stood still. Behind him a young woman looked past him out the window at the sea. The winds were gentle off the balcony at that high level and she felt pleasantly cool.

"It's a mystery," the young man added.

He raised his binoculars again but this time turned them on the streets below. Slowly he scanned every section of the main avenue running parallel to the beaches. The young woman sat down on the bed and stared off into the afternoon.

"You're not a sailor." she said.

For an instant the wind rose and blew through the curtains into the room, causing papers on a nearby desk to scatter. The young woman was about to get up to retrieve them when her friend suddenly raised a hand.

"Here comes one," he said in hushed tones.

The young woman quickly seized a pad and pencil from on top of the bed and made ready to write. The young man grew tense and concentrated on two vehicles speeding up the avenue.

"It's Quevedo," he said, "in the first car . . . mark the time."

"Two twenty one," the woman noted.

"No . . . wait!" the young man exclaimed, "that may not be Quevedo after all. It's Quevedo's staff car, but the escort behind it belongs to Major Villalobos. That means the hoods inside it are also Villalobos'. That means Villalobos is riding in Quevedo's car."

"Very good, Roberto," the woman smiled, "you're getting good at this."

"Put a question mark by the entry and jot down my comments," he continued, the excitement fading from his voice.

"Yes . . . Comandante," she replied, scribbling down the remarks in shorthand.

When she had finished she raised her head to watch him as he followed the vehicles with his binoculars to where they disappeared behind a corner of the building. She saw him snap the binoculars back up the long stretch of avenue to see if anything else was coming, then drop them on a chair beside him.

"Another piece for my puzzle," he said, turning his eyes back to the horizon. A wisp of smoke remained where the ship had been and dull calm was setting in for as far as the eye could see.

For some time the young man alternated sitting in the chair and standing up. He would raise the binoculars quickly as traffic approached, then lower them to his side with each passing false alarm. The woman behind him waited patiently as he watched, now and then doodling on the pad. She wanted to sleep but kept her eyes open. Amidst the rising sounds of traffic below, and the now and again voices of the family above, she heard the sometimes soothing strains of the kitchen radio, volume set on low.

"Roberto," she asked, "just what do you hope to accomplish?" The question brought the binoculars back up to his eyes, but Roberto didn't answer. The woman leaned her head back for a moment and looked up at the clock. When enough time had passed, she went on.

"I saw Ramiro Ruiz this morning at the Super. He asked about you. He thought you had left the country to study. He has a beard now and looks interesting. He made me laugh."

She smelled gas from a cooking range in the vicinity and instinctively looked over at the kitchen.

"He said something about a party next week. I said we'd see if we could make it."

A child began to wail somewhere upstairs. Its cry brought sharp reproach from an attending mother. There was an eggshell poised on an impossible angle at the top of an overflowing heap of trash in the kitchen wastebasket. It could only have maintained that precarious position, she knew, if dried egg had stuck to the paper sack in the plastic bucket. That had been a breakfast egg, maybe from the day before. She closed her eyes and tried remembering the event. The breaking of the egg. Someone took it out of the icebox, cracked it open, then tossed it into the hot oil . . . then pitched the shell.

"This isn't fun anymore, Roberto, it's getting hard to help you with this. I've done my best."

Slowly, deliberately, Roberto lowered the binoculars and placed them in their leather case. Taking a deep breath, he scanned the ocean horizon once more and stooped to pick up something half-hidden behind the curtains. The woman watched him again from the bed and closed the note pad she had worked on throughout the day. She heard snaps unsnapped and saw him taking something up into his hands.

"I don't blame you, Eva," he said.

In a moment the something transformed itself into a reality clear enough. Roberto produced a rifle barrel in two parts and began to screw it together. Its soft bluing shined quietly with each movement of his hands.

"You asked where our savings went," he mumbled, finishing the barrel interlock and looking back down at the case by the curtains. "I guess you could say they were invested."

Eva sat straight up on the bed and watched him intently. This, to her, was brand new.

"What . . . the hell is that?" she asked.

Roberto reached down and brought up the stock. He examined it for a few seconds, then proceeded to fasten it to the rifle.

"It is a gun," he replied, "a special kind of gun."

With a flourish of hands Roberto connected the two parts and raised the barrel to the balcony light. After inspecting it at length, he smiled.

"A reminder," he said, still eyeing the weapon, "just a reminder of what Mario told us that day after we left Gorgona. You remember. He knew what the papers hadn't printed, all about what happened to my friend Hugo. . . ."

"Roberto!" the woman interrupted, standing up beside the bed, "God this is an obsession with you! Forget it, please! The man is dead! There is nothing we can do about that, and we are alive!"

He now had a scope in his hands and was attempting to connect it to the top of the barrel. He hesitated a moment, then slid the piece up to where it locked in and clicked. Lifting the whole weapon up he pointed it out the open balcony at the sky and looked down through the scope. The woman tossed the note pad off to the side and walked up behind him.

"It is astonishingly accurate," he said as she approached. "I have fired it many times on Cerro Azul."

Roberto turned to look at her and smiled.

"The dry runs are over, Eva."

She stood looking on as he pointed the rifle first at one object below, then at another.

"You are going crazy on me," Eva said, "completely crazy. Put that thing down and let's go out. For God's sake, this is madness."

"Madness," he answered, "is doing nothing. Madness is letting these bastards get away with what they do, day after day after day after day!"

There was a loud click as he squeezed in the trigger. She saw that the weapon had been pointed at a man on a sidewalk far below.

"You are one man, Roberto," she said, "you are not a movement or a political party or anything like that. You are one man who has become obsessed with the death of a friend. Why did you study so many years to become an engineer? So that you could throw it all away for some stupid revenge?"

"Stupid?" he repeated, opening his eyes wide and lowering the gun. "Stupid?"

Roberto looked at her and turned around to face her.

"You know what they did to him, and you call this stupid? Do you know about his agony? Do you. . . ."

"Enough!" Eva shouted, throwing up her hands. "Yes I know! And I know you can't change that either! God has made the time pass and that is over. He does not feel it anymore! If you feel it then do something for yourself! Not for Hugo, he is no more!"

"You know," Roberto replied, now face to face with the woman, "you know there will be others like him, if there haven't been many already! It is up to me to put an end to this terror. I am the one who can and will do it! I am the one who will avenge the horror of my friend!"

"Roberto," she said, backing off and regaining her composure, "I do not believe you even care about others. I believe this is an personal thing of your own. I feel that the same evil you see in these people you hate has now possessed you as well. It has consumed you and will go on ruining you until you get some help. Get rid of that terrible weapon and let's get back to living."

Roberto, stern, watched her walk back to the bed and sit down. Leaning the rifle up against the wall, he went back to looking out off the balcony.

As the afternoon turned to shadows the traffic picked up on the avenue below. Cooking smells began to find their way to the light airs around the balcony, and a long way off toward the city on the sea, small lights were beginning to appear. Eva lay sleeping and Roberto sat gazing off into space.

* * * *

"My Captain, do you have a moment?"

"What is it?"

"Just something I heard this afternoon at Headquarters, Sir." Captain Arias lowered his drink and looked up at his lieutenant from the easy chair where he sat.

"Yes?"

"When we were leaving, there was an old man outside, they had thrown him out but he was still there carrying on. Do you remember?"

"Yes, I do. What about it?"

"He was ranting and raving about something . . . it's probably nothing at all. . . ."

The Captain looked at him and motioned with his hand.

"Yes, yes, go on."

"The old man was shouting something about . . . about a treasure. Some map or something . . . I thought nothing about it at the time, especially because they were smashing him in the face . . . but. . . ."

"But what?" Captain Arias had begun to drum his fingers on his knee in impatience.

"But I knew I had seen the old goat somewhere, at least I thought I recognized him. And the more I thought about it, the more I remembered. You know, that old man used to be a government official out in Penonome. I think he was a notary. I know because when I lived there, I used to see him now and then. I wonder, why the hell was he at Headquarters bothering the Colonel? If I remember, he was a somber man, a sober type, you know. . . ."

Arias grabbed a newspaper and lifted his drink again. Glancing at the front page, he took a healthy swallow and pursed his lips.

"My Captain," the lieutenant asked, "don't you think that is strange?"

"It's stupid," Arias answered, "I've got important things on my mind. Good night."

The lieutenant nodded his head and began to move away. He saluted once, then headed for the exit. Arias placed his drink on a side table and spread the newspaper wide. His eyes passed over article after article, page by page, until sleep was on him.

The lieutenant was awakened suddenly in the middle of the night by the ringing of his bedside phone. Switching on a light, he noticed it was past three a.m.

"Yes?" he asked when he'd picked up the phone.

"Find out why the old man was bothering the Colonel."

"Yes, Sir . . . I. . . ."

He heard the other end hand up before he could continue.

Nombre de Dios
Audiencia de Panama
Viceroyalty of Peru
December 9, 1543

4

"We believe these things are for you, Father Silvera. They were possessions of a Holy Caravacan Brother who traveled with us, and he spoke of you on a few occasions."

Father Silvera gazed down at a large canvas bundle on the wooden floor and reached out to receive a red velvet wrapped scroll. Before him stood a group of Spanish sailors.

"What happened to the Brother?" he asked, now eyeing the scroll.

"He disappeared one night as we rounded Hispaniola. We found no trace of him. There was talk among the crew that a sailor on board, a Basque, knew something about it. Some of the crew accused him murdering the Brother, but the Basque denied it."

"Basque be damned," muttered one of the other sailors, "he was an Englishman."

"English?" Father Silvera asked, looking up from the scroll.

"His mother was English, or something like that. I don't know," the first sailor answered.

"Where is he now?" Father Silvera said, again studying the scroll.

"He, too, disappeared one night. We encountered a terrible storm just after Hispaniola and our ship was driven off course. We ended up anchoring off a small island near Borriquen. That is where the Basque disappeared."

"Just in time," the second sailor added, "he'd have been acquainted with a noose had he stayed."

Father Silvera walked over to the small church altar and continued to examine the scroll. Beads of sweat were beginning to form on his brow as the morning heated up. Carefully, he untied the black cords of the velvet and removed the scroll. Then he hesitated.

"The seal is broken," he said, holding the scroll up to a window's light. "Someone has opened this document."

He looked at the sailors.

"Was it one of you?" he asked.

The sailors all began shaking their heads. The first sailor held up his hands.

"God forbid that we would do such a thing." he replied.

"Do you swear by the Virgin and all the saints that you have not read this document?" Father Silvera insisted, taking a step toward them. He looked slowly at each of the men before him.

The Spanish sailors protested their innocence with gestures and pious denials. Several swore oaths.

A long moment passed. Father Silvera lowered his head and began to nod.

"Very well," he said, returning to the alter with the scroll. Go with God and return for vespers. We will celebrate your safe arrival to Nombre de Dios. Now go."

As they hurried away the holy father lay the scroll on the altar and closed his eyes.

5

"Why me?"

A young American stood with his hands outstretched in Bob Friedan's study in Panama City. Bob sat at his desk and fooled with his tie.

"Because I said so," Bob answered.

The air conditioner made a loud, clunking noise and both men looked over at it. In a moment it was back to whirring smoothly. The young man coughed and held his hand up to his mouth.

"You know these people, you've been here for years. For God's sake, Bob, I'm supposed to just walk in and lay a bombshell like that on them? I'm a junior staffer here. What the heck is this?"

Bob Friedan pulled a drawer open and looked for a bottle. Then he remembered he'd emptied it the week before. He slammed the drawer shut.

"I can't get involved in this deal right now, there's too much at stake. They're saving me for . . . other stuff, even heavier stuff. Just go do as I say. They're not going to bite you."

The young man loosened his tie and walked over to the window. He shook his head.

"Just walk into the military headquarters, sit down with Quevedo, and lay this on him. Christ, Bob. What if he up and shoots me."

Friedan laughed.

"It's not that kind of game, Phil, that's not how it's played. We all earn our keep here, and we all prove ourselves. Years from now you'll look back and remember it as a proud moment. Join the club. Just walk in the door, ask to see Quevedo, and tell him the news. But do it today. Washington wants it done right away. If anything happens to you, I'll see to it that we launch a major protest."

Phil looked at him with astonished eyes.

"Oh, thank you, Bob, that's reassuring."

"Don't mention it," Bob laughed again, now standing up and walking to the door. "Señora," he called out, looking down the hall. "Señora, venga Ud. aqui, pronto."

The young man sat down by the air conditioner.

Children were off somewhere in another part of the house reciting a Spanish lesson. Their voices were audible in the study and at times the young man could make out what they were repeating. Presently a maid appeared and Bob Friedan gave her some instructions. She walked away and Bob returned to his desk.

"It has to be you, Phil, you'll understand these things as time goes by. You don't send in your front line troops with heavy business. They don't, and we don't. I have to be available for the diplomatic stuff. You get dirty as a junior around here. But don't worry. By the time you're a senior, all the faces will have changed. Then you'll be able to enjoy some of these, shall I say, privileges."

"Then let me get this straight," Phil said quietly, "You want me to get an appointment with Colonel Quevedo, sit down with him, and tell him that he now has zero support among the gringos. All life support systems gone."

"You've been chosen," Bob said, "because of your winning ways and your Spanish. Quevedo can't speak any English. Don't tell him nicely. Lay your cards on the table and sit there watching him. If he asks you any questions, tell him that the decision was made way up at the top. You're just a messenger."

"Nothing official, nothing unofficial, right?" Phil asked. "He's sure to ask me what unofficial lines remain."

"Tell him 'nada'. Tell him he's on his own. Tell him," Bob said, leaning forward, "that he's fucked. Time to pack it up and head into exile. He knows the deal we've set up. Don't let him bargain. Stand firm."

"What deal?" Phil asked, looking puzzled.

Friedan sat back in his chair and grabbed at his tie again.

"He knows, just tell him what I said."

Phil looked down at his hands and gently clasped them together.

"I see," he said.

The air conditioner clunked again and Bob Friedan cursed softly.

"Damn thing."

From that other place in the house the Spanish lesson continued. Phil heard verb conjugation drills and marveled at the childrens' clear pronunciation when their voices rose to carry on into the study. The maid appeared again, this time with a tray of cold beer and cheese snacks. The woman offered Phil first choice but he declined with a wave of the hand. She waited for a polite moment, then served Bob behind the desk. Bob picked up a beer and and fistful of cheese and motioned to the woman to set the tray down on his desk. She nodded, set it down, and gracefully backed away. When she had left, Bob spoke. He had a mouthful of snack in the way of his tongue.

"Politics," he said, wiping his lips, "I hate 'em too, Phil, but you've got to have them. That's what makes the world spin around. You'll learn."

"I never liked this bunch," Phil replied, "not from the day I got here. But now that I've got to go and do this, I wonder why I'm the lucky one. You've been their buddy-buddy for so long. All those promises, the damn gifts and parties. I remember that even after the Congressional investigation you went on baiting these bastards, telling them that the whole thing was posturing. I don't understand, Bob."

Bob swallowed the beer and cheese mush in his mouth and eyed his junior counterpart.

"You see," he said, holding the cold, wet beer bottle up to his cheek, "you can't cut people off when they're still powerful. Somebody has to keep the pipeline open. They gave that job to me. How the hell else do you think we could communicate with them? Damn, Phil, I don't like this way of doing things any more than you do. But get smart, this isn't idealism. They're hoods. They're animals. We are a legitimate government. You need a Bob Friedan to keep the train on the track. Now it looks like they're out. When they were united, we couldn't do much. But now we're watching them fight it out amongst themselves. If there's a barracks revolt, nobody's going to come out on top, that's our best information. That means chaos. We can't have chaos. That's why you're delivering this message. When they get it, they'll move fast to end the damn thing, everybody for themselves. You'll see. That's when we move in to back legitimate interests. Bob Friedan is a friend of democracy. I just work in strange ways."

He lifted the beer bottle, savored the bouquet, and quaffed. Phil shook his head.

"There's a lot I don't understand here, Bob," he said, "and there's a lot I don't agree with. It sure seems like you're the one who should be going."

"Damn you!" Friedan said, spitting out beer and slamming the bottle down. "Don't you understand? Coming from you the news is final. It's cold and final! From me it's another line of bullshit." Friedan stood up and pointed at Phil.

"Just do as I say and do it now. You don't have the experience to question my decisions. Walk out the door, get the limo, and get over there. That's an order!"

Phil looked at Friedan calmly, then pulled his lanky body out of the chair.

"I'll go," he said, matching Friedan's stare. "I'll go because I'm a good, loyal member of this team. I still don't understand though, why me and why now. This message should have been delivered long ago."

"Yeah, right, right," Friedan muttered as Phil departed. Bob watched him disappear down the hall and waited until he heard the front door crack open and close. He looked down at the telephone for a moment, then picked up the receiver. Dialing a few hasty numbers, he looked out the window across the room.

"Overseas operator? Yes, get me Zurich. I want a local operator . . . yes, yes, English speaking, of course. . . ."

* * * *

"Roberto, I'm going out for groceries. What do you want for lunch."

Roberto lowered his binoculars and turned around.

"We don't need food, we have plenty in the icebox."

Eva searched in her purse for something or other.

"There are some things we don't have here," she said.

He stood looking at her, letting his binoculars dangle from their cord while he placed his hands on his hips.

"There's enough of everything. Stay and help me with my work."

"There are some things we need," she repeated.

Outside the sun had risen to the midpoint and the apartment was as hot as it got during the day: not too bad, but stifling in the absence of the morning and afternoon airs. Roberto had waved off the notion of a fan as trivial. She remembered his speech on the value of proletarian virtues. It wasn't bad speech, but he was somehow too serious.

"Stay here," he said.

"I'm going out," she replied, snapping her purse shut. "I need the air and I need a walk."

Eva looked up at Roberto and smiled.

"And I'd like you to come with me. That would be the best."

Roberto's eyes flashed as he turned back to the balcony window and lifted the binoculars up to his chest. He gazed out over the city and said not a word. Eva watched him and shouldered her purse strap.

"I'll be back soon," she said, making for the door.

It wasn't until she had reached the elevator that Eva felt the weight of her move. She kept watching the apartment door as the ride approached, fully expecting to see Roberto open it and demand her immediate return. The car arrived sooner than she expected, though, and with a sense of relief she stepped inside. An old grannie dressed in black sized her up as she entered. Eva smiled and pressed the lobby button. Only after she had pushed it did she realize it had already been pushed.

"Ya, hija," she heard the old woman say.

The door eventually slid shut. Thankful of the moment, she had not even thought of her usual elevator thought. Not until she was reminded.

"Last week the Señora Rodriguez was trapped in this elevator for six hours," the old woman said.

Eva winced and closed her eyes. The old woman continued.

"It's because they skimped on proper materials, and the building inspectors are all brothers and cousins of the contractor. That's why."

Scraping noises from one side of the descending elevator opened Eva's eyes again. She felt her heart beat once out of sync.

"I'm sure the elevator is fine, Señora," she replied.

A loud thump from below marked the arrival of the elevator not to the lobby, as Eva had hoped, but to a lower floor. The doors opened and a short, chubby man entered the car. He looked Eva over from head to toe before the doors closed again, pausing for an extended inspection of her hips.

"Señorita," the old woman said, looking up at the floor indicator. "I am Señorita Marquez, if you please."

Eva nodded her head.

"Señorita, I'm sorry," she said, now backing off a step from the little man. He was conducting a survey of Eva's chest.

The car continued to go down, swaying gently from side to side. Eva crossed her arms over her breasts to hide from chubby's penetrating stare, but the man kept on looking. The old woman coughed loudly.

"It's like that woman downtown, you know what happened to her."

Eva sighed. She was afraid to look up at the floor indicator.

"She got her long hair caught in the elevator doors. When the elevator went up, it scalped her. I know. I read about it in the newspaper. Newspapers don't lie. She was bald when she reached the sixth floor. A bloody mess."

The little man had taken a half step closer to Eva. His chin almost rested on her forearms. He was now looking intently up at her eyes.

"That is terrible, Seño . . . ah, Señorita," Eva said.

When at long last the car came to a halt, and the doors opened to the brilliant light of the lobby, Eva pushed past chubby and headed out toward the building's front door. She could hear the little man's crisp steps on the stone floor behind her. When she reached the door she was almost running.

"Extra! Extra!" Eva heard once safely exited and out under the noonday sun. She glanced up briefly at what the tabloid had to offer but quickly looked away from the scene of a train-bus collision. Across the way two Guardias were arguing with a truck driver and a woman had dropped a pitcher of fruit juice on the hot pavement. A car somewhere was leaking gasoline. Eva rounded the first corner and looked way up at the high rise. Too high. The angle was too steep from where she stood. Waiting for the right moment, she darted out between two parked cars and crossed a busy street, dodging car and bus alike before making it to the other side. Once arrived on the opposite sidewalk, she took one last look up at the high rise. The sun got in her eyes and she could not concentrate long enough to see the upper floors. Eva turned and began to walk into a small market. She stopped. No, she hadn't come to shop. A car horn behind her began to honk furiously and a man was shouting. From across the street came the sound of sheet metal beaten with an iron rod. Eva made a left-face and marched away. She was heading for the ocean when she ran into a roadblock coming the opposite way. Instinctively she grasped the towering object and held on, the alternative being a head-over-heels spill. When she had regained her balance, she looked up.

"Eva Icaza," she heard a voice say.

"Angel . . . Mendez . . ." she answered, now firmly in the grip of the roadblock.

From above she saw a regular smile and a glowing set of white teeth.
"Nice to see you, I'd forgotten you were around,"
Eva smiled but gently pushed away.
"It's been a while, Angel," she said, "but it's good to see you."

The two made conversation for a moment, Eva looking away, her old friend looking on with an intent but friendly expression. With cars and such roaring by it was hard to hear.
"You are still with Roberto?" she heard him say.
Eva nodded and pointed up at the high rise across the street.
"Yes I'm with Roberto," she answered.
"Then we must get together, soon," the man replied, "at my place or at a party, I will call you."
Eva nodded again and looked up into his face.
"Soon," she said.
Angel grasped her shoulders and lowered his head to her eye-level.
"Very soon, I hope. You should stop by any time. Here is my card."
Eva took a simple white card with black lettering.

CAPT. ANGEL MENDEZ
3rd BATALLION
24-34-80 FFDDP

"Call me soon," the tall man said, caressing Eva's hair.
He was off before she could say good-bye. She watched as he got lost in the crowd, head above the tallest shoulders for almost an entire block. Suddenly she glanced up at the high rise across the street. As before, it was too bright. Eva shielded her eyes and started off again toward the Pacific. She looked at her watch. One fifteen p.m.

* * * *

"Sir."

The Colonel looked up from his work at the Lieutenant in the doorway.

"Yes?"

"Sir, some of Captain Arias' men were just here. Outside the headquarters, I should say. That man who has been coming here in the mornings and afternoons, the one we have chased away . . . they took him away."

"Took who away?" the Colonel asked.

"That man, Sir, the one we have been telling you about. The old raving fool with no hair. We've tossed him out on his ass three times now." Colonel Quevedo leaned back in his chair.

"What?"

The Lieutenant shrugged and grimaced.

"Sir, that old man who had been coming here, you always ordered us to kick him out, you must remember. He has been a pain in the ass."

The Colonel sat up and looked worried.

"Just why was this old man here so often, what the hell is this?"

"He said he had a big secret for the general, but he blabbed a lot of it. Something about treasure and some damn map."

"Did . . . Arias' men hear anything about this?" Quevedo asked.

"I guess so, Sir. They were leaving yesterday as we were punching the old fart out."

Colonel Quevedo looked off to the side, then back at his Lieutenant.

"Follow the sons of bitches," he said between his teeth, "if it's not too late. If you can't follow them, go straight to the captain's hideaway. They'll likely end up there."

"Yes, Sir," the Lieutenant answered.

"And . . . Oh . . .," Quevedo went on.

"Yes, Sir?"

"Let me know as soon as you know . . . just what this is all about."

"Yes, Sir. And one more thing."

"Yes?"

"Sr. Phil Travis is here from the American State Department. He will not tell me what he wants, but I gather that it is important. He is wearing a storm cloud."

"Send him in, Lieutenant," the Colonel said. He held his chin with one hand and pushed some papers out across the desk.

6

There were too many people hanging around for them to do it right. That was a lesson they had learned from ample experience. And even though the people were among the trusted few, far better to keep the secret from even them. So with a wave of the hand the Captain's senior lieutenant began to chase the idle loungers away. They offered no complaints as they rose from their chairs and tables. The lieutenant was serious. That was plain to see. It wasn't a joke. To a man the sergeants, privates, and corporals headed for the doors of the large mountainside mansion. They would either regroup at the pool outside, or load into staff cars to return to the city. The occasional women with them scurried away with their men. They were also conscious of a coming "business" encounter. Nobody asked questions, nobody lingered. When the fun ended, it ended.

"Andale," the lieutenant smiled at the last few to leave. When they were safely outside he locked the patio glass doors and drew the curtains. In a moment another lieutenant arrived, then a sergeant. Then a man was led in, an old man with a grave expression. They motioned to him to sit down at the bar.

The air conditioning in the place was superb. It was cool, perhaps 65 degrees. As the drawn curtains darkened the room, one of the privates who had ushered in the old man flicked on a light by the bar. When everyone was comfortable, a civilian arrived. He was a short, dark man, quite chubby and sloppily dressed. He walked up to the old man and held out his hand. The old man hesitated, then shook it. He felt a clammy, limp mitt.

"Mucho gusto," the little fat man said, coughing and holding his free hand to his throat.

"Mucho gusto," the old man replied with a slight bow. He half stood up from his seat at the bar but was held back by the fat man, now switching his greeting hand from the old man's palm to his chest.

"Ah . . . please stay seated," the fat man said.

His smile was something chilling to see.

". . . Of course," the old man said, looking around the room. The fat man loosened his tie and pulled a cigarette out of his breast shirt pocket. Snapping his fingers in studied self reproach, he then offered it to the old man.

"A cigarette?" he asked, eyebrows raised.

"No thank you," the old man answered, motioning with an outstretched hand.

The fat man closed his eyes in acknowledgement and slowly turned his back to his "guest". The old man sat watching him.

"Mind if I smoke?" the fat man asked.

Someone in the background chuckled, but the fat man shot him a furious glance. The chuckling stopped abruptly as the source understood the message. The fat man stood rigid, cigarette in mouth, match lit in his hand. After a moment he went back to lighting up.

"Can I get you a drink?" the fat man asked, turning around to face the old man. Again his eyebrows were raised in convincing sincerity. The old man shook his head.

"No thank you," he said, looking around.

The fat man nodded and blew out a puff of smoke. Squinting, he approached the old man and began to examine the latter's face. There were bruises beneath the eyes and one cheek was very swollen. His nose looked crooked, though that could have been an artifact.

"Who . . . did this to you?" the fat man asked, raising a finger to the old man's cheek.

"The sons of bitches at the military headquarters," the old man replied. "Your people, of course."

The fat man looked shocked.

"My people?" he said, holding a hand to his chest and standing straight up.

"I don't know whose people," the old man answered, "just some soldiers. They beat me up twice."

The fat man shook his head and made a clicking sound with his tongue.

"Dear me," he said, "these were not *my* people, you can be assured of that. Look around me. Are these the people who mistreated you?"

The old man put on a look of disgust.

"Look," he said, "I was told that I could talk to the General here. Where is he?"

"The . . . General?" the fat man asked, stepping back.

"Yes the General!" the old man replied, now irritated. "Where is he?"

"I . . . don't know," the fat man said, taking another drag off his cigarette and looking innocent. "Where is he? Do you know?"

The old man turned red.

"I want to see the General," he said, "and I want to see him now. Tell him it is important."

The fat man nodded.

"Yes, it is important, I agree. So let's talk."

Toward the back of the room the few soldiers sat smoking. A sergeant by the drawn curtains poured himself a drink. Outside there were occasional noises from the pool. A woman's laughter rose now and then to highlight the fun. The fat man watched the old man and continued sucking on his cigarette.

"Come on, tell us what you have," he insisted.

The old man shook his head.

"I want to speak to the. . . ."

"Enough!!" the fat man shouted suddenly stepping forward. "That's enough!! Talk to me!! Now!! I will decide if what you have is worthy of the General's time!!"

The fat man looked into the old man's eyes and stared. The old man looked away. The fat man snorted and went on.

"I mean, we know you were talking about money, and we know you were the notary in Penonome. We know a lot about you, Mr. Vazquez, just come to the point. What is this all about?"

The old man looked surprised.

"You know . . ." he began. Looking around again, he went silent.

"Yes we know," the fat man said, drawing closer. "We know all about a number of things you have been saying. Just spit out the details, then I'll bring in the General. He does not like to be bothered by the details."

The old man was now bewildered.

"It's the map," he said, "the map I found in the archives. And the notes. I can lead him to it. I just want my share, that's all."

The fat man came to a halt and opened his eyes wide. He took another drag off his smoke and cocked his head to the side.

"Yes," he said, "the map . . . where is it?"

The old man held onto his chair and tried to empathize with his questioner.

"You understand, I cannot go there alone. I need the General's help." The fat man tossed the cigarette aside on the floor.

"No I don't understand," he said, rubbing his hands together. "Why can't you go alone."

"If you know," the old man said, "then why do you. . . ."

"Just tell me!!" the fat man screamed, now almost perching on the old man's chest. "Tell me and we'll help you!!"

The old man leaned back in fright. Seeing the futility of threats, the fat man slowly backed off. He turned and walked away a few steps.

"Tell me what you know," he mumbled, searching for another smoke. A corporal had extinguished the first with his boot on the hard tile floor. The old man grasped his throat.

"Millions in gold and silver," he said unexpectedly.

The whole room took notice.

"What did you say?" the fat man asked, turning back to his "guest."

“I said . . . millions in gold and silver. I’ll take the General there. But I’ll only take the General. Tell him that.”

The fat man eyed the old man and tried to strike a match. He broke it in half.

“Where?” he asked.

The old man smiled and crossed his arms.

“That’s where I come in. I want to speak with the General.”

He sounded final. The fat man drew out another match and scratched it quickly on his pants’ zipper. It flashed and lit up.

“Clear the room except for you, Lieutenant Cruz. Everybody out.”

His orders were promptly followed.

Panama City later that day. . . .

"That's what they told me, my General, I am only reporting what they said . . . no, not Friedan . . . it wasn't Friedan . . . it was a young man, I have never seen him before . . . or maybe I have . . . he was a gringo like the rest of them . . . no, no, not him, this was a tall, young man . . . yes, Phil Travis, or something like that. . . Yes, my General, nothing official, nothing unofficial, I asked him several times . . . I don't know what this means, except, I'm sure it's serious . . . yes . . . yes . . yes, that's right . . . I . . . my General, I don't know why they delivered the message to me. In the past they have done it, you know . . . sometimes, perhaps they were afraid of you, I don't know. . . Yes Sir. I will certainly do that. I will go to. . . Yes, Sir I understand. . . .

". . . dear Jesus, yes, of course . . . I do understand the gravity of the situation, my General, let us meet to discuss it . . . you can count on me. . . ."

"It's me, Bob, Phil, message delivered . . . how'd he take it? With a stone face, that's how. He didn't . . . what? Yeah, he asked questions, sure. . . . Right. He asked me if the news was official or unofficial. He hardened up a little when I told him it was both. He kept asking about you. . . . No, not scared, just . . . how should I say, interested. Not scared . . . that wouldn't be the right. . . . Huh? . . . no, he didn't say anything like that. From what I gathered, it's life as usual. Nothing had happened by the time I walked out . . . what? . . . hell, Bob, I don't know. That's supposed to be your realm of expertise . . . no, I'm at the casino on . . . sure, I'll tell him. Boy, that was scary. I'll tell you, Bob . . . right . . . but I'll tell you something else that happened, just after I got there. Half of Quevedo's men went running out the door after I arrived. Real strange. Yeah, dead run, right out the door, right past me . . . right out the door . . . looked like something was cooking, something's up. . . ."

Above the City

Eva closed the apartment door behind her and took a moment to look in a mirror by the doorway. She tossed her hair up with her fingers and turned her face for a lateral view. Then she turned away from the mirror and proceeded to walk back out of the kitchen to a small living room-bedroom beyond. Roberto was, as always, on the balcony looking out. Eva sat down on the bed.

"I sat by the ocean," she said. "It was nice."

Roberto appeared to lean forward to get a closer look at something down below. Eva noticed he had uncorked a couple beers in her absence. The empty stood by Roberto's feet. A half-full bottle sat on the balcony ledge. She recalled that a beer set there had once been knocked over the ledge. It had fallen six floors to a lower balcony flower box where it had exploded with the force of impact. A brief note had appeared in the elevator the following day. Even Roberto had laughed. "To the clumsy beer drinker above . . ." it had read. Eva looked over at her possessions on the oversize dresser and remembered her days at the university. Shared possessions they had been. Missing lipstick, powders half gone. She saw her bottle of medicine and noticed that the pills were more than half gone.

"Any sightings?" she asked.

He didn't answer.

A photograph attracted her attention briefly. It was the one she had taped beside the dresser mirror showing Eva and her three college roommates. "The uglies," they had called themselves. For the picture one of them had pinned horns in her hair. Another had a moustache. Eva was wearing funny looking sunglasses belonging to a kid down the hall. They were hilarious. She looked over at Roberto again and lay back on her elbows.

"If you shoot someone, they will come and kill you, too. Of course, you know that. Are you ready for that?"

"I am ready for anything," the statue replied.

Eva was mildly surprised that he had answered.

"Then you agree that this is madness."

"I agree, that my friend Hugo was tortured and killed . . . no, more than tortured," Roberto said, turning around. "More than tortured, Eva, he was. . . ."

"That's enough, Roberto, I've read it and heard it a thousand times, what more can you add. Yes it was horrible. And I repeat. You are alive. I am alive. Can we go on living?"

Eva rose from the bed and stood facing him.

"Hugo . . .," Roberto began, then paused. He stood with his mouth open for a moment, then sat down in the chair by the balcony. "You . . . were with . . . who . . . down there? I saw you. Who was that?"

Eva thought quickly but could think of nothing smart.

"Who where?," she asked lamely.

"Down there, by the shops." Roberto went on, "you stopped to talk with a man. Who was he?"

"Angel Mendez," she said. "That was . . . Angel Mendez. He asked about you." Why not. It was the truth.

Roberto looked on impassively, mind almost vacant.

"He is a military man? Didn't he join the Guardia after school? That Angel?"

"Yes, I guess he did," Eva said, "so who cares."

Roberto crossed his arms and looked back out the balcony.

"So now he's a pig, too," he said. "Did you tell him that?"

Eva looked back at the "uglies" photo and smiled.

"Yeah, I guess he's now a pig, too. Let's go out for dinner. I have ten dollars stashed away. You need a break."

"I need," Roberto said, "a little time to figure. Why don't you stick around and help. There are some calculations I need to do."

"Why don't you make love to me," Eva asked, unbuttoning the top buttons of her blouse. She unsnapped the front latch to her bra and began to expose her breasts.

Roberto watched her for a few moments, then shook his head.

"I have work to do."

Slowly he stood up again and walked back to the balcony. He took up the binoculars and began to scan the avenue below.

"I saw first Arias' men speed past, then Quevedo's not long after. I think something unusual is under foot."

Eva hung her head, then stiffened up and tossed her hair back. At last account she had been considered beautiful. She was beginning to doubt the very thoughts that most inspired her in her hours of trouble.

* * * *

"My Captain, a regrettable accident has occurred."

"What?"

"The old man, Sir, he, uh. . . ."

"He what?"

"He died, Sir , we think."

Captain Arias stood up quickly.

"What the hell do you mean, 'he died'?"

"I think . . . he was frail . . . it seems that an unfortunately placed blow did him in. In any event, he is dead."

"And the body?

"Taken care of, Sir . . . but Sir . . . there's something else. . . ."

"What?"

" . . . The old man said something about monies. I thought I should tell you."

The Captain turned his back to the fat man in civilian clothes. He picked up a cigarette from a silver case on the table by his chair and tamped at the tobacco at one end.

"Monies?" he asked, one eyebrow raised.

"Yes, Sir monies. Something about . . . but no . . . that's crazy."

Arias stuck the cigarette in his mouth and flicked at a lighter. The flame didn't take. He looked over at the civilian.

"Come to the point," he said quietly.

He let the hand with the lighter drop to his side and watched the civilian raise a fat fist to his mouth as he cleared his throat.

"Millions in gold and silver, at least, that was what the old man claimed."

The civilian laughed. Arias did not.

"What?"

"Millions," the civilian went on, striking a match and offering its flame to the Captain. The Captain stared and did not light up. The civilian put on a serious expression and lowered the match.

". . . The message wasn't clear. The old man was choking."

Captain Arias flicked his unlit cigarette away. It landed on a nearby sofa.

"Tell me, you son of a bitch," he said, "just what the old man said."

The civilian came to attention and cleared his throat again.

"At some damn place . . . out on the road to Aguadulce, past Penonome. The old man said he had a map, he said the map showed everything, but then he croaked. The map was not on him. A fortune in ancient bullion and coins, sounds like a fantasy . . . and yet . . . no . . . just the rantings of an old fool."

Captain Arias fumbled for another smoke in the silver case. The civilian quickly offered him one of his own, yelping suddenly as the burning match in his hand singed down to flesh. The civilian tossed the smoking wooden stick aside. The Captain refused his cigarette and finally managed to extract one from the case. He brought it up to his lips. The civilian was busy with another match.

"Somebody thought he was the notary in Penonome," Arias said, now leaning forward to accept the flame.

"I believe that was what they said," the civilian replied, finally connecting his light to Arias' tobacco.

The Captain took a long, thoughtful drag.

"Get out to Penonome, Mr. Santos," he said. "Lieutenant Cruz will go with you. Search the old man's house and conduct an "inspection" of the Civil Register. Find out what you can. If it's the senile babbling of an old man, so be it. Go tomorrow at dawn. Now get out of here and send Cruz in."

"Yes, Sir," the civilian said, bowing slightly in obeisance as he backed away. When he had exited the door, the Captain sat down. Lieutenant Cruz appeared at the doorway shortly after. The Captain waved him in.

"You . . . will go with Santos tomorrow morning to Penonome. Keep an eye on him, a close eye. Don't let him out of your sight."

"Yes, Sir."

Captain Arias calmly finished his cigarette with Cruz standing close by.

Nombre de Dios
July 29, 1572

7

"Father Silvera! Corsairs! The English have landed! They're advancing on the town. The defenses are crumbling and our forces are in retreat!"

The Spanish father rose slowly from the altar where he had been at prayer and turned to face the panting man who had entered his church with the news. The man rose the altar steps to stand before him.

"I have been expecting them," Father Silvera said calmly. "Leave here at once and go to the jungle to hide. These intruders are not kind."

"But Father," the man said, looking over his shoulder, "is there something you want me to take, some favor in the name of the Virgin or God. Say the word."

Father Silvera shook his head.

"As quickly as they came, they will leave. Go with God. I will look after the holy church."

The man hesitated a moment, staring at Father Silvera.

"Go, I say," the priest repeated, now pushing the man gently with his frail, seventy eight year old arms.

The man turned and departed.

"Look lively, lads! Up with you, now, keep low, keep your heads!"

A number of English sailors scrambled up the beach under the watchful eye of their leader. Musket and harquebus fire mixed with the cheers of the invaders as the battle grew fierce.

"Keep moving, now!" the English leader shouted.

A fresh group of sailors were sloshing through the surf from the skiffs that had brought them ashore. Most were half covered with wet sand by the time they reached their leader.

"That's it, boys!" he continued to shout, "move and keep down, keep down!"

Off in the distance he could see the ships that brought them rising and falling with the swells. Whitecaps tossed the remaining boats of sailors coming ashore. The English leader sheltered his eyes from the fierce bright sun and attempted to survey the town past the beaches.

"Go to the government houses, lads, secure them quickly!"

Suddenly a cannonball whizzed overhead. Several sailors scampered off to a protected dune. Away near the trees at the entrance to the village, they saw two Spaniards working the piece that had authored the insult. Two English sailors dropped down on their bellies, knives between teeth, and slithered off in that direction. In a minute, they reached their mark. Two screams signaled the end of Nombre de Dios artillery.

"You there," the English leader barked to the sailors on his left, "over there! Go!"

He was waving in the direction of a large cluster of wooden structures near the middle of town.

"The rest of you," he said, turning around, "follow them in as a second wave. Set up a rearguard and don't let them cut us off from the ships. Go!"

The leader put his hand on the shoulder of one young sailor who was starting off in the direction of the second group. Then he motioned to another.

"We . . .," he said, stroking his moustache, "are going to church."

The young sailor at his side looked up in puzzlement.

"Church, Sir?"

"That's right," the leader said, now gesturing to the other sailor to follow him.

The three of them made off on a right angle from the rest of the invading host. As they cleared the high dunes they saw a church cross rise above a grove of thin trees. With the sudden roar of attacking men off to their far left, they ran down into a rocky gully beyond the sands. The church lay before them.

In the church, Father Silvera knelt at the altar and stared up at a window at the top of the church. He was aware of the battle in the city. He heard the frenzied sounds of the invaders and the defenders alike. But they were remote. What made him close his eyes and say one final prayer was the soft scraping sound of shoes he heard directly behind him at the entrance to the church. Kissing the silver cross he wore around his neck, he slowly rose and turned to meet his visitors. They had stopped, he observed, at the first row of pews. One sailor looked at his leader, then at the priest, then nervously removed his cap. The leader of the men smiled and took a few steps toward the priest.

"Good cheer, Holy Father," he said in Castilian.

The priest remained silent and stared at him. The two sailors accompanying the English leader moved off to the side a bit.

"I come to ask you some questions," the leader said, coming to a halt. "Perhaps you can answer them."

Father Silvera shook his head.

"I have no answers. Now leave and respect the sanctity of this house of God. I believe even the English have a God. . . ."

The English leader began to advance up the aisle again, smile broadening.

"Were it such a simple thing, I would leave immediately," he said, "I have no desire to violate the sanctity of these premises."

He paused a moment near the middle of the church aisle and changed to a somber expression.

"You do know what I mean?" he asked.

Father Silvera looked at him impassively.

"I have no idea what you mean, now go before the Lord strikes you down."

The English leader nodded slowly and lowered his head.

"I'll take that chance," he said, starting up the aisle again.

Then he stopped cold, eyes trained on the wooden floor.

"Search this place, lads," he ordered, "turn up every board and holy stone, look into the vestry and up into the rafters, there's treasure here, don't doubt that."

The sailors hesitated for a moment, looking at each other in disbelief.

"You heard me!" the leader said, half turning around, "go to it, boys!"

"No!" the priest said, raising his hands. "Stop!" His words were in English and his heavy accent troubled the sailors even more.

"Damn it!" the leader shouted, looking at the sailors. "We haven't come a thousand leagues to this hot hell to whimper about in a wooden shack. Move!"

"Stop!" the priest repeated, but now the boys were moving. Taking opposite side aisles, they hurried toward the altar end of the church, eyeing everything they passed. Their leader watched them go and looked back up at the priest.

"Sacrilege!" the priest shouted as the sailors began to ransack his church. "You will rot in hell!"

One of the sailors looked back at him for a long moment, then at his leader. He went quickly back to his work. The English leader sat down on a wooden pew and watched them for the better part of a quarter of an hour.

The nervous, high-pitched shouts of war soon gave way to the shouts of looting and revelry in the distance by the town. The English leader's eyes had scanned every inch of the church, and his men had turned over everything in the place before they were done. Once, one of them brought his leader a golden chalice. Examining it, the English leader tossed it aside.

"Gold, laddie, not bronze, the metal we want is heavy."

Father Silvera, composed but furious, stood there looking from the altar steps. From time to time he tapped his foot. Otherwise, he showed no impatience. The sailors returned from the hidden compartments behind the altar and shrugged. Their leader watched them come to a standstill below the priest at the foot of the steps.

"So I give up," the English leader smiled again. "Where is it?"

"Where is what?" Father Silvera asked.

"The gold, Holy Father," said the Englishman, "the gold. Twenty years ago I heard it from a dying Spaniard . . . he swore this church would make me rich. Where's the gold?"

Father Silvera began to smile himself. Then he chuckled. Then he laughed.

"A . . . Basque? . . . Whose mother was an Englishwoman? Don't tell me. I knew him too. He was a crazy fool, a storyteller." Father Silvera laughed again.

"And he has made a fool out of you, my young friend. Nombre de Dios is what you say it is. A hot hell. It is nothing else. You have missed the real gold and silver shipments by months. The royal fleet was here and it has gone. The gold of Peru has been shipped across this isthmus from Panama City and loaded on sturdy ships . . . the kind a dog like you would never dare to attack. So go look elsewhere, my friend the fool. Here you will find a poor church and a tired old priest. Go while you can. His Imperial Majesty Philip has a fondness for his gold, and these waters regularly see galleons too mighty for corsairs and puny skiffs. God forgive you."

The English leader heard some sort of cheer from the town. Then he heard another. Likely that would be the discovery of wine casks. He stood up and walked slowly toward the old priest. Suddenly, his eye came to rest on a large dual cross on the altar. He squinted in the dim church light and attempted to get a good look. Father Silvera followed his stare but carefully avoided either moving his head or showing any type of emotion. The Englishman began to walk up the altar steps to where the priest was standing. He came to a halt beside him. The cross was dark gray and black, almost green. With the utmost of calm, Father Silvera turned his head to follow the Englishman's stare. When both were looking at the cross, the Holy Father spoke.

"You are interested in bronze, Admiral? We have much of that here in Nombre de Dios. You want the Crucifix? Good. Then you shall have it."

Father Silvera turned to walk toward the altar but the Englishman cursed and began to depart.

"Come on, lads," he said, briskly descending the steps, "let's leave this wretch to his sweat and fevers."

The sailors quickly followed after.

Father Silvera watched them go. From the town he heard renewed cheering and guessed why the Englishman had set out in that direction. But no matter. The reason was not important. Slowly he returned to the altar and knelt down to pray. After a long silence he lifted his eyes to the crucifix. He swallowed hard when a ray of the day's advancing light gleamed for a brilliant instant from a speck of unpainted surface near the brow of the Christ.

As the English leader arrived to the town he stopped for a moment and looked back at the church. Eyebrows knit in puzzlement, he surveyed the now distant building's spire and lofty white cross. Then an urgent call returned him to his immediate duty. It came from a seaman rapidly approaching him on the road.

"Sir! We have discovered great quantities of gold and silver in the Customs House. But the metals are cast in heavy ingots, at least four stone or more in weight. It would take us a day to get them to the ships."

"We have a day," the English leader remarked calmly, now walking toward the center of the town and the main contingent of his men.

"Sir, I beg to differ," the excited seaman said. He was pointing to the woods beyond the village limits. "The Spanish have regrouped, over there. And there are reinforcements arriving from other settlements. I fear they will launch a counterattack soon."

The English leader stopped and studied the situation carefully. As he had suspected, a good number of his men had found the supply of wine.

"Then go directly to the government houses. There should be a goodly supply of coin there. It will be easier to move. Get going, man! Stir those sluggards off the porches. Tell them that any man caught drinking by me will be shot!"

"Yes, Sir!"the seaman replied, scampering off in the direction of the invaders.

The English leader started walking again, then broke into a trot. Yes, it was true, the Spaniards were reorganizing just beyond the far clearing.

"Lively, lads!" he shouted as he entered the main plaza. "Get the coin and jewels, get them back to the ships! Forget the ingots. They'll weigh us down!"

Three sailors struggling along with gold bars listened to their leader, then stared at what they were carrying. Mournfully, one after the other, the seamen let their treasure fall to the earth. Each ingot landed with a dull thud and a cloud of dust. Following their commander, they sprinted toward the government houses.

"You, and you!" the English leader shouted, "form a guard from the men there behind you, station yourselves between us and the Spanish over there. Get ready to shoot. You there, you by the wells!"

A sailor crouching by a stone well stood half-way up and watched his leader closely.

"Get with the others over there and form a guard around the government houses. You will be our second line of defense . . . look lively, lad! This is no social on a Sunday's morn'!"

The man and others near him first formed a group to discuss the matter, then chased off toward a low wall, a good position for defense. The English leader nodded slowly and continued to walk toward the government houses.

Before he arrived, however, a number of his men rushed out dragging bags behind them.

"Coin a'plenty, Sir," one of them said in passing.

Three more men exited with bags, then two after them. The English leader stood in the doorway and watched over the operation. Then suddenly a loud roar issued from the far edge of town. There was no surprise in the face of the English leader as he saw a goodly sized band of Spaniards rushing toward them across the clearing.

"Show some speed, now!" he barked, "step to it! Here they come! Get what's to be got, then let us leave . . . orderly like, now!"

Gunfire sounded in harsh spurts from the direction of the Spaniards. The English leader looked that way, then signaled to the advanced guard. A solid volley of shot sounded and in the distance, the attacking line faltered . . . but then continued. Uneasily, the English leader assessed the returning enemy's strength.

"There are too many of the bastards," he muttered, glancing nervously at the sailors still inside the government house. "Move, get your asses out, now!" he commanded.

Several men shot out the door in front of him, but a few more lingered.

"Move now!!" the English leader roared, "it's now or the Spanish torture, move!!"

The advanced line of defense fired off one more volley, then beat a headlong retreat back toward the second line. Once they had passed their waiting comrades, the second line fired. When the smoke had cleared, the English leader looked very worried indeed. The Spaniards were still coming in a wild rush.

"Pull out, boys!" he shouted to the second line of defense.

Without a further word of prompting, the second line obeyed. Some didn't make it. The Spaniards were within firing range now and a few English sailors lurched to the tune of direct hits.

"These are regulars!" somebody screamed as he ran by the English leader. And in fact some were. The English leader could already make out the characteristic dress of Imperial troops, men who had served in the wars of the Spanish European conquests . . . Flanders, the Germanies. Veterans. When suddenly he was struck. Someone's stray ball had struck him . . . squarely on. The English leader let out a muffled shout, then seized the door frame. The worst flashed through his mind, then the unspeakable. As the world became a dizzy whirl, he felt nausea, then horror . . . he would be taken prisoner . . . alive. Too much. The English leader grasped the door frame even harder. In desperation, he pulled himself up straight.

"I . . .," he began.

"Don't worry, Sir, just hold on!"

From somewhere welcome a stocky sailor grabbed his leader and hoisted him over his shoulder. Amidst the smoke of the fleeing English muskets and the hot fire coming from the Spanish counter-attack, the sailor leaped over logs and low bushes on his way back to the beaches. Now partially recovered from the initial shock, the English leader, bouncing up and down on the strong shoulders of his crewman, wrenched a pistol from his belt. He waited until a Spaniard was closing from behind, then fired. The sound of the pistol shot startled the sailor who was carrying him, but only for an instant. The man resumed his run as the Spaniard behind them lay dead on the earth, bullet hole seeping blood from the middle of his chest. Above, from the vantage point of shoulders, there passed a fleeting image of a church in a fresh, shallow glen. He caught himself as he was passing out, and with a final burst of energy, the English leader opened his eyes wide to study what he was passing. Between the fury of the battle around him, and the inviting world that beckoned with the heightening of his pain, the English leader saw a dual cross with the figure of a sad Christ nailed to its wide expanse. A cannon shot and an English cheer were the last battle sounds he could remember.

As the English sailed away a solitary figure on the prow of the lead ship gazed off into the night. Oblivious to the stars and the splendid night sky, he studied the waves as they broke across the bow. The winds were picking up and his hair lifted and blew in soft, undulations. He had earlier been aware of the arrival of another, unexpected English ship upon their departure from Nombre de Dios. The ship had tagged along as they left, but now its captain had come aboard. The captain and a few other sailors were approaching the solitary man reclining on prow.

"Commander," the newly arrived captain said from behind him, "I wish to express my sorrow with respect to your wounds. May they heal quickly. I also wish to warn you. We have just now come from near Cartagena. There is a large Spanish Imperial fleet in the vicinity. I saw them only two days ago. They were slower ships, but they were headed this way. It is well that you make for the north. I know there is talk of returning, talk of gold you were forced to leave behind."

"Thank you," the man on the bow said without turning his head. "I will take that into account. Please excuse me, my wounds have diminished my strength."

"Of course, Commander Drake, we wish you a speedy recovery. I will return to my ship now. Perhaps I can join you in a few days."

"That would be fine," the English leader replied.

As the captain and his people shuffled away, the Commander looked up at the sky, then suddenly clapped his hands.

"Damn!!" he cursed out loud. "Damn it to hell!! Of course!!!" Muttering a dozen oaths, he winced and attempted a feeble kick at the bulwarks. Then he clapped his hands together again. Turning suddenly in the direction of Nombre de Dios, he looked out expectantly, then let his head droop.

"God damn!," he repeated, "of course! I am a fool. . . ."

In Nombre de Dios Father Silvera held a special mass and smiled as the last celebrants filed out of the church. He turned to the crucifix on the altar and offered a private prayer of thanksgiving. The Christ he prayed to was the only part of the holy relic they had been able to clean in the interim, and it softly sparkled in the candlelight.

Central Panama
Dawn, May 28, 1987

8

A bird screeched in the hollow in the first light of the day. Leaping furiously from twig to twig, from branch to branch, it shook the entire side of a lush, green tree. Then it took flight and soared up to a point even with the very top of the tree. It hovered for a moment, eyeing something directly below, then dived straight down into the high grasses. The bird screamed and beat its wings violently as it rose and swooped down continuously to the same place in the grasses. Finally it flew back to the tree and sat again, wings outstretched in watchful agitation. It took to screeching again but eventually smoothed its feathers out and stood still. From its perch it kept an eye on events below. An armadillo scurried up out of the hollow, sniffing at the morning air as it rambled along. It had rained before dawn and things were still plenty damp. The armadillo stopped for a moment and stuck its nose into a patch of soft earth. Then it snorted twice and disappeared.

"They're moving," a man with binoculars mumbled from atop a jeep. "Looks like Santos . . . Cruz . . . and six regulars . . . they're taking two cars. Get ready."

Around him several soldiers in uniforms and plain clothes scrambled to get in cars and the jeep. The man with the binoculars concentrated on the scene below.

"They're leaving," he said, "they're on their way."

"Do you want me to call Headquarters?" a young soldier in the jeep asked. "The mobile phone stands ready, Lieutenant Roma."

"Not yet," the man with binoculars replied. "Hold on."

In the valley he watched cars speed out of Arias' driveway toward the mountain road beyond. They would pass just below him on the road and he didn't want anyone to be seen.

"Get the vehicles out of here," he said loudly, gesturing with his free hand.

Roaring engines behind him confirmed that his order was obeyed. A sergeant was back there barking instructions.

The Santos and Cruz cars had vanished behind dense tree lines directly between them and the observers. The man with binoculars attempted to calculate just when the cars would reappear.

"Steady, boys," he said, adjusting the focus.

Then in an instant the cars appeared below him and raced up the sharp incline to a point not twenty meters away.

"Steady," he whispered as they rushed past.

They had seen nothing. For a fleeting instant he had seen the faces of the men inside the two cars, and nothing. They were gabbing.

"Now!" he said, waving a hand in the air.

One of the cars behind him revved up and spun out of the wet sand to follow the high road trail above the Santos and Cruz cars. It sped along the rough stretch, pitching and leaping with the bumps, then crossed down on a tractor lane to the low road. It now followed the observed vehicles at a distance of about half a kilometer. The man with the binoculars picked up a walkie-talkie and pressed the transmitter button.

"In sight?" he asked.

He waited a moment for the reply.

"In sight," he heard in scratchy tones from the radio.

"Move!" he shouted to the rest.

In minute's time all vehicles were on the road.

"We've got an intelligence report here, Bob, it's pretty fresh. Here, read it."

Phil entered Bob's study with a thin document in his hand but was surprised, when he looked up, to see Bob packing a bag. Bob stared at him for a moment, then fumbled clumsily at the bag's zipper to close it up. When the zipper stuck toward the middle of the bag, he cursed and stood up.

"Who let you in? Isn't there such a thing as knocking anymore?"

Phil looked at him and stopped in his tracks.

"I'm sorry," he said, lowering the document and holding it to his side. "We had this meeting planned. . . I think. . . ."

Bob struggled with the bag and tried to push it behind his desk. It was stubborn, though, and hung up on the leading edge of a carpet. Bob shoved it twice, but no use.

"Damn," he muttered, looking back at Phil. "What day is it?"

Phil looked up at the ceiling, then back down.

"It's Thursday," he answered.

"So what do you want?"

Bob Friedan stood up and wiped at the sweat on his brow. Phil raised the document and began to study it casually.

"I want to show you what intelligence has been on to."

The house was strangely quiet that morning. Phil had a feeling that it was completely empty when he walked in. He remembered his heels clicking on the polished floors as the maid had showed him back through the halls to Bob's study. The flowers in the house seemed unusually fragrant, the air unusually heavy. Then he noticed that the air conditioner was off. Bob bent down and picked up the bag. He lifted it around in back of his desk.

"Going somewhere?" Phil asked.

"Maybe to San Carlos, to the beach house," Bob replied.

He waved off the report as Phil began to hand it to him.

"What does it say?"

"It says," Phil said, opening the document up and looking at its contents, "it says that plenty of jockeying has begun in the ranks. Quevedo may be on his way out. They don't see him as an effective strong-arm. The General may be looking at younger officers to take control. That means an upheaval."

"That's not news," Bob sighed, sitting down at his desk, "that's been coming for a while. What else does the damn thing say?"

Bob was reaching for a cigarette by the telephone.

"It has an addendum," Phil remarked, leafing to the last two pages. "There's talk, yesterday and last night, of some intrigue between Quevedo and Gustavo Arias, a Captain with the Fourth Infantry Division, but more involved in G2 intelligence operations. Seems they're up to something."

"Up to what?" Bob asked, leaning back and lighting up.

"I don't know, Bob."

Phil shook his head and closed the report. He looked up at Bob and smiled.

"Maybe up to a drug war, who knows."

Bob Friedan blew out a puff of smoke.

"Meeting's over, I've got a ride to catch. See you later, kid."

Phil looked down at the report, then over at Bob. A few drops of muggy rain pelted the window.

"Enjoy yourself at San Carlos."

* * * *

"West . . . the bastards are heading west! They're not going back to town."

From the wooded bluff where his jeep had come to a stop, Lieutenant Roma followed the two cars before him on the plain as they picked up speed on the two-lane highway. At the crossroads below he saw his own lead car stopped and waiting for instructions.

"Turn east," he said into his walkie-talkie.

He watched as the car slowly wheeled out onto the main road and followed his instructions, heading off in the opposite direction.

"Get on the mobile phone!" Roma shouted. "Get the Colonel and tell him they're headed west, we need a progress report on the sons of bitches. Muñoz!" he shouted into the radio.

"Yes, Sir," he heard over the receiver.

"Take the lead, follow them at a kilometer. If they stop, go by."

"Yes, Sir."

Lieutenant Roma raised his binoculars one last time and watched the cars wind off into the distance.

"What the hell is this?" he mumbled as they dipped into a valley and out of sight.

* * * *

"Going somewhere, Bob?" the American heard from behind him as he stepped up to a ticket counter at Omar Torrijos International Airport. Bob turned around and saw three civilians with sunglasses watching him closely. He smiled nervously and stepped forward to meet them.

"To . . . Isla Contadora," he replied, "time for a vacation."

"Wrong airline, Bob," one of the men in sunglasses smiled back. "And besides, we know a shorter route."

Bob saw a pistol flash beneath a sports coat rolled up on the man's arm.

"So why don't you come with us," the man said.

Bob looked around quickly, then picked up his bag and loosened his tie.

"Sure, why not."

9

Dull, lifeless winds swept up the sands at Chame. Low clouds rolled off the waters spreading more of the same, damp heat that had ruled the day. Occasionally the clouds would bring a spattering of bloated raindrops, never more than a handful, and at times they would clear just long enough for the sun to sear through for an unwanted moment. On the beach a child remembered what a ninety year old man had once told him under the shade of a scraggly palm, that the shores of Chame had provided much of the sand the gringos needed for the Pacific locks. It wasn't a particularly interesting fact. The old man hadn't made a big deal out of it. It was just something remembered. A shark's fin appeared above the surf about fifty meters offshore and turned in a long, lazy arc back out to sea. It looked to be a big shark from the size of its fin. A flash of lightening slipped silently from a cloud on the horizon to the distant waters below.

"Shame on you, Bob," a bespectacled man in tropical dress said from the chair where he sat. He smiled as he watched Bob Friedan from behind his partially shaded lenses. Bob cast an idle eye on the man's loose-fitting, stylish tan pants, matching jacket and soft pink shirt. Bracelets and gold neck chains hung off his wrists and neck. He wore several expensive rings.

"Shame on you. Our friend and loyal companion, sending us such shocking news in this our hour of need."

The man spoke English exceptionally well with just a hint of a Latin accent. His smile grew broader and he reached for a tall drink.

"We, your steadfast allies, abandoned at the capricious whim of yet another misled administration. Shame on you, Bob, we have reason to believe that you engineered this. . . this catastrophe."

The man picked up his drink and sipped at it. Peering down at the beverage, he licked his lips and turned his head to speak to a tall man behind him.

"What an excellent mix," he said in Spanish, "where did you find the recipe?"

The man behind him cleared his throat and looked nonchalant.

"It's called, "Planter's Punch", in English."

The seated man looked puzzled and glanced back at his drink. He studied it for a moment, then sniffed it.

"Then you've got the ingredients all wrong," he mumbled. "What's in it?"

"What the hell am I doing here?" Bob interrupted. He asked the question in Spanish. The man seated across from him looked up from his drink and smiled again.

"Why are you here, Bob? Why?"

He swirled the liquid in the tall glass to mix it with the crushed ice, then set the drink aside. He answered Bob in English.

"Because of the dirty trick you just pulled on us. Imagine. Pulling out the carpet from under our feet. The American government is too fickle a friend to count on in this day and age. All those nice things we did for you, all those favors. . . now this. You send a rookie over to tell poor Quevedo that it's finished, that the ball game's over. Come on, now, Bob, we all knew it was you. Uncle Sam needs us. It seems you've convinced him otherwise."

Three hoods stood in a far doorway and two more were sitting at posts behind Bob in another room. Bob looked away and frowned.

"Don't bullshit me," he said, "you know what's going on, this thing's just as hard on me as it is on you."

"Not quite," the man said, fingering his drink, "not quite. You could die today."

Bob looked back at the man and sucked in his lower lip.

"Don't fuck with me, Matos," he replied, "what do you have in mind?" Matos smiled and rubbed his hands together.

"I mean it, Bob, you'd better say the right things today. You remember the Spadafora thing. You could go the same route. There are boys here who would love to do it."

Bob's eyes wandered around the room at the goons in waiting. He went to his breast pocket for a smoke but Matos sat up quickly. Bob paused with his fingers in his pocket as he watched the startled man in the seat across from him. Matos, whose face had gone rigid.

"It's a cigarette, pal," Bob Friedan said, extracting one and holding it up in plain view of his captor.

Matos leaned back into his chair and watched Bob light up. He watched the smoke rise up from its lit end and closed his eyes as Bob exhaled. Outside the rain came again, again descending in a few excited spats, again subsiding before it got started. Bob looked around for an ashtray.

One of the men in the room behind Bob stood up and walked over to a far door. He opened it and gazed out at the green, misted fields. Matos had assumed his relaxed position again and was calling softly for a refill, a fresh drink. The man who had whipped up the first concoction whisked the partially emptied glass away to a room hidden from Bob's view. Matos clasped his hands and looked serious.

"All this time we have worked together, Bob, you for your insignificant 3 percent of the gross, we for the good of the patria and our beloved people. And I know the 3 percent wasn't all yours, Bob, you have people to pay, bills to settle, rents to keep in order, we know. American generosity is limitless, Bob, such a small part of the take. How can we thank you enough. And you've done your job, you've kept Washington in line for years. That's good. We don't know who got those 'extra' payments, and we don't care. But this we do know, Bob. Either you help us today, or I will personally see that you return to your flowery estate in Maryland . . . without balls and with the New York Times in full possession of your dealings with the Cubans, with the Colombians, with the Contras, and with the goddamn Sandino . . . in beautiful detail. The deballing I will personally supervise here today."

Bob looked up at the hoods behind Matos and looked away. He flicked an ash on the floor without thinking and buried his face in his free hand.

"I'm a reasonable man," he said quietly, "what the hell do you want?"

Matos was smiling again.

"That's better, Bob," he said, reaching up for his fresh drink, "that's better."

He took a sip and made a satisfied "ahhhhh" sound.

"You told me," Matos continued, "that you had a 'contingency' plan worked out for us. That's not good enough. I do not consider shelter in Dutch West Africa a viable alternative to the life I have in Panama."

"Gabon," Bob corrected, rolling his head back and staring at the ceiling.

"Fuck you," Matos replied, sipping at his drink again. "We're making a bid for Panama. Now listen closely."

Bob Friedan closed his eyes and nodded.

"Shoot."

"We make hay of the Nicaragua thing again, Sandino beating down on the respectable republics of Central America. Panama is still considered to be friendly to the average Joe in his beer cockpit in front of the American television. We're not Communist, we're not perverts, we're good, old-fashioned banana republic stuff, a dark glassed, cocked hat military fucker in control. That's what they want."

"Not in Congress, but go on."

Bob was now back to looking at his old acquaintance. Matos paused, then went on.

"Of course not to Congress, but that doesn't mean a thing. To the nine to fiver we're o.k.. Admit it."

Bob closed his eyes again and shook his head.

"The nine to fiver ain't in control," he replied.

"Listen to me," Matos persisted. "The Nicaraguan thing always gets 'em. I read a report that even though they don't like the Contras, they like Sandino even less. True?"

Matos looked at Bob expectantly. Bob shook his head.

"You can't wave that flag any more, it's a worn out, tired piece of shit. They won't bite. You're through, Matos. The President wants your little pal out. Pronto. What the hell can I do?"

Matos grabbed his drink and held it before him, both hands squeezing the glass.

"That's where you're wrong, Bob. Make no mistake about it, no. You're in big trouble, so are we. I swear to God I'll see you in little pieces before we go down. I swear to God. . . ."

"I don't doubt it," Bob said, "what's this all about?"

Matos stood up and waved the goon squad away.

"Vayanse afuera," he said loudly, turning to say it in all directions.

When the men had sauntered out and closed the doors, he faced Bob again.

"This time, a Sandinista inspired Panamanian radical kills your beloved Senator Dodge on a visit to our lovely land. There's talk of a coup-d'etat and a Communist takeover, and guess who steps in to smash it up. . . ."

Bob looked at the man with an astonished expression.

"What . . . the hell. . . ."

"You do it our way," Matos menaced, "or we do it to you."

Bob thought for a moment, then crushed his smoke out on the arm of the chair.

"How do I fit in?" he asked.

"One million in cash, and a free trip to Paraguay where you've set up your retirement . . . that assumed name and all. When the police rush in to investigate the shooting, they find incontrovertible evidence that the assassin has acted on direct orders from the Nicaraguan government. They find letterhead and messages to the effect, maybe cables and tapes lying around, phone bills. . . can you swing it?"

Bob relaxed for the first time and even relinquished an echo of a smile.

"Too crude," he mused, "too . . . amateurish. They're not fools. But I have some ideas. . . ."

Matos clapped his hands.

"Good old Bob," he murmured, looking on, "I knew it, you bastard."

Bob was almost lost in thought.

"You have a candidate for the rap?" he asked.

"A ripe plum for the pudding," Matos replied.

Bob smiled out loud.

"Tell you what," he said, reaching for another smoke, "I'll take a look at what I've got in dirty tricks . . . just let me out of here . . . in one piece . . . and I'll get back with you soon. I promise."

"You . . . promise, Bob?" Matos asked, sitting down again. "Sure, that's right, you . . . promise."

Matos gently picked up his glass and sniffed at the liquor inside.

Bob held up his hand as if to offer some kind of oath.

"Good, Bob," Matos said, sipping at his drink, "you'll work with my men 24 hours a day. They'll keep an eye on your slippery hide day and night. One slip-up and you're dead . . . no, worse. Mutilated. I saw your face when my boys talked about how Spadafora died. You felt horror. That can happen again. Easily. I'll. . . ."

"Let's get this thing over with," Bob interrupted. "How the hell are you going to swing the murder?"

"Leave that to me, good friend, leave that to me. In the meantime, get to work."

Bob Friedan crossed his legs and lit up. Blowing out the smoke, he patted his cheek and tapped his shoe on the rug. Then he laughed.

"Good. But I'll tell you right now, get me the hell out of Chame. I want a headquarters in the City. Air conditioned and the works. I'll need an unrestricted phone and a staff of trusted crack artists. And the million deposited you know where. If not, no deal. Ball-less or whatever, I'll take my chances."

Matos looked on with a somber expression. Bob laughed.

"I'll have to see this to believe it," he chuckled.

As the cars departed with Bob inside Matos stood in the doorway watching. A raindrop splashed off his nose and mixed in with the sweat on his cheek. He raised his tongue up to his upper lip and tasted the salty residue. Behind him a short, paunchy man appeared in the shadows. His face, in its fifties and bearing the marks of a ravaging acne, was strangely equanimous in the harsh grayness of the day.

"This has to work," he said to Matos in a forceful but quiet way.

Matos turned to look at him, then looked away.

"I understand, my General," Matos answered, placing his hands on his hips.

Nata, Panama
May 28, 1987

10

"Father Sandoval, may I speak with you a moment?"

". . . Of course, Miguel. What is it?"

The rough looking, middle-age priest had just settled into his study chair at his desk and looked mildly surprised at the appearance of his assistant. The man standing before him looked troubled.

"Something occurred while you were away," the man said, "and I thought it best to approach you about it the moment you returned."

Father Sandoval cupped his bearded chin in the palm of a large hand and watched the man for a few seconds, waiting for him to go on.

"Yes, Miguel, I'm listening."

"A man came here about a week ago, just after you left. He was an old man, a notary from Penonome. He told me he had a document that needed translating, a document that had something to do with our church here at Nata. He handed me the document and explained that it was written in Latin. As he had some knowledge of Latin, he had translated parts of it, but there

were numerous, lengthy gaps in his rendering, and not a few inaccuracies. So I invited him inside the rectory and we sat down here, in your study. As I examined the document and began to translate it, I realized that it was special. Now, however, I am very worried."

Father Sandoval continued watching the man. His deep, brown eyes took in every detail of his assistant's countenance and demeanor. Now fully relaxed and sitting back in his chair, he was indeed a commanding figure.

"Go on," he said, eyebrows narrowed.

"It was an old document, Father, exceedingly old. It dated from the Colonial epoch, from the latter seventeenth century. The script was clear and legible, but there were stylistic devices peculiar to that period, some were difficult to decipher. As my translation progressed, though, the task became easier. I completed it too quickly, perhaps not paying enough attention to the content of the text. It was not until I had reached the end of the document that I realized its full meaning. It was . . . a packing list, Father Sandoval, a list of sundry items shipped from the old City of Panama to Nata de los Caballeros. For some reason, a government official was involved, that is how the document came to rest in the notarial archives of Penonome. It bears the seal of an administrative official, a Corregidor, I believe, and an inscription by the hand of the same: "There Are No Copies". The old man stated that he had come into possession of the document during a recent renovation of the Civil Register."

"Where is the document?" Father Sandoval asked, slowly closing and opening his eyes.

"I do not have it," Miguel replied, "the old man took it away with him."

Father Sandoval changed position in his chair and looked away.

"I see," he said quietly.

Miguel continued.

"The packing list was extraordinary, Father, absolutely unbelievable. Gold and silver in abundance, chalices, candelabra, ornamental works of art exquisitely fashioned by colonial Spanish artesans, the document described some of them in detail. The list went on and on, gold chests with intricate lace designs, an archbishop's personal service, completely in silver, a large confessional, Holy Father, a carved mahogany confessional the height of a man with gold trim and a polished gold face plate . . . and so many other things . . . I cannot even remember them all. . . ."

"Except for one," Father Sandoval said, staring past Miguel.

Miguel stood mute for a moment. He looked back at his superior and attempted to smile.

"Yes, Father Sandoval, one item I can remember well. It was the last one on the list . . . how do you. . .?"

"Where is the old man?" the priest asked, now exceedingly dark and somber.

"He . . . left in a hurry when I had finished. He thanked me and went away . . . this is why I am so worried. There was something else attached to the document. . . ."

Father Sandoval watched and waited in the silence.

"Some kind of map. All I noticed on it was the location of our church, but there was a good deal of detail I did not examine. I tried to talk to the man after I had finished the translation, but it would not stay. He made excuses and left. Then, two days later, I made a discovery in the morning as I went to our wine cellar to store a delivery. The chamber off the cellar that has always been sealed, the one with the old, thick wooden door . . . the door that has almost disappeared with the dust and age . . . the hasp was broken and hanging from its hinge. The door was ajar."

Father Sandoval sat up with a start.

"Ajar? You mean it had been opened?"

"Yes, Father, someone went in there. I opened the door and looked in. There were footprints in the dust."

"Was . . . there anything . . . was anything you saw disturbed?"

Father Sandoval looked at Miguel intently.

"Not that I could tell, Holy Father, but of course, I have never been in there, never. All I could see were footprints, nothing else. There were racks of dust covered objects, cobwebs, and stacks of unknown things, all unrecognizable. The light was very poor, it seems there are no windows to the place, I didn't go far in."

"How could you tell that no one was in there?" Father Sandoval asked.

"Because there were tracks out as well, Father." the man answered.

"In any event, I sealed off the chamber again, quite securely. If there was anyone inside, he is still there."

The Catholic priest relaxed again and closed his eyes. He let his hands drop down off his chair to his sides and rolled his tongue up under his upper lip.

"The document bore a warning, Father, it was at the very end. I read it to the old man, and he listened closely."

Father Sandoval nodded.

"To all who may read this," he began as Miguel looked on, eyes wide, "all join the Devil's Legions and forsake the Lord of Light thee who wouldst interfere with the Holy Works of the Knights of Caravaca. Now prepare ye for thy certain death."

The powerful man looked up at Miguel.

"Go quickly," he said, "go sound the bell and summon the initiates. They will be surprised to hear the ancient piece toll, it will take them a while to collect their thoughts."

"Yes, Sir," Miguel replied.

"And Miguel," the priest added, motionless in his chair.

"Yes, Sir?"

"Prepare a High Mass for this evening at 9 o'clock. Bring out the robes of the Order we have kept so long in the vestry alcove. See to it that they are presentable in their old age."

Miguel nodded and backed away. He turned to depart and had reached the door when he stopped and turned around.

"The old man . . . he is . . . he will be back, Father?"

Father Sandoval shook his head.

"He is already dead. Those who will return will come from the dark depths of Hell, now go."

Penonome, Panama

"So, nothing in the Civil Registry. What the hell, this sounds like another stupid wild goose chase."

Santos stepped out of the lead car and surveyed a white brick house before him on the rural street.

"We've still got the house to check," Lieutenant Cruz said, coming around from the other side of the car.

The Lieutenant strode up the small walkway to the wooden front door. Looking around, he reached down to try the latch.

"Locked," he said, "it's locked. Now what?"

"I have a key," Santos said from behind him, "out of the way."

The fat civilian motioned to a formidably built tall soldier at his side. The soldier walked up to the door and with a single tremendous kick smashed it in. The door wobbled freely on the single hinge that remained and swung around in a ridiculous open arc.

"After you," Santos gestured, half bowing and pointing to the entrance.

Cruz strutted in. Santos winked at the "key."

"Good work," he said under his breath.

He then followed the Lieutenant in with the rest of the troops and came to an abrupt halt just past the doorway. Cruz was standing there staring at an extremely attractive young lady seated on a couch in the living room. She wore a skirt well hitched up to reveal a nylon stocking's top gartered to points above.

"Who the hell are you?" Cruz inquired.

The young woman smiled and puffed on a half-smoked cigarette.

"You just broke down my door," she answered, "I guess maybe you had better tell me."

She looked up at Cruz and fluttered her eyes, glancing down the length of his tall frame in an interested way. On the way up she met his eyes.

"General," she said.

Cruz coughed loudly and looked back at Santos. Santos shrugged and smiled, then lit up a smoke.

"I am *Lieutenant* Cruz," the military man said, "4th Infantry, investigating on behalf of Captain Arias. Who are you?" he repeated.

The woman stood up and walked toward the Lieutenant.

"I am a private woman," she smiled, "second cousin to the Notary Public and Official of Archives of Penonome, I keep his place looking spiffy, he lets me stay here. But let's talk about you. What do you want?"

She placed her arms around Cruz's hips and nudged up to his uniformed body. Cruz looked back at Santos again, then down into the eyes of the magnificent creation before him.

"I'd like . . ." Cruz began, pausing to place his hand on the woman's shoulder, "I'd like . . . to get to know you better, cousin."

"Fresh!" she gurgled, placing a finger to Cruz's lips.

The rest of the contingent looked on as Cruz led her away to the nearest room. They watched the couple enter, then exit just as fast. Not in the kitchen, Santos guessed.

"That Cruz," the civilian muttered with a gesture of respect, "the man just knows all the moves, lucky dog."

A soldier standing beside him scratched his head, and another started to ask a friend what the hell was . . . when Santos motioned to them all.

"So . . . the Lieutenant is 'busy', but life goes on. We've got a job to do, boys, you'll be looking for some old pieces of paper with some crazy writing . . . may be a torn up piece of shit, that doesn't matter. If you find anything old and written, bring it to me."

"Here's a Reader's Digest," one of the soldiers said immediately, raising the magazine above his head.

Santos looked at it and closed his eyes.

"Not exactly what we had in mind," he said in measured tones, "keep looking."

The soldier looked at the Digest and laid it down, pausing to flip through a few pages. Santos was already into drawers.

* * * *

In a field, on the outskirts of the villlage of Nata, a mechanic rose from beside an old tractor at the first sounds of the ancient church bell. Resting his free hand on the tractor wheel, he wiped the sweat from his brow with the forearm of the other, the hand that held his wrench. For a moment he just stared. Inland seagulls flocked around a planting between him and the distant church, and gray clouds pressed down on the humorless, sultry day to imprison it even more. As bells continued to toll, he laid the wrench on the tractor seat and walked over to a large spigot in the center of the field. Still looking in the direction of the church, he stooped down, turned on the spigot, and turned the hose on his warm face and shoulders. He let the cool water pour over his open shirt and chest, flinching a bit as it reached his waist and hips. Then he doused his entire head. The bells were still tolling, and he dropped the hose and pressed back his long, wet hair. With an expression of mixed curiosity and apprehension, the sturdy man set off walking through the field. As he reached the village, he was joined by an old friend, also walking in the direction of the church. They saw two others crossing the plaza before them.

* * * *

"Is this what you're looking for, Mr. Santos?" a soldier asked, showing the civilian an old parchment document and two other yellowed papers.

Santos reached out to receive the papers, examined them briefly, then shook his head.

"Nope," he said, "these aren't the ones. Keep searching."

"Yes, Sir," the man said, returning to the pigeonhole desk he had been looking through.

Santos held the papers behind his back for a minute or so, rocking on his heels as he watched the soldiers move from shelf to shelf, from drawer to drawer. Slowly he rolled them together, waiting for the soldiers to move off to other rooms before acting. When only one soldier remained, back turned toward him, Santos suffered the roll into his shirt and pants. He coughed and pulled a cigarette out of his shirt pocket.

"Nothing here," he heard from a back room.

He heard frantic breathing and moans from another, a thrashing of a bed.

"Keep looking," he commanded in a loud voice.

* * * *

Eva Icaza watched Roberto button his shirt at the door, then turn and look at her briefly.

"I'm going to the University," he said tersely, "I have a meeting." Eva smiled weakly and watched him leave. After five minutes or so of leafing through an old magazine, she rose and walked over to the door. She opened it, looked out, and saw no one in the halls. Then she closed it again. Walking over to the balcony, she looked out at the ocean and another ship on the horizon. Slowly, almost without thinking, she picked up the binoculars and brought them to her eyes. After staring out at the day for a while, she lowered them and walked back to the kitchen. She placed the binoculars on a counter and picked up the phone, then dialed a number she had thought of often.

"I am calling for . . . Captain . . . Angel Mendez," she said." . . . Yes . . . I'll wait."

Eva gazed at a torn "The People, United, Will Never Be Defeated" poster on the kitchen wall and pressed her ear closer to the receiver. Presently she perked up and turned in a half circle to face the door.

"This is Eva you remember? Hello. I just called to say it was nice . . . seeing you the other day. I thought we could have a cup of coffee and . . . now? . . . sure, but I . . . o.k., sure . . . but let me meet you there. Yes, there's a little place just off the Avenida Balboa . . . Tio Pato, it's called. . . .

" . . . fifteen minutes? . . . yes, but . . . sure, o.k."

Eva hung up and stood leaning on the wall for a full minute. Someone upstairs was beginning to argue in a loud voice.

* * * *

"What did you find?" Lieutenant Cruz asked, walking out of the bedroom and zipping up his pants.

"Nothing," Santos replied, frowning and tossing a cigarette butt out the door. "There was nothing to it. Let's get the hell back to the Capital."

Cruz paused in the middle of the room, giving his pants a final hitch up and looking around. The place was upside down. Two soldiers exited from the back rooms and walked toward the entrance.

"Let's pack it up and leave," Santos urged.

Cruz nodded and joined the soldiers on the way out.

"The day wasn't a total waste," Cruz mumbled, rubbing his hands together.

As he reached the front door the young woman appeared at the entrance to the bedroom. Santos watched her impassively. When Cruz was outside he smiled and waved.

"Adios," he said.

"And this?" she asked him from across the room, holding up a key.

"Toss it in the river," Santos replied, now turning to leave himself.

"There'll be a package in the mail for you in the next few days. What we agreed on and a little more for your good work."

"Good-bye, Señor Santos," she said.

Cars were revving up to leave in the street outside.

Nombre de Dios
December 28, 1595

11

An elegantly dressed gentleman in breeches and silk stockings stepped cautiously through the abandoned shambles of a weathered wooden church he had known before. Stopping in the middle of the structure, he looked up at the hanging rafters and wondered at its state of disrepair. Light filtered in through more than one hole in the roof and white stains marked where the birds were now nesting. He shook his head and placed a pinch of snuff between his lip and his gums. Outside the hot sun bore down as always and the unhealthy damp winds continued to circulate and blow off the top of the warm water surf. Through a window in the side of the church he made out his brig rising and falling at anchor in the bay. Suddenly he turned his eyes to the front of the church to locate the source of an unexpected noise. He saw a elderly man dressed in loose-fitting tropical white cottons come forward to meet him.

"What do you want?" the man said, coming to a stop.

The elegantly dressed man watched him for a moment, then stepped up a little closer.

"I am here to see . . . Father Silvera, the old priest who used to be here."

The elderly man in white shook his head.

"Father Silvera?" he asked incredulously. "Father Silvera has been dead for many years."

"I was told he was still alive," the elegant man said in cold tones.

The man in white smiled.

"Then he would be a phenomenon of nature," he replied.

Outside there were faint shouts and voices carried in on the wind. The words were unintelligible. The elegantly dressed man looked up at where the altar had been and saw nothing. Just small piles of rubbish and an occasional empty wooden box. He lowered his head, then looked back at the elderly man.

"What has happened to Nombre de Dios?" he asked.

"Gone," the man answered, "left to the tropics as a place that should never have been civilized, left to the heat. Nombre de Dios is no more."

The elegant man stepped forward even closer.

"You are telling me that the Spaniards now have no shipping terminus on the North Sea, this is true?"

"Wrong," the old man said, pointing to the west. "The main contingent has now relocated up the coast in a harbour known as Portobelo. If you are a seafarer, you must know of it. You see, my friend, you and your English comrades have burned Nombre de Dios down one time too many."

The elegant man stroked his beard.

"Portobelo? Then, the church is there also?"

"Yes," the main in white said, smiling again. That is where they relocated the church."

"And everything that was in it?"

"Yes, and everything that was in it."

The elegant man paused and studied the elderly man in white. Then he nodded and turned to leave.

"Thank you," he said as he walked toward the door.

"Dearest God, Brother Francisco, you've sent that scourge to Portobelo?"

A tall, gaunt man had rushed up behind the old man in white after the visitor departed. The old man looked around at him and placed a hand on his shoulder.

"He doesn't have far to go," the old man said, "not far at all."

He walked out to the center of the church and looked out the same window the stranger had looked out earlier. The gaunt man followed him to the spot and looked over his shoulder. In a few minutes, they saw the long boats pitching through the breakers on their way back to the ship.

"Perhaps he will wish to settle there," the old man whispered.

A sailor leaned up against a cannon block and looked out across the sea. He saw a low island, perhaps a reef, about a league to starboard. It would appear, then disappear briefly with the passing of increasingly larger waves. Beneath him the decks were beginning to groan and above him the rigging was already singing. A young mate was barking orders to the crew behind him as the winds freshened and the sails bulged. He turned to watch the quartermaster strain at the wheel.

"All hands, trim sail, storm's a comin'!" he heard.

In a moment the entire ship's crew was on deck, each man hurrying to his post. Some manned lines at the base of the masts, others scrambled up top to work with the sails. They worked in perfect unison and before long they had finished. The brig soared up over the white-capped swells and surged along in the water, charging into troughs and exploding through them to the other side. Rough going.

Down below a cabin boy watched as his master lay down on the bed.

"Fetch the ship's surgeon, boy," he heard him say.

Standing for a moment to see what was wrong, the boy noticed that his master's shirt was soaking wet.

"Go now!" he heard.

The boy quietly exited the stern quarters and made his way forward in the darkness of the below decks. At length he reached a cabin about amidships. He paused outside the door, then knocked.

"Who is it?" he heard from within.

"Master Robert," he replied.

For a moment he heard nothing. Then the cabin door flew open.

"Yes, lad, what is it?"

"It's Lord Drake, Sir, he is ill. He asked that I summon you at once."

The surgeon looked up the passageway in the direction of the after quarters.

"Let me get my bag," he said.

12

In the Cuartel Central

"When they got to Penonome, they went straight to the Civil Register. We watched them for about an hour, maybe a little more. From where we were we couldn't see much, but after they left, I had a couple of men stay to find out what they were up to."

"First things first," Colonel Quevedo interrupted, resting his chin on the thumbs of his clasped hands. "Are you sure they don't know you were following them?"

"I'm positive," the lieutenant answered, glancing behind him at the office door.

His men were stationed just outside. Beyond them, everything was calm at Headquarters.

"We followed them at a safe distance and they never stopped. I have no reason to believe that they knew we were there."

"That's good, Quevedo nodded, "go on, Lieutenant Roma."

"The people I left at the Civil Register said that Santos and Cruz searched the place. They wanted to know where a certain notary's desk was, and where the notary filed his documents. His work stations, you know. It seems that the notary disappeared a few days ago and hasn't been heard from since."

"That would be the old man you were telling me about, the one who tried to get in to talk to me, but go on."

"Yes, Sir. It seems they didn't find what they were looking for, so they headed over to where the notary lived, a house on the west side of town. We followed them there, too. When the boys I'd left to ask questions at the Civil Register caught up with us, I guessed it must be the notary's house. We called the Register to confirm it."

"Using somebody else's name, I hope," Colonel Quevedo said, leaning back in his chair and picking up a glass of water.

"For all they know, we were part of the Santos/Cruz group."

"Good. Keep talking, this is absolutely crazy," Quevedo said between sips of water.

"They stayed at the house for about a half an hour. Then they took off. They came straight back to the Capital. They turned the damn place upside down, it was a mess."

"But . . ." Quevedo said, sitting up, "found nothing, evidently."

"I don't know, Sir, I have no idea. There was something, though, something very peculiar."

Quevedo sat watching.

"A young party girl by the name of Lucia Prados walked out of the place after they split. A couple of my men recognized the bitch. We didn't see her go in. She must have been there."

"Who is Lucia Prados?" Quevedo asked, finishing his water.

"She's a camp-follower," the lieutenant replied, "used to be a Paredes girl until the General made his move. Then she dropped out of sight. She's beautiful, I'll give her that much."

"A Paredes girl?" Quevedo said, turning in his chair. "She used to hang around with Ruben Dario Paredes?"

"The same," the lieutenant said, nodding his head.

"That means she could know Santos," the Colonel mumbled, looking out the window.

He sat for a moment, working his lips with his finger, then turned back to Lieutenant Roma.

"That's it," he said, "she's a Santos connection."

The lieutenant looked behind him again at his people at the door. One was reading a daily paper. The other was staring stupidly off into space.

"Keep an eye on Santos, where are they now?"

The lieutenant cleared his throat and replied.

"At Captain Arias' place, Sir, we have them under surveillance, don't worry.

Colonel Quevedo looked up at the man and frowned.

"Worry?" he said, shaking his head and slowly standing up. "I am not really worried about Arias, Cruz, or Santos, Lieutenant, I have other very real things on my mind. Just keep me informed, that's all. You may go, Roma."

"Yes, Sir," the lieutenant answered.

Behind him there was commotion and he looked back. Across the great hall he saw Major Villalobos coming straight toward him with a contingent of men. The man looked mad as hell.

"With your permission," he said to the Colonel, saluting and backing away.

"You may go," Colonel Quevedo said quietly.

* * * *

Eva Icaza had only been seated a few minutes at her table when she saw him come in. Angel Mendez cast a shadow on the sparse crowd as he walked in. He attracted every eye in the place as he paused by the cashier to look around. Eventually he saw Eva. He smiled and gracefully eased his six foot, four inch frame through the closely placed tables and chairs.

"Hello, Eva," he smiled as he approached.

She looked up and once again marveled at the way God had put that man together.

"Hello, Angel, it's good to see you."

She looked down at the table and picked up her purse. As Angel got seated, she stashed her purse beneath her chair. When she looked up again, she saw him motioning to a waiter.

"We'd like a menu," her old friend said.

Angel Mendez was a profoundly Latin looking man with straight dark hair and bronze skin. He had perfect teeth and features to go along with a box office hit. He had been the most popular guy in town for as long as Eva could remember. They had grown up together in Paitilla in modestly well-to-do homes, and they had been friends from childhood. Eva's father's business misfortunes, however, had seen her move away from the neighborhood to an apartment in a less exclusive suburb as she graduated from high school. She had lost contact with Angel during college, as he had gone to West Point to study for a military career in the United States. It had been seven years since she had seen him before their chance encounter on the street in front of the high-rise. Angel had said many times that Eva would be his bride. She had met Roberto at the University, and had stayed with him ever since. Not married, but as close to man and wife as a couple can be. Roberto had also grown up in Paitilla, though he and Rogelio had never gotten along. Roberto had always been given to study. Angel to the social life and practical matters. His move to the military had been a practical decision.

"After all these years, my love calls me on the phone. I'll have you know I was engaged in an important discussion, a matter of state. A Major had ordered lunch and it failed to appear. We were interrogating a carry-out driver."

Eva smiled.

"It's good to see you," she repeated.

The waiter finally showed up with the menus and Angel corrected the man, gently insisting with a sweeping gesture that the lady be given the menu first. The waiter raised an eyebrow and offered Eva first choice. She refused it and asked for a cup of coffee. The waiter shrugged and looked back at Angel.

"I'll have the same," he said.

Angel half watched the waiter return to the kitchen as Eva changed positions in her chair. Some one dropped a cup on the floor in a far corner and the small restaurant resounded with the shrill smashing noise.

"She should be in better places than these," Angel said mindlessly, looking over in the direction of the accident. Eva looked a bit resigned. She raised her eyes to view the street entrance, then looked at Angel.

"What are you up to in the General's army?" she asked.

Angel turned his eyes on her and cocked his head slightly.

"I'm up to making a living, just like anyone else. How about you. How's our friend Roberto?"

Eva smiled, somewhat less than convincingly, though. Angel was atuned to the message in the smile.

"He's fine, Angel," she said, "he's just fine. He's at the University now."

Angel leaned back in his chair and began to study nearby customers.

"The University, Eva? What is he, a professor?

Eva shook her head.

"No, he's not. He's still studying. I think he's attending a meeting today. There's a protest scheduled for tomorrow. He's very much into that sort of thing, ever since his friend Hugo was killed. That affected him a lot."

Angel's eyes suddenly froze on an object off to the side. He remained motionless.

"Why . . .," he asked, "would that have affected Roberto?"

Eva saw the waiter coming with their coffees. She followed him with her eyes as he approached.

"Because Roberto was an admirer of Hugo. He considered himself a disciple. They had many a discussion, the two of them, and when Hugo Spadafora died, Roberto couldn't get over it. He thought of it as something personal."

Angel Mendez glanced up at the waiter as he arrived at the table, then calmly watched as he served Eva.

"I see," he said, nodding gently as his turn came.

The waiter placed a slightly chipped cup in front of him and poured in a less than steamy brew. Angel waited until he had departed before he spoke again.

"And just what does Roberto plan to do about Hugo's demise."

Eva took her first taste of coffee and pursed her lips. Bitter. She looked up at Angel and suddenly remembered who he was.

"How about you? Are you married? Do you have children? It seems you always wanted a million bambinos playing around your feet."

Angel laughed.

"I never said any such thing, Eva, that's pure 'invento'. I am a single man, and a single man I'll stay . . . that is . . .," he paused. ". . . That is, until you give me the word. I remember a cool night on the Pacific and a long Icaza kiss. I have always wanted another."

Eva laughed.

"That was not Icaza. You were drunk. I think you must have been with the 'muskrat', she was following you around that night. In fact, I know it was the 'muskrat'. I was spying from the dunes."

Angel put on a serious expression.

"Just facts, ma'am, I always tell the truth. That was Icaza sending me off into orbit. I have never returned."

They both laughed.

"This coffee is wonderful," Eva said, eyeing the stale liquid. "How about another cup?"

"No thanks," Angel replied, pushing his cup away.

For a moment he looked down at the coffee, then stopped smiling. He fiddled with the spoon, then looked over at the windows in the back.

"You know I still love you," he said softly.

Eva glanced down at her watch, then followed his gaze to the windows. A newspaper vendor had stuck his head into the restaurant and was shouting something about an explosion in Chiriqui.

"I have to go now, Angel. Roberto is sure to return soon. I have to make supper. It has been wonderful seeing you again, and I think of you, you know, as one of the dearest people to me. And that's the way it will stay. So excuse me, I'll be on my way." She rose and Angel rose and the latter, bending down to kiss her outstretched hand, said farewell.

"So long for now, Eva Icaza," he smiled, rising to look into her eyes, "you know the number."

Eva smiled back, paused, and was off. She walked briskly to the entrance as Angel dropped a couple bills on the table.

* * * *

"Bob Friedan, it's good to see you. Say, where the hell have you been? I've been trying to call you since this morning. Your maid told me that you'd left town for a few days. Nobody at the station knew that."

"My maid is nuts," Bob replied, "I told her I was going out with an old girlfriend on the Q.T. So what the hell brings you here?"

Phil looked down at his muddy shoes, then back at Bob. He was as he often was, seated in his study chair, feet up on the desk.

"Bob," Phil said, "we have a lot of business to transact. I have a brief-case full of it. Are you still a member of this team? You're supposed to be in charge."

"First things first," Bob said, biting off the end of an expensive cigar. "Get today's intelligence report and give me a rundown."

Phil sat down in the easy chair and opened his briefcase. He shook his head.

"Nothing more on the Quevedo business," he remarked, pulling out a neat, thin binder. "The General went off into hiding yesterday, to Chame, we think. It's hard telling sometimes, especially when he uses the old three car routine."

Phil referred to the General's habit of sending out identical cars in the morning, each in a different direction. You never knew which one he would be in. . . if in any one of them.

"Why Chame?" Bob asked coyly, threading his tie through his fingers.

"Who knows," Phil answered, turning the first pages of the report over in crisp, exact fashion. "What counts is that Quevedo's people didn't know where he was going. That's the third time this month that they've been kept in the dark. That means the General is taking him less and less into his confidence. And that means. . . ."

"Yes, brilliant," Bob said, lighting up and swinging his feet off the desk to an open drawer about a foot lower. "So Quevedo's on the way out. I've been saying that since December. What the hell else have these brains found out."

The cigar glowed scarlet for an instant, then Bob blew out the smoke.

"Only . . . that some of Captain Arias' men took a side trip to the city of Penonome this morning, then came back. Quevedo's people followed them and pulled into town just after. . . ." Bob surprised Phil by knocking a ledger off into space from on top of his desk. The book came to rest with a loud 'wham' in a corner of the room.

"Petty intrigue," Bob said, now placing his feet on the floor. "Tell me something important."

Phil looked up and stared. Bob puffed twice on his stogie and stared back.

"When Senator Dodge comes here on Monday, what the hell is the agenda?"

Phil winked his eyes and looked blank.

"That hasn't been completely decided," he replied. He won't meet with the General, though, that's for sure. He may even court the old man of Panamanian politics. That's a possibility, Bob. I'll tell you, the President's pissed off. He wants this bastard out before he hits the happy trails of retirement. He said Marcos, and Baby Doc, now this other dragon in the closet. The message you had me deliver to Quevedo was quite explicit . . . that is your wish, too, isn't it?"

Bob nodded and stood up.

"Yeah, I've been saying that all along. Get this asshole out. Bring back democracy. I'd like to plan a businessman's luncheon for the Senator, maybe at the Marriott up Balboa, you know, get all the middle class kingpins in to represent the 'people', Dodge would like that, wouldn't he. Something separate from the military, something they're not invited to. Should piss 'em off and make our message clear at the same time. The U.S. sides with business, the white collar stiff making a buck on commerce. What do you think, Phil?"

Phil raised his eyebrows and smiled broadly.

"Bob, that's just the thing. Good idea. We'll make our point and show the world where we stand. We'll invite the entire business community, but not the General or any of his hoods. He'll turn green and have a fit."

Bob smiled at Phil and hitched up his trousers.

"That's right, son," he said, "a real coup d'etat, Dodge will like it. You set it up, top to bottom, and I'll stamp it o.k. Just one thing."

Phil looked on, stuffing the intelligence brief back into his briefcase.

"What's that, Bob?"

"Get me a complete map of where the motorcade will travel. Personally, I'd rather they come up the Avenida Balboa to the Marriott. Keeps us in the, well, better part of town."

"Sure, Bob," Phil answered, clasping the case. "I get 'ya, keep the ol' Senator away from any possible harm."

"That's right, Phil," Bob puffed from behind the cigar. "Security, you can't beat it, not with a stick. Talk to you tomorrow, but not here. I'll meet you at the golf course. Ten o'clock fine?"

"Fine with me, Bob," Phil smiled.

13

For four hours the rains came sweeping down the crests of Cerro Azul. The tropical forest was wet to saturation with its dense foliage dripping from top to bottom, from the high trees above to the ferns and flowers under drooping wide-leaf shelter. As a prelude to the rainy season this strange day had begun as a muggy hot affair, but changed its course in the afternoon's passing as a coolness arrived from the oceans. The heavy clouds came in on the refreshing winds to pour out their soothing waters and everyone, from east to west in the winding isthmus, felt much relieved with their coming. In the mountains, not far from the city, a man lay back in a fresh, comfortable cot; to rest as the rains rolled off the canvas roof of his unfinished dwelling. And as evening slowly arrived, the man drifted in and out of a peaceful sleep, awakening but not moving each time the winds rose and the rains came harder. A most satisfyhing light breeze seemed to make its way up to his bare arms and face as he lay there deciding what to do. He would feel its cool touch in the gray and the quiet, and he would sleep again. Water was trickling down on a pile of stones at the edge of the dwelling nearest the almost jungle thickets at the border of his clearing. The sound added to his rapture.

In the city a group of children played on a makeshift porch as their mother fixed supper behind them. Cars splashed through the streets behind them and an occasional airplane or jet cruised through the skies overhead. The television was playing an American action drama with voices dubbed to Spanish. The children's mother watched as a crack team of adventurers infiltrated the dangerous realm of a Middle-Eastern fanatic and brought him to his knees. A group of Arab patriots were thanking the heroes as they boarded their plane to leave. Some street vendor or other was whining from a covered cart across the way, one of the children noticed and went over to the porch screen to take a look. Mother than called them to supper and the hungriest of the bunch took off running. A couple others stayed playing with their toys on the porch. In the kitchen they switched mother's channel to a cartoon.

Soon it was dark in the city and dark on the slopes of Cerro Azul. The man was sleeping deeply and would stay that way throughout the night and the shifting rains.

"You have come here tonight," Father Sandoval said, looking over the group of twelve, "to participate in an ancient and perpetual ritual of initiation. You have come here to lend your good minds and youthful strength to the cause of the Father. Tonight you will become Knights of Caravaca, and as such, you will take your places alongside some of the most illustrious gallant men in the annals of Christian history. To you, tonight, I offer the Light of our Holy Cross of Caravaca, and to your souls, eternal salvation. I offer you peace for the remainder of your lifetimes. Now hear, 'Semper in animo sapientis est placidissima pax', tonight you will learn."

Father Sandoval turned to light a candle on the altar. When the flame had passed from a flicker to brightness, he slowly turned back to face the twelve. Beyond them he saw the rains pouring from the eaves over the entrance. He heard the rains falling on the roof of the church. Miguel stood off to the side, quietly looking on.

"Do not think," Father Sandoval continued, "that it will be at all easy. It will not be. But you were chosen by the preceding generation, elders who watched you in your childhood and hand picked you as you grew in manhood. Your special treatment, the special masses, the instruction given apart from that given to the others, our retreats and the endless hours spent on history, which you so dearly loved, to a man, save the frustration of the questions we could not answer . . . for reasons you will now know . . . has been preparation for this our final hour of training. You are ready to guard the secrets we will now divulge. Listen carefully. First we will address the mind. Then the soul. The latter will require all of your great energies, for you will be taken to the limits of your concentration, to the extremes of your endurance."

The Holy Father paused and looked up as the rain intensified for a moment. He then looked over at a dark window and gazed sightlessly out into the night. The men before him were silent.

"When the bells tolled this afternoon," Father Sandoval went on, "the elders wept."

He looked down at his feet and smiled.

"They are awake now, looking out their windows, out their doors, in this direction. . . asking God why it hadn't been them. So be thankful," he said, raising his eyes to meet the staring faces before him, "you are the chosen, the blessed in God's eyes, and to you falls the task of perpetrating the glory of the Order. I will lead you where I can, but you must lead yourselves where I am not a worthy guide. You have said a full, high mass, you have each confessed, and you have each meditated at length in the way in which you have been instructed. Now we shall begin. All kneel."

The twelve knelt down on the hardwood floor and continued to watch Father Sandoval. Miguel disappeared momentarily from the altar area, then reappeared. He carried a number of red velvet robes trimmed in black to the participants kneeling before him.

Arias Hideaway

"I vote for the one with the big tits!" a private squealed, lifting his mug to his face and spilling beer down his chin.

"The dark one with the nice ass," another yelled from up front.

A well-dressed man standing beside the line of smiling, naked women, stretched his hand out triumphantly to his covey of beauties. The troops by poolside laughed and cheered. One of them, dressed only in a bathing suit, did an exaggerated swaying dance up to a tall woman in front. As he reached her, he extended his hips to rub his expanding penis on her shaven lips. The two gleefully mashed to the rhythm of rock music in the background, backs arced and bottoms at play. The rains rolled harmlessly off a canopy above.

"Take her by the pool, wild man!" somebody shouted.

"Show, show!" another yelped, half coughing on a mix of rum and coke.

"The best is yet to come!" the man in charge of the girls called out, attempting to stem the flow.

He raised his hands above his head and smiled without smiling.

"Hold on, boys!" he said as loudly as he could without screaming. In the nick of time a beefy sergeant stepped in between the troops and the girls, exhorting the enlisted men to control themselves. Enough did to return the event to a semblance of civilization. The girls began their dance again and wiggled past the pool. From the mansion a solitary man looked on from a second level room. He stood at the curtained window and watched the antics below.

"Ay!!" he heard one of the girls shout. "Ayyy!!! Get that, get it out of there!!!"

A sneaky bastard had crept up behind her and buried his finger up between her legs. He held her stomach and plunged it. The girl writhed and struggled to get loose.

"Stop that this instant!" the man with the women shouted, taking a bold step in the direction of the fracas.

The troops roared their objections as their sergeant advanced in the same direction.

"Stop it!" the sergeant barked as he approached. With both hands he pushed the buffoon into the pool.

The dancing girl scooted off to the side, walking bowleggedly as she complained loudly and rubbed at her intimates. The man watching from the second floor window turned away and motioned to a man standing in the doorway to come in. The man in the doorway hesitated, then entered.

"Yes, my Captain?" he asked.

The man who had watched from the window sat down and lit up a smoke.

"We have a big day tomorrow, of course, get these bastards into bed at a reasonable hour."

"Yes, Sir."

Renewed cheering from below and increased volume from the poolside stereo made the man glance back at the window. He smoked his cigarette for half a minute, then returned to give Lieutenant Cruz his full attention.

"So get to it."

"Yes, Sir, I'll go down below."

Captain Arias watched Cruz wheel and head for the door, then stopped him as he arrived.

"Cruz," he said softly.

The lieutenant stopped to listen, back still toward his superior.

"Yes, Sir?"

"Send me Santos, I'd like to talk to him."

Cruz slowly turned around.

"Santos left this evening, he went on a brief vacation. He said that he'll be back in a few days."

Arias choked on his cigarette and stood up quickly, grasping his throat.

"He what?"

"He . . . went off to see some relatives in Darien, said he would be back soon."

The Captain regained his control and swallowed. Crushing out the cigarette, he approached Cruz in the doorway. Arias stopped and studied the man for a moment.

"He isn't due for a vacation," the Captain said.

Cruz put on a serious expression, stern and officious.

"He's on vacation," he repeated, trying to avoid Arias' eyes.

Arias stared for an exceedingly uncomfortable minute.

"Was there . . . any time, Lieutenant Cruz . . . when Santos was separated from you in Penonome? I mean, did you let him out of your sight . . . as I asked you not to. . .?"

Cruz grew stiff.

"Maybe not, my Captain," he replied, wiping his mouth.

Captain Arias waited.

It sounded like a riot was breaking loose down at poolside. There were mixed male and female shouts and screams and someone had turned the stereo up full blast.

"Maybe for a minute," Cruz said, stepping up to his tiptoes and feigning interest in the celebration below the window. "I got . . . how shall I say . . . sidetracked once."

"For how long?" Arias asked.

"For maybe a half an hour," Cruz answered, following the ancient credo that when things are going bad, truth rights a listing ship.

"How?" Arias persisted.

"By a girl," Cruz snapped. "I fucked the notary's second cousin on his bed. But they didn't find anything. I know. My men would have told me."

Arias glanced over at the window and heard the revelry below, a score of whooping troops engaged in drunken battle.

"Your men," Captain Arias said, "your men."

Someone was smashing glass somewhere on the patio. Captain Arias sighed.

"The notary's second cousin . . . she just happened to be there?"

"Yes, Sir, quite a broad if I don't say so myself."

"Shut your fucking mouth," Arias replied, leaning up against his second in command, "and find Santos. Go now. Take as many sober bastards as we have . . . you asshole, the old man was on to something."

Cruz's eyes darted from side to side.

"Where . . . is he?" the lieutenant asked.

Arias steamed.

"Where the hell else? Get out to Penonome, to that damn Register. Find Santos but don't kill him. I have a better idea."

"Yes, Sir."

The rains continued to fall, shouts muffled in the lull, peaceful sound.

Panama City
Before Dawn
May 29, 1987

14

"My Colonel, I hate to keep bothering you with this nonsense, but it goes on and on. Last night Santos slipped away from Arias' place. He was alone. The boys lost him on the road back to, I suppose, Penonome. It was raining like hell. And now they tell me that our people in Penonome can't locate him. I have them spreading out all over Cocle. He's gone. The sleasy bastard has disappeared. I'm at a loss."

Quevedo had just finished his morning coffee and he was relaxing in his window chair. His back was turned to the lieutenant standing in the doorway. Quevedo rubbed his eyes.

"You say he left alone?"

"Yes, Sir. I am informed that he seemed to be sneaking out of the compound. He certainly did not make any farewell speeches. There was some kind of party going on. I am worried that we have lost him. He's good at hiding."

The Colonel poured himself a tall, cool glass of water from a jug on the window ledge. He examined the drink, then wet his lips.

"It's five thirty, Lieutenant, when was your last report?"

The Lieutenant glanced at his gold watch.

"I heard from them at two, my Colonel, I have not been back to communications since then. Why do you ask?"

The Colonel brushed at some lint on his pantleg and sniffed loudly.

"You'd best go back to communications. You're missing the best part."

The lieutenant squinted and looked puzzled.

'Pardon me, Sir?"

"Your people are following Arias' men now, Lieutenant Roma, at least I hope they are. You needn't find that pig Santos. Arias' people will lead you right to him. Get back on the horn and find out how far they're gone. If I'm not mistaken, this is something big. Keep me informed."

"Yes, Sir," the Lieutenant said, backstepping out of the office.

Seeing no further reaction from the Colonel, he hurried away to a back chamber of the building. When he was long gone, Colonel Quevedo picked up the phone and waited patiently, receiver at his ear, eyes staring out of the still dark morning window.

"Get me Captain Angel Mendez," he said at length, "get him right away. Tell him to report here immediately."

Later that morning. . . .

"There's a bigger picture here, Congressman," Bob managed through a mouthful of bloody Mary, "you've got to see the whole picture, everything in its context, it's not a simple who's right and who's wrong. That's not the world anymore."

The youthful, well-dressed man sitting in front of Bob looked on impassively as the latter tried to make his point.

"I mean, Congressman, I know the President wants this little jerk out the door, and I don't blame you for supporting him . . . the President, that is . . . you do agree with the President . . . I assume."

Bob winked and smiled, chilled glass in hand. He was seated in a splendid old chair at the edge of a huge indoor patio. Behind him spread the beautiful depths of the embassy, from room to hallway to lovely after lovelier shadowed chamber, the quiet good taste of some bygone artist. The Congressman showed no signs of amusement at Bob's crack about support. Bob took another drink and smiled.

"Sure you're a Democrat, Congressman, we all know that," he said, "and it ain't fashionable liking what the Pres likes, but you've got to agree with the old man. The sawed off pot-bellied cracker isn't making us any friends. It's just the timing I don't like, and that's where you've got to be flexible. With the goddamn Sandino blowing up in our face, and the Canal thing boiling, and the druggies and the M-19 crawling around in Colombia, and the whole Cuban geriatrics crowd looking for that one last haymaker . . . say, you've got to get on board here. I say, it's prudent to hold off a few months, let the thing rest for a while. What we don't need is a brand new explosion on our hands. Tell that to the President. I know you're an independent mind. The President doesn't make policy. That's up to the Congress, men with a vision like you and your fellow Representatives. We're all in agreement, but why rush in?"

The Congressman sat and stared.

"I'm not ignorant, Mr. Friedan," he said, "I keep myself informed. This is my area of specialty. Excellent sources have advised me regarding this whole rotten mess in power down here. These people are animals, Mr. Friedan, they are not human beings. I have read the Spadafora investigation ten or twelve times now, and it turns my stomach more with every reading. I have it from several reports that the man in power engineered General Torrijos death, rigged elections, jockeyed two other military people in and out of power, and now rides roughshod over a drug empire that expands south to Bolivia, and north to my constituency. What kind of man is this?"

"A bastard," Bob answered, swirling the ice in his drink, "a real honest to god bastard, the type that won't be easy to boot out, you'd better that that straight."

The Congressman looked away at an approaching maid with a tray of drinks.

"I'm no pansy, Mr. Friedan," he said with an air of security. "I can play as rough as the next man, and I'm in an excellent position to do it. No two bit dictator in his right mind would fool with me and my committee."

Bob smiled at the maid and reached up for a bloody Mary refill. The Congressman politely refused.

"No gracias," he said to the elderly Panamanian woman.

She nodded and backed away. From her style, Bob guessed that she'd been around for a long, long time. He remembered seeing her at a few embassy occasions.

"You've been working on your Spanish," Bob mumbled, following the woman away with his eyes.

"My Spanish is almost fluent," the Congressman corrected.

Bob agreed with a sweeping nod and went for the refill.

"Cheers."

They were getting closer, Bob Friedan understood. As he rubbed his finger up and down the bloody Mary he remembered how infrequent a junior Congressman's visit had been. In those days only the big boys had spoken out on marginal issues, such as . . . Panama. Nobody cared. Even through the thick and thin of Nicaragua, no one had even raised an eyebrow. Not even with the aid brigades to Sandino, the protesting en masse about Salvador . . . not through all of that had anyone as much as sneezed about . . . it hadn't been fashionable. It still wasn't, he conceded to himself, and at least he had that . . . but the old days were gone. He looked up at the suited thing in front of him and wondered at the peanut mind that powered the lanky frame. Bob knew he was a sinner, and he knew it was winding down to a desperate finish, but to have to listen to a pompous idiot. . . .

"I'm going to insist on some changes, Mr. Friedan, immediately. This can't go on. Whatever resources are needed, we must provide them. The good people of this land can't be abandoned in their struggle for freedom. Solidarity, that's the word. I'm in favor of a solution."

"Me too," Bob nodded, gazing out at the patio. He had often admired the peace of the place. There were flowers there he hadn't even seen anywhere else.

"Fill me in," the Congressman said, edging forward in his chair, "you are intelligence here. Who killed Torrijos?"

Bob slowly turned his eyes back from the patio to look at the man. He smacked his lips and studied the Congressman.

"I don't know," he replied.

Bob's guest waited for an elaboration. Seeing that Friedan would not continue, he went on.

"Fine, I'll take 'I don't know' for an answer. Who killed Hugo Spadafora?"

"Some drug lords, Congressman."

Bob again grew mute after the terse answer. The Congressman shifted position in his chair.

"So, Mr. Intelligence, then who rules the narcotics kingdom in these parts?"

"Your good old American idle rich, Congressman, they're the buyers. Without them, coke would sprout, bud, leaf, wilt, and wither. No denying that simple fact of life. You want to control coke, you put the fear of god in your small town doctors and lawyers, your businessmen on the fast track, your kids in school. These people are supplying the alcoholic with his booze. You don't ban liquor. That didn't work at all. I know who killed Spadafora, and I know why. He'd been busy fanning the flames of a hot war that cost a lot of good kids their lives, running back and forth from Panama to Costa Rica with his words of wisdom. He was fucking around in a jungle. He got eaten alive. That's what you must tell yourself very clearly every day you go out to do something dirty; the shit may end up on your own face. And when it does, you bite your dead lips and kiss your ass good-bye. People who live that way accept it. He didn't. He figured he was special. When the devil called in his chips, and Spadafora was riding on one, the whole world should have known, should not have wept. You play with fire . . . count old Omar Torrijos as one of the key players. For him, it ended fast. So fast he never knew the end had come. Lucky bastard. . . ."

Bob caught himself and noticed the Congressman's expression, somewhere between astonishment and anger. He ended the oratory and sipped at his drink.

"Sorry, Congressman, I got carried away. A hood named Santos killed Spadafora, he was an intelligence agent under Captain Gustavo Arias, Fourth Infantry. *Is* an intelligence agent, I should say . . . there were several other hoods present, but what's the diff', it could have been anyone. The murder was ordered by Colonel Anastasio Quevedo, the actual order probably came from higher up. It took six hours for Hugo to die, that wasn't part of the order . . . it was to be shocking, but cleaner than that . . . things got out of hand. The Torrijos death was caused by a bomb placed in a radio transmitter on the plane he was flying. The drugs we haven't been able to crack, but signs don't point to the top, here. They point to foreigners."

"Bullshit," the official snapped, "bullshit and you know it. The ugly little strutting man on top is guilty, and I aim to prove it."

"I wish you luck," Bob replied, now partially glassy eyed. He didn't like to get that way in the morning, but sometimes it was inevitable.

"Senator Dodge is coming soon," the Congressman went on, "and we expect to get some action then. We're counting on your organization to carry the ball, if you know what I mean."

Bob looked up and leaned back into his comfortable chair.

"Who else knows about this?" he asked, "other than you, Congressman?"

"Just a chosen few," the Congressman answered, straightening his tie.

Bob lowered his head and cleared his throat.

"Good, Congressman, we'll be standing by to help out. Count on me."

The Congresssman stood up and, buttoning his suit jacket, strode off toward the hallway. Bob licked his lips and placed the bloody Mary remains on a table beside him.

* * * *

"Colonel, you were right, Arias' men hit the road just after my last communication. They're all headed to Penonome, so it seems."

"Then follow them, Lieutenant Roma. Go personally and meet your men wherever they may end up. Find out what's going on and tell me as soon as you know something. Go. Go now."

"Yes, Sir, I'm on my way."

The lieutenant had to salute twice on the way out. Once in exit to his superior officer, and once on the way by a smiling Captain Angel Mendez.

"You called for me, Colonel?"

"Yes, sit down, Captain, we have much to discuss."

Panama City
Seat of the Audiencia of Panama
Viceroyalty of Peru
November, 1670

15

"The bastards are coming! They're coming here! We saw them! They're on their way! Damn you, why won't you listen?!?"

"You'll hold your tongue!!" the high official and object of the verbal assault answered, half rising from his chair and leaning out across the table to shake a finger in the face of the speaker. Several guards half raised their pikes and their sergeant stepped up beside the angry young man now staring the President of the Audiencia in the eye. The young man lifted his chin stiffly, then backed off. Pulling his coat lapels together, he glanced haughtily at the Sergeant of the Guard and resumed speaking.

"It would be a crime to remain silent, Your Grace," he said, looking at the President again.

Don Juan Perez de Guzman eased back into his chair and studied the man before him, a young officer recently arrived in Panama from Cartagena.

"These are the same animals who stripped Dona Agustina de Rojas of Portobelo after their treacherous invasion," the officer went on. "They put her in a tub, filled it with gunpowder, then threatened to touch her off if she didn't reveal the whereabouts of her jewels."

"I am aware of what happened at Portobelo," the President said, stroking his silk collar. "I needn't be reminded."

The officer's eyes lit up again. He took a half-step forward.

"Then if you are aware . . ." he said incredulously, "what are you going to do about it?"

Don Juan tilted his head to the side and motioned to the Sergeant of the Guard.

"I will begin by tossing you in jail for a week or so, perhaps you will learn something about respect . . . take him away, Sergeant."

"Yes, Sir," the Sergeant replied, seizing the young officer with the help of his guards.

The man continued to stare at the President as he was dragged out of the chamber.

When calm had been restored, and the judicial chamber almost emptied, the President adjusted the buttons of his robe and summoned a remaining soldier to stand before him. The soldier walked quietly over from his position and bowed.

"Yes, Your Grace."

"Go find that Corregidor who came over from Portobelo last year. I wish to speak with him."

"Yes, Your Grace, immediately."

The President watched the man walk away and turned to look at a military officer and a clergyman seated together at a far end of the table. The President waited for a moment, then spoke.

"So their presence is confirmed?" he asked of the military man.

"That is correct, Sir," the man answered, "their invading fleet advances in nearby waters, they are not far from San Lorenzo on the other side of the isthmus."

"I see," the President mumbled, looking down at the table. The heat in his chambers was beginning to grow uncomfortable. He usually ended his hearings before that hour, but that day was an exception. Soft winds curled around the structure outside blowing the leaves of trees in the windows. The air was not moving inside, however.

"How many of them are there?," Don Juan Perez de Guzman asked. The military man shrugged.

"A few ships, maybe two or three hundred of the corsair scum, no more, certainly no more. They are here adventuring, nothing more."

"Adventuring?" the President asked, turning his eyes to the military man again. "After what happened at Portobelo, you call this a band of adventurers?"

"Corsairs," the military man answered, "not an invading army. This is not a group that would or even could cross the isthmus to attack us. They are seafarers, and as such they would have to sail down around the deadly horn to reach us, a journey I do not believe a buccaneer would relish. Portobelo was there for the picking, what with its defenses all unattended and its soldiers off carousing and hard pressed to stay sober. They rolled the place over. I do not compare that sleepy hollow to the City of Panama."

The President cleared his throat and loosened his collar just a bit. He was beginning to feel queasy from the heat.

"Gentlemen, there is a need to continue this conversation, but I am inclined to remove it from these sweltering halls. Shall we walk together to my seaside patio?"

The two at the far end of the table expressed their instant approval by nodding and scraping their chairs noisily across the floor as they rose. It seemed that they were anxious to make the President's words a fait accompli before he could change his mind. Slowly, with dignity, the President stood up from his chair and smoothed his clothing. Setting his jaw firmly, he gestured in the direction of a stone arched door facing the sea. The three filed out together.

On that limpid fine day the waves were taller and more agitated than usual. The surf broke in surging white thrusts and the winds were fresh and gusty. Sparkling white clouds rushed in from the ocean and the place had a hopeful look, a look that teased the minds of dreamers and quietly refreshed the warm faces of the working city crowd. It was as if Panama had entered into a new era, now abandoning its sticky, hot past. Tomorrow one could expect more of the same.

"Let's sit here," the President said, holding his hands on his hips.

Before him were a half dozen or so stone tables, all beautifully crafted. The President's two companions arrived at one of them, but remained standing in deference to their superior. Don Juan Perez de Guzman motioned to them to sit down. While they seated themselves, he looked out at the ocean and frowned.

"A nice day," he muttered, grasping a chair and lowering his stiff body down. "A nice day."

Three soldiers had followed them and now stood at a distance of about twenty meters, discreetly out of earshot should a sensitive matter be discussed. The company sat in the shade of a stand of palms. Salt air rose around them.

"Exactly why did Henry Morgan sack Portobelo?" the President asked, studying the distant horizon.

The military man, the recipient of the question, shook his head.

"You cannot predict the actions of these lowlifes," he said, "they are illogical and ungodly, who knows what they think."

The President raised an eyebrow.

"They exacted an enormous sum in ransom from my . . . predecessor, I'll give them credit for that, even though ransom was an afterthought. But why," he continued, "why Portobelo when he did? It was empty of valuables. The great fleets had come and gone, the gold and silver had already been shipped to his Majesty in Spain. Then, in the in-between, along comes a pompous Englishman looking for gold. It doesn't make sense. If he'd asked anybody in Jamaica they would have told him. The Imperial Fleet's coming and going is no great secret. Here for years I thought the English had spies tracking the fleet's every move. Six days every so many years, that's when Portobelo's alive . . . no, let's give it two weeks, what with all the loading and unloading. . . ."

"A month's activity," the military man said, now also looking out to the sea, "a good month in all."

"Exactly," the President insisted. He had brought his eyes back from the coastal waters to look at his companions. He leaned forward in his chair.

"Just a month. But Morgan doesn't show up for the fat catch . . . he shows up during the doldrums . . . the town was empty . . . there was nothing there, nobody around."

Two seabirds squawked overhead, gliding in the winds and trying to peck at one another. The third partner, the clergyman, looked up and watched them.

"Maybe he knew all about the fleet's movement, the gold shipments, the Portobelo Fair," he said.

His words caught the attention of both the President and the military man. They looked at the clergyman and waited for what followed.

"Maybe . . . he was after something else," he concluded.

"What the hell else could a corsair want than gold and silver?" the military man asked.

The clergyman remained silent, looking down at his feet and then away to the waves. Don Juan Perez de Guzman watched him closely.

"Yes . . . what?" he prompted.

Too long a moment passed and the President grew impatient.

"Go on, Lord Bishop, what are you getting at?"

"Nothing," the military man intervened, "the question doesn't need an answer. When the gold is shipped from Panama City to Portobelo across the isthmus, when Peru has sent us its wealth, the entire Spanish armada is here to protect it, with thousands of men and guns to blow a puny lad like Henry Morgan into a million smithereens. It's no secret."

The clergyman, the Bishop, smiled.

"Yes, that's true," he said. "No defying that logic. And the English have contented themselves with scraps from the table. Mansfield, Parker, even Drake. Sir Francis attacked a mule-train in the isthmus one night thinking he was on to a gold shipment. His cutthroats slashed open a dozen or so sacks of grain . . . flour or something. He left much chagrined. But now Drake lies buried in a lead tomb off that dead, hot port, away down deep beneath the waters. Drake was a Knight of the English Crown, and a rich man, besides. What brought him here again after leading the English to such an astonishing victory over our Armada Invincible? Ask yourselves that."

"The Armada Invincible was not defeated," the military man interjected. "That was a skirmish, an impromptu battle in unfamiliar waters."

The Bishop smiled.

"Get to the point, Your Reverence," the President said, now very much absorbed in the mystery at hand.

"The point is," the Bishop said, "that there is something else these sturdy hearts are after. Something infinitely more attractive than your run of the mill plunder and rapine. I believe these scoundrels are after a prize so great they would risk their souls to get at it. That is my belief."

The military man shook his head and mumbled something inaudible but plain. The President sat there staring, engrossed by the remarks he had heard. Soon, though, he was distracted by an announcement from behind.

"Don Francisco Luna, Your Grace, Corregidor of Portobelo."

The President turned and looked, then acknowledged the newcomer's presence with a slight nod. The Corregidor performed a deep bow, arm sweeping in a wide half circle before him.

"Don Juan," he said on the way up, "I am honored."

"Come join us and sit down," the President replied.

A servant had arrived with refreshments and a light lunch. The man served the Bishop first, then moved on to the military man, who accepted a beverage but waved away the solid nourishment, slices of cold meats with relishes of different varieties in a ring around them. Like the military man, the Corregidor took a beverage, but declined the meat. While taking his first sip from the drink he produced a perfumed handkerchief and patted at his cheek. He was a man in his mid to late fifties, slender and well-preserved. His manners were exquisitely those of a courtier, and his bearing was deference. The President thought him effeminate. He studied the Corregidor closely.

"What happened at Portobelo, Don Francisco, tell us in your own words."

The Corregidor brushed at his lips with his handkerchief and assumed an attentive pose.

"You have read . . . the report of His Majesty's 'Visita', I am sure," he said tentatively.

Don Juan Perez de Guzman frowned and repeated the question.

"I asked . . . tell us what happened at Portobelo. Of course I have read the report of His Majesty's official 'Visita'. Much finger pointing and a lot of evasive answers. I want it in your own words. You were there. You have much to tell us. The bastards are back, now. What can we expect?"

The Corregidor raised a finger and studiously made a point.

"You are exactly right, Lord President, much tattling on others and few straight answers, I was appalled at the. . . . "

"Can you just tell me," the President asked, also raising a finger, "what happened at Portobelo?"

The Corregidor cleared his throat and swept his handkerchief across his forehead.

"Yes, of course. I shall never forget it. We were warned of the corsairs' presence in the North Sea by a letter from the capital, here in Panama. I showed the correspondence to the Mayor of Portobelo, Don Andres Fernandez, but he was not interested. I then approached the Castellan of Santiago de la Gloria. Again, no interest. Then one morning I was confronted by a young soldier by the name of Benitez. He and his comrades had been out on a scouting mission up the coast in a supply yawl. It seems they had seen many corsair ships."

The Corregidor, now aware that he occupied center stage amidst the small group, paused to examine his handkerchief.

"I knew immediately that his information was accurate," he said. The courtly man lowered his handkerchief and put on a serious expression.

"It was no use. I could not convince the Mayor or the Castellan that the danger was real."

"Why?" the President asked. "Why wouldn't they believe that danger was imminent?"

"I believe," the Corregidor began, again raising his finger, "I believe that they had grown so complacent that the mere thought of trouble was alien to their essence. My exhortations were of little consequence. When the moment came, the dog Morgan was upon us. There was little to the defense."

The President sat back in his chair and look amazed.

"Portobelo . . .," he said, "was designed by the finest military architect of the epoch. It has three major forts and a number of other, lesser fortifications. Good Lord, San Jeronimo, the Castle of Santiago de la Gloria, San Felipe, the Iron Castle, those structures are monuments to military genius. The port is impenetrable. Properly defended, Portobelo could laugh at the entire English fleet. Nombre de Dios was another matter. It was a pushover. But Portobelo . . . what do you mean there was little to the defense?"

The Corregidor shook his head.

"Little that *manned* the defense," he mused. "Wet gunpowder, no one at their posts at the onset of the hostilities, the complete lack of a plan, the fortifications proved ludicrous. Morgan attacked by land, not by sea. He came across from somewhere near the Chagres . . . I don't know."

The group was silent in the breezes and the pleasant, lovely day. The Corregidor went on.

"He descended on us in the early hours. Everyone was asleep. By daybreak the bulk of the matter was over. There was a siege of Santiago Castle, but the castle fell before midday. The rest was savagery. Houses were looted, women violated, gentlemen tortured for information regarding their personal wealth . . . horrible."

"Where did Morgan go first when he arrived?" the Bishop asked.

The Corregidor looked over at the holy man and produced his perfumed handkerchief again.

"He . . . went to the church, Your Reverence. That is what I have heard. They later made the church a prison for the people. But come to think of it, when I arrived at the church, it had been turned upside down. Everything inside it was a shambles. Strange."

The courtier puzzled on the observation as the Bishop lowered his head.

"Did Morgan find much . . . gold and silver in Portobelo?" the latter asked.

"No, he did not," the Corregidor replied. "His only gain, so to speak, was the ransom money sent over from Panama after the invasion. I saw Morgan many times. He was aggravated by the circumstances. There was little gold and silver in Portobelo when he came. I explained to him about the ships and how they come and go in fleets every two or three years, but he seemed to know all of that."

"You fraternized with Morgan?" the military man asked, suddenly sitting up.

The Corregidor waved his hand aside and closed his eyes in disdain.

"Of course not," he replied, "I was only . . . collecting information for the Royal Crown, I was one of the few present who spoke English."

"You know what I think," the military man began, but he was interrupted by the President.

"Quiet," he said. "Tell me, what was at the church that Morgan could have wanted?"

The Corregidor looked thoughtful.

"Nothing of great value," he answered.

The Bishop now sat gazing off at the sea. Slowly, with seemingly great effort, he rose from his chair and smiled weakly.

"Forgive me," he said, "I must go now. I have . . . preparations to make."

The President, Don Juan Perez de Guzman, rose with him and leaned out to kiss the Bishop's ring.

"God be with you," the Bishop said, making the sign of the cross in the direction of the others. He departed along a path leading down close to the seaside. The assembled company watched him go. When he was quite a ways away, the President turned to the military man and rubbed his hands together.

"How many Spanish soldiers would you need," he asked thoughtfully, "if you were planning to raid and destroy the City of Panama?"

The military man threw up his hands and shrugged.

"What kind of question is that, Don Juan, I. . . ."

"How many men would you need to take the City of Panama?" the President insisted.

The military man grasped his chin with his hand and uttered a "hmmmmm" sound.

"Four or five thousand men, I believe. But why do you ask such a question?"

He looked up at the President. The President looked back at the Bishop, now only a silhouette in the distance against the afternoon bright sea.

"Then the English are coming with two thousand men. They're coming here, to the City of Panama. Organize the defense."

"But Don Juan," the military man protested, "Don Juan, they must first deal with the fort at San Lorenzo, and I swear they shall not pass."

The Corregidor opened his eyes wide and discreetly viewed the two men before him. Behind them in the city the laborers were preparing for their early afternoon slumber.

The President had a final question.

"The young soldier . . . Benitez? That was his name."

"Yes, My Lord, Benitez."

"What happened to him. He died in the defense?"

"Uh . . . no, My Lord, he did not. It seems young Benitez went over to the corsairs and joined forces with Morgan. The last I saw of him, he was marching away with the Englishmen."

The President stared at the Corregidor and grimaced.

"You there! Yes, you!"

The military man's sudden outburst surprised the President and the Corregidor. They looked in his direction and followed his gaze and pointing finger out to a young woman standing a short distance from him on the edge of the patio. The military man turned in his chair and quivered.

"Seize the wretch, the vile spy!" he was saying to the Majordomo, a tall mestizo directing the servants.

The woman had been sweeping.

"Sir," the Majordomo said, taking an uncertain step toward the woman. "I do not understand."

"I said, seize her!" the military man shouted again. "She is a spy and a traitor! Seize her!"

The Majordomo bowed and together with two other male servants walked over to the woman in question. She dropped her broom and stared at the military man. The servants took a hold of her arms and marched back to where the military man was seated.

"What is the meaning of this?" the President asked.

The Corregidor look on curiously.

"This woman, this low life mulatta, she was here behind us all the while. She is a spy, I tell you, she was listening in on state secrets." The Majordomo looked puzzled. The other servants stood by nervously and watched the scene.

The woman, approximately twenty-four years of age, was dressed in the typical style of tropical courtly service, white, full-length dress with short, airy sleeves and a small bustle. Yet the Corregidor, before the President, saw something remarkable in the unfolding occurrence. The woman was very lovely, very graceful and dignified of bearing. She looked at her accuser with troubled dark eyes.

"What in heavens name can this be all about?" the President insisted.

The military man looked up at the woman and sneered.

"I don't know," he said softly, "but we soon shall find out. Take her to my residence, my good man."

He motioned to the Majordomo.

"Yes, Sir."

"My Lord, I am not a. . . ."

"Silence!!" The military man interrupted her in mid-response and motioned once more to the Majordomo.

"Away, get her out of my sight! We shall see later just what evil plans she had in mind."

The Majordomo and his company dragged the woman off. The President look astonished.

"Extraordinary," the Corregidor remarked, sitting back into his chair and marveling with an amused smile.

"I still don't understand," the President said.

"Believe me," the military man replied, holding up a hand, "I know about these things. You can't be too careful. I had my eye on that scoundrel from the moment we walked out here."

"I'll bet you did," the Corregidor mumbled to himself.

"Just leave it all to me, she'll cough up her secrets before I'm done."

A sea breeze pushed by them gently and the sound of breakers rose to their ears in the silence. Behind them near old Panama a church bell tolled and a donkey brayed twice, loudly, far enough away to make the noise pleasant.

"But as I was saying," the military man continued, "the scum will die during the seige they will wage on the castle at San Lorenzo. I shall be expecting good news."

"As shall I," the President agreed, watching the young woman being hauled off by the Majordomo and associates, "as shall I."

8 p.m.

It was the right time of the tropical night for one's customary walk outside, that fulfilling of an urge to take advantage of the only real coolness the steamy hotlands had to offer. That night the sky was close and dark overhead, and there was an odd sense of slow, cumbersome movement in the clouds. The occasional bonfire in the thereabouts of the city reflected off a kind of oppressive ceiling, a weighty, tiresome stagnant mass. The heavens spilled thickly from the skies onto the rooftops and the lanes. Old Panama was ready for a walk. In one residence, however, there was no thought of leaving. The stuffiness of the air inside the stale mansion, made all the more intolerable by the smells left over from some foul meal, kidney, no doubt, gave rise to some manner of desperation.

"Why don't you tell me your name, young lady," the military man said quietly, raising a cup of red wine to his lips.

The mulatta woman stood calmly before him and met his gaze with a defiant stare.

"Aurora," she said tersely.

"Aurora, splendid!" the military man chortled, wine caught up somewhere sticky at mid-throat.

He took a moment to cough and arrange his voice. Then he smiled, teeth gleaming.

"And what, pray tell, is your surname?"

"Alvarado," she replied without hesitation.

The military man nodded and took another sip of his wine.

"And . . . you have a mother?" he asked, eyeing his find. "Do you . . . have maternal lineage?"

"Drake," the woman snapped, again without pause.

The military man looked surprised. He lowered his cup of wine and wet his lips.

"Drake? But how marvelous, how marvelous . . . that is a joke, no doubt. . . ."

"Drake!" she repeated.

A native servant cleaning up around the dinner table stopped what he was doing momentarily and looked on.

"My name is Aurora Alvarado de Drake," the woman went on, "now may I leave, my Lord? I have done nothing and I wish to return to my house."

"Not so fast," the military man smiled, fingering the wine cup and examining its contents. "You will remember who you are talking to, and you will show some respect . . . you do know who I am?"

The woman looked around and made a face.

"You are Don Francisco de Haro, many know of you."

"Yes," the military man replied, "many know of me, and for the present, we shall discuss your presence on the patio today and your insolent spying on affairs of state. You could be hanged for that, you know? . . ."

"May I leave, your Grace?" the woman asked again with the same defiant tone.

Don Francisco shook his head.

"Of course not," he said bluntly. "Get used to it, this will be your home for some time to come."

He glanced over at the servant looking on.

"And what are you staring at?"

" . . . Nothing, my Lord, I . . . was just finishing up."

"Get out of here and leave us alone."

"Yes, Sir, immediately."

"And close the door to this room."

"As you wish, your Grace."

The military man watched him back out of the room, securely latching the doors as soon as he had left. In a moment he looked back at the young woman.

"The night is long, you are here for as long as I would like, and you had best get used to it."

Aurora looked down at the floor and softly sighed. She closed her eyes and her shoulders went limp.

"Sit here on my footstool," the military man said.

The woman slowly raised her eyes to follow his pointing finger.

On at least one balcony the heat wasn't so bad. Two servants, seeing their master preoccupied with affairs of state, stole upstairs and found their way in through the darkness to a breeze that moved the curtains silently in the night. In whispers and hushed tones of giggles mixed with notes of caution, the couple tiptoed out into the fresh air and surveyed the quiet city. Away in the distance they made out the center of the town and the lights, the many lights, that told of life in progress. He held her close and she held him back and the two were soon in rapture in retreat from the drudgery and hot management of a clean, proper house. Soon they were kissing, and soon his hands made an anxious pass to where they shouldn't have. . . .

"Mario, ya!"

He muttered something and she gave him a stern look.

"Es que, yo. . . ."

"I, nothing, behave yourself."

The young man frowned and kissed her on the bridge of the nose. The young woman caressed him tenderly and smiled.

"Eres mi amor," she murmured, eyes alive and full of mischief.

The young man pulled her even closer and gazed off into the night. No moon, no stars, just a carpet of thick, dense ink and rolling steam above. He closed his eyes and smiled.

"Ya pronto," he whispered.

The fragrance of flowers rose up to the balcony from below and lingered in their presence.

"I am from Portobelo," Aurora said quietly, "that is my home. But my family is from Nombre de Dios. We are simple people from the coast. That is all I can tell you."

The military man sat watching her.

"So . . . why are you here?" he asked.

The woman stared at his skinny stockinged legs and buckled leather shoes and shook her head.

"Because the corsairs came and chased us away," she said.

The military man poured himself another drink of wine and listened intently. Holding the fresh cup up to eye level, he stared off through the cup to a point well beyond it.

"You would not have been mistreated . . . I mean, the corsairs have a liking for . . . white women . . . they much prefer them to women of color . . . why did you flee? . . ."

"You see color in me," she said, "and nothing else. . . ." She paused. The military man looked back at her.

"And beauty," he said.

Aurora arranged her skirt and looked him in the eyes.

"Some corsair liked women of color, or are you blind as well as stupid?"

The military man shot her a furious glance.

"Best hold your tongue, you harlot," he snarled, "you are in the presence of a Knight of the Crown."

Aurora took a deep breath and leaned back on the stool. She continued watching her new master.

"How did you come to Panama?" he insisted.

"On foot," Aurora answered, "in the company of an old friend, also of color. . . ."

"You will," the military man said with a determined stare, "learn your place . . . or I will have you hung . . . tonight . . . now answer my questions. Why are you here?"

Aurora looked desperate.

"Because the corsairs came, my Lord, they overran and sacked Portobelo, they killed many and hurt many more. What more reason do you want?"

"I saw . . .," the military man said, now rising to his feet, "a most unusual expression cross your face when the Corregidor of Portobelo mentioned the name of one Benitez, a turncoat gone over to the corsair filth. Your eyes fairly popped out of your head. Now what was the meaning of that emotion?"

Aurora grew uncomfortable and shifted away from the military man's penetrating stare.

" . . . I fail . . .," she said, "to understand your Grace's remarks."

"Then I shall repeat the question," Don Francisco said. "Why did you look so surprised when the Corregidor mentioned the name of this Benitez? Do you know him? Is he your friend? He was from Protobelo, like you. Now, however, he is in the service of the enemy. What is this all about?"

Aurora nodded her head.

"Yes, I know him," she remarked casually, regaining her presence. "He is from Portobelo. He was a good soldier."

The military man squinted and leaned out toward the young woman seated in front of him.

"Go on," he said calmly.

Aurora was now watching a far window.

"There's nothing more than that. I last saw him the night the pirates were arriving. He ran off to the city's defense. He was gallant and a soldier, a loyal subject of his Majesty. I do not believe this nonsense about his going over to the English."

"But the Corregidor confirms it," Don Francisco said, sitting down.

"I do not know why," Aurora replied.

A candle on the dining room table sputtered and cast an eerie shadow on the two. The military man glanced around and saw that other candles were also burning down. He cleared his throat and sat back a bit in his chair. Raising his cup, he finished off the wine. In a moment he reached over to a nearby table and grasped a fine glass decanter holding a splendid French brandy. He lifted the decanter, poured himself a little more than one would normally pour, and returned the vessel to its place.

A procession of low-lifes passed close by the house on a lane not far away. They were singing and carousing in the way of the village people, and their voices played crisply through the dense air and warmth of the night. The military man at first look irritated, but as the group passed he eased back in his chair and closed his powdered eyelids. Aurora watched him relax. He soon began to smile.

"Not the last, mind you, but the time before, the convening of His Majesty's fleets at Panama, the silver shipments from Peru . . . not much gold anymore . . . you should have been there . . . but you are so young. You were just a girl. What a celebration. The entire vice-regal court in passing . . . from Lima to Spain. The music, the pomp, such as this city has never seen. It was a week to remember . . . ah, me."

The man remained there for a long minute, eyes closed, body slumped back, mind off on a journey in time and fantasy. A hearty but now distant cheer brought back the merriment outside for an instant, but the night closed in on the inner room of Don Francisco de Haro's mansion, leaving Aurora alone with the spindly man and his dreams. When he opened his eyes again, and came back to the stuffiness of it all, Aurora was looking at him. Don Francisco took a deep sip of brandy and sized her up. Arrogance returned to his expression.

"I sense this vagabond was your lover. You were a kept woman." Aurora's eyes flashed.

"He was a gentleman, and he was my friend," she said.

"And you, are a harlot," the military man remarked, taking another sip.

"You," Aurora began, rising to her feet, "are a beastly liar and an improper gentleman. My family is free and I am not a servant or a slave."

"An educated slut," the pretentious man mused, closing his eyes again. "Let me guess, the missionary school."

Aurora was furious.

"I am a free woman and by law I need not be here. I demand that you let me go."

"You are in a position to demand nothing," Don Francisco laughed, "you are here at my command, and this is an interrogation. This Benitez, he is leading the English scum to Panama, is that not correct?"

Aurora stared at him. She was breathing hard and her lips quivered.

"If he is, my Grace, then find shelter," she said in a low voice. "From what I saw at Portobelo, and from what I am looking at here tonight, the Englishmen will take you at breakfast time, and dine here in your quarters on the eve of the same day. And if I am here when they arrive, you had best hope that Armando Benitez is not with them as his Grace the Corregidor predicts. Then I would pity you."

The military man came alive suddenly, eyes opening wide, muscles stiffening. He sat us straight, then rose from his chair. He put the brandy down and walked up to the woman before him.

"Do you really think I am afraid of a turncoat and a band of illdisciplined, ungodly cutthroats? I have campaigned in Europe, you filthy whore, and I have supped with His Majesty Charles in the Royal Court, how dare you insinuate that I am less of a man than a rowdy in the service of a corsair?"

The two stood face to face. Aurora backed off not an inch.

"Words, Don Francisco, wine and words, so cheap." His expression changed from stern, to angry, then to wildly irate. Don Francisco de Haro's hand shot up through the air to slap the young woman's face. She ducked, though, and he missed. Stumbling forward, he almost pitched head first onto the floor. At the last moment he seized a table with his hand. Aurora, who had shown remarkable agility, stood beside him. She backed off a step as the Spanish gentleman recovered his balance.

"Slow, my Lord," she laughed, " you'll have to do better than that!"

"You'll pay for this," the military man said, standing up straight.

"I'm sure I will," Aurora said calmly, "but I have to make an effort, otherwise, it wouldn't be right."

Livid, Don Francisco advanced toward her.

"Harlot," he menaced, "daughter of a whore, daughter of a whore's whore, it must be in your blood!"

Aurora evaded another clumsy feint, then smiled again.

"One more generation, my Lord, back to my mother's mother's mother. There's the whore."

"You will obey me!!" the man screamed, lunging in her direction.

Aurora moved quickly, turned and lifted her skirts. Don Francisco missed again, this time landing full force on a low table and crushing it with his weight. Slightly stunned, the wind knocked out of him, he lay there staring at her, gasping for breath.

"Drake, you filthy swine," she whispered, "back again, how about that?"

The young woman lifted her left hand and examined a heavy gold ring on the index finger, a ring way too large for her hand.

"Guards!!" the military man bellowed, oblivious to the young woman's words, "Guards!! Here!! At once!!!"

Aurora clutched the ring and glanced around. It was useless. The windows were everywhere barred and sealed.

Suddenly, guards rushed in. Their leader, a young man Aurora's age, sized up the situation. Tense when he had entered the room at a run, the of-

ficer relaxed a bit and lowered his head. Don Francisco was pulling himself up off the floor and cursing. Aurora stood there watching the man get up.

"My Lord," the officer began.

"Seize the whore!" Don Francisco shouted.

The officer reluctantly summoned his men with a wave of the hand and walked over to the young woman. Slowly, almost apologetically, he reached out and held her arm. Don Francisco strutted up, brushing off the dust.

"Take her to my quarters," he said firmly. "Bind her and leave her there. Then you may go."

"Yes, Sir," the officer sighed, leading her away.

The guards looked at one another, at the woman, and at Don Francisco.

"What . . . is the meaning of this?!?"

The servant lovers, startled in their embrace, looked from the balcony where they held one another to see Renaldo, their master's head housekeeper. In the dim light afforded them by the single candle inside the bedroom, and the low, reflected light from the city, they saw the slender, proper man standing there over them, mouth puckered in pious disapproval.

"Using the Master's balcony as a nest for filthy lusting? I declare, this is disgraceful!"

The young male servant looked at the effeminate butler and frowned.

"Get lost, Reynaldo, this is a private thing."

"Private?" Renaldo repeated, holding his head back, eyes opening wide, "in our Lordship's very chambers?"

He looked down at the girl.

"With bosoms exposed and skirts half way off? Private? Why, you ought to be ashamed of yourselves! Outrageous! Simply outrageous! If I were you, I would leave here immediately! The Master could return any minute now!"

He sniffed loudly and turned to go, pausing for an instant to adjust the curtains. With an unceremonious yelp and a little leap straight up into the air, he reached back and patted his bum. It seems he had received a little pinch.

"How . . . dare you!" he barked at the young servant on the balcony, turning to confront him.

The young servant laughed. Beside him his companion had completely removed her blouse. The butler looked shocked and put his cupped hand to his mouth. The young servant followed his gaze to the woman's breasts. He laughed again.

"Disgusting, isn't it?" he asked. "But you could not possibly be interested in that. Leave us alone."

"You just wait and see!" the butler gasped, backing away. "The Master will be by soon, then you'll pay for this impetuous behavior."

"The Master will be by when he is finished with his bottle," the servant smiled, returning to the task at hand, "either staggering or on the back of a guard. Either way, we'll long be finished."

"But not too quickly," the young woman chirped, laying an arm around her lover's shoulders.

The butler cursed and shuffled off through the bedroom.

"Rowdies!" he called out softly as he headed for the door. In a moment, he was gone.

The Corregidor found himself in an unusual place that night. Wandering out late, he took an old pathway that led down to the seashore. There he walked slowly along, just above the gentle, breaking surf, looking out to sea at the dark swells and rollers advancing toward his shores. Stopping for a moment, the Corregidor squinted at something farther out, something that seemed to bob and rise just at the limit of his vision. A ship, perhaps a small boat, the light was far too faint for him to discern exactly what was there. The Corregidor looked down at his shoes and a bit of foam that had made it to his feet. Then he sighed and moved along.

Behind him in the city he could still hear shouts and an occasional peal of merriment, no doubt remnants of the earlier evening celebrations so customary of the city's cooling after-hours. From seaward there were no sounds save the waters tossing in the darkness. Above there were no birds, before him only a furtive scurrying albino crab or two safely beyond all danger. The Corregidor walked on and on along the beach. Seaweed and a castaway ship's timber kept his eye on sands approaching his feet.

In distant Oviedo the Asturianos were sitting by hearths in the chill evening quiet. Day done, they would be recounting a price in the market, an excellent trade, a deal gone sour and an aftermath of bad tempers. Somewhere someone would be lamenting the demented state of the poor bewitched king and the maneuvers of his 'loyal' courtiers for influence and power in the absence of authority. And somewhere far, far away, perhaps in Cadiz or Seville, a file with the Corregidor's name would be tucked away neatly in an archive of overstuffed folders and unread transcripts of events unnoticed but eternally recorded for the watchful eye of whoever cared. . . . The air in Oviedo would be filled with lovely, hazy smoke from poorly ventilated stalls and leaky rooms. Its smell would be everywhere. Some vagabond children would be chasing up the street at that ungodly hour to the shock of mothers who happened to be looking out . . . and one small face would be two stories up watching them, wishing he were there . . . to run and be a famous source of mischief for the gossip the new day would bring. Two child's eyes looked on as the children disappeared down a small alleyway across from his father's house.

The Corregidor stopped suddenly and looked out at the dark sea. Then he lowered his head and examined the waters at his feet.

Back in the city, the servant's final romantic overtures were cut short by the unexpected and riotous arrival of a struggling group of guards dragging a woman he had seen downstairs in the dining room into the Master's bed chambers. As the party crashed through the door, falling and rolling across the floor, first the woman on top, then the men, the young servant reached carefully up to the curtains and pulled them slightly farther toward the mid-point to conceal his precarious rendezvous. His sweetheart scrambled to cover herself with clothing in a hopeless scattered disarray around her. Fortunately, the balcony where they lay was darker still than the inner chamber. There could be no escape, but they could possibly avoid discovery.

"Damn!" came a shout from within the room. "Damn, the bitch bit me!"
"Hold still, sister!" another man complained.

The battle was furious. It took the entire contingent more than five minutes to subdue the woman. The servant on the balcony placed his hand over his friend's mouth in an effort to squelch her worried moans.
"Be still!," he whispered loudly in her ear, "damn it, we're in trouble!"
His lady closed her eyes, chest heaving and body rigid.

"Get her on the bed! That's right! Tie her down!"

The crew inside, now in control of the situation, lifted the young woman onto the bed and began to bind her. She wasn't screaming, but her shrill remarks were penetrating, sharp and to the point. With remarkable composure she alternately scolded and cursed her captors, reminding them of their cowardice. The group of guards binding her did not reply to her remarks. Instead, they went about their business with the greatest efficiency possible; quietly, tense but mindful and well-trained in duty. When the young woman was completely bound, they paused a moment to catch their breath. Each man stood up and stared at the woman on the bed. Two or three tended to wounds on their faces and arms. None of them were talking.

"Faggots!" the woman shouted, lifting her head up, black eyes darting in the dim light.

One by one her captors filed out, the first two slowly, the next two at a brisker pace. The last two took a moment to rest, one looking over at the balcony. The servants crouching there froze.

"Let's go," the guard looking at the balcony said, "let's get the hell out of here."

"Right," the other guard mumbled.

"Traitors!" the woman taunted from the bed, watching them leave. When they were gone, she collapsed back onto the pillow and began to weep. Outside on the balcony, the pair in hiding came alive.

"They're gone! Let's get out of here."

"Shhhh! What if Don Francisco comes?"

"I don't care, let's go."

The woman moved first, nervously glancing around, then pushing in through the curtains. She was quickly followed by her boyfriend. The two began a dash across the bedroom, but came to a halt about half way across. The young woman tied to the bed groaned and twisted. They stood and watcher her. First out of morbid curiosity, then out of pity.

"You go on," the servant woman said to her friend, buttoning her blouse and motioning with her head to the exit. "Stand outside the door and watch for Moors on the coast. Do what you must if they show up. Go!"

Her friend didn't need much prompting. With a brief look back, he shot out the door and disappeared. The servant woman approached the bed and put her hand on the bound woman's forehead.

"Lay still," she said, bending over to examine the situation. Carefully, with an eye on the door behind her, she undid the hurried knots set in place by the guards. In less than a minute, the captive was free. Now untied, the young woman did a quick roll and slipped off the bed. The two hurried to the doorway and departed.

Outside the young servant heard them coming and turned to say something. The two women shot by him, though, on their way down a long passageway leading to the far side of the mansion. The man watched them vanish down the corridor and shook his head. Then suddenly he heard someone coming up the stairs. Looking around, he quickly ducked into an adjacent

cubby and hid in the shadows. The clickity-clack of hard leather soles on the stairs allowed him to approximate their wearer's moment of arrival. The young man was sure it wouldn't be someone he was fond of seeing . . . but then the visitor appeared. It was . . . Reynaldo! The butler was back to sneak another look, possibly hoping to catch a glimpse of the servant as Adonis on the balcony. The servant watched him peek warily into the bedroom chambers from the hallway before him. Then he had a grand idea. As Reynaldo tiptoed into the room, the servant tiptoed after him, hardly able to suppress his laughter. Once inside, and hot on the trail, the servant snuffed out the candle.

"Hey! Hullo!" the butler called out turning around to see who was there, unable to do so in the darkness.

* * * *

"Ho, there, the watch is relieved. Go tend to matters of sleep."

The guardian at the edge of the forest looked back at an approaching shadow and felt thankful. The journey from Jamaica had been rough for him and he was exhausted.

"Good, good," he muttered in thickly accented English.

He turned his eyes once more to the high crest across the broad River Chagres and the sturdy fort that commanded its entrance from the sea. He still could not comprehend its taking by land assault. But then, the British had surprised him before, and he knew what the Spaniards might offer in the way of defense.

"What news?" the approaching man asked from behind him.

"No news," the sentry replied, "no news, nothing."

"Wonderful," his relief smiled in the darkness. "Perhaps the night won't be so long after all."

Somewhere close a dull flapping sound signaled the passing of a large bird. The night had closed down in its usual hot way. It was close, and it was humid, and all around there were pesky insects and gurgling swamp sounds. It may have been the last place anyone would have chosen to live. At least that was the thought on the mind of the sentry as he unceremoniously surrendered the watch to a hefty man now standing beside him.

"And am I relieved?" the sentry asked.

"Yes, you are relieved," the hefty man said.

The latter had a rum smell about him that somehow seemed to blend in with the tropics; at least it was natural. The sentry shouldered his long musket and sighed.

To both of their surprise, a cheer arose a ways off behind them through the forests. The buccaneers were being less than discreet after their thirsty voyage. But who cared. The Spaniards knew they were there. No doubt about that.

"How far to Panama?" the hefty man asked his associate.

The off-duty sentry looked up into the darkness on a line that would parallel the River Chagres in the light of day. He took a moment before answering.

"I said them, they did not listen. This is dry season. The river low, the going very bad. Ten days, Bad, bad days."

The hefty man laughed.

"They're used to bad going. And the castle? Tough?"

The sentry shook his head.

"Could be. Damn thing is well-built. Hard to attack. Maybe a very hard battle. Depende. . . ."

"Depend-e on what?" the hefty man asked, slapping at a mosquito.

"Depende . . . of how much willing to fight, how much men inside, could be very much, could be easy. Don't know."

A little heat lightening flashed and lit up the sentry's face. The hefty man saw a muscular, intense-looking youth in his mid-twenties staring off in the direction of San Lorenzo across the Chagres. Soon it would be midnight.

"Who they got in charge of the place?" the hefty man continued asking.

The sentry swept his hand across his neck to chase the bugs.

"A good man . . . a valiant man . . . but a foolish man," the sentry answered.

Away across the Caribbean horizon a series of lightening flashes skimmed the distant waters. The two men remained silent for a while.

Buccaneer cheers continued to rise from the main camp in the forest. The sentry wondered what would happen if the Spaniards were to sally forth on a midnight raid, who would defend the place with a cutlass, rather than a rum bottle, in hand. But then he banished the thought and almost chuckled. Rodomontade, he knew, midnight raids and Spaniards . . . past their bedtime.

"Who's defending Panama?" the hefty man asked.

The sentry shook his head and smiled.

"The Virgin and the Saints, and probably a black man or two . . . they are made to fight, you know. The Spaniards put swords in their hands. They say . . . 'you there, Constancio, fight for His Majesty Charles . . .", then they watch to see what he do."

The hefty man laughed.

"Seriously, what's this going to be like?"

The sentry turned slowly and began to walk back to camp.

"It's going to be hot, hotter, hottest, so I hope there is gold in the pot we been promised. Maybe Lorenzo, the rest fighting not bad. . . ."

"Good night, sailor," the hefty man said, trying to make out details on the Chagres.

Armando Benitez first lost the path back, then he found it. He almost didn't make it back for the heaviness of the sleep on his eyes.

"A toast to Spanish ladies!" came a cheer through the thick trees.

"Hear! Hear!"

"To Charles, Charles the Bold!"

"Another brandy, my Lord?" a young, male servant asked his Grace, Don Francisco, upon passing through the dining room. The military man looked at him and made a sweeping gesture.

"Get out of my sight!" he snapped at the servant.

"As you wish, my Lord," the servant replied, moving off.

The military man rubbed his hands and began to stand up. He lost his balance momentarily, then caught himself with a firm hand on a swaying chair. He looked up at the second floor and sized up the walk that would take him from his chair to the stairwell.

"Now the bitch will learn discipline!" he laughed out loud. Firming up his position, the military man set out for the stairwell. He took the final few steps on a wavering run. At last he was in possession of the means of going up. He seized the banister and pulled his way slowly, stair by stair, up, up, and up.

When at long last he reached the top, he walked out down the hall to his bed chamber. He reached out, opened the door, and entered. As always, the candle was lit, the room was how he wanted it . . . and tonight, his special treasure was beneath the covers in an odd-shaped high mound. The military man laughed again and approached the bed.

"Bitch!" he exclaimed as the covers moved over the squirming form beneath. "Tonight you will . . . perform! See what I have in mind for you!"

Drawing his sword with an unsteady hand, the military man pushed it through the covers beside the hidden form and, with a hearty heave, lifted them up and off the figure tied to his bed. But lifting the covers, he saw not what he hoped he would see. Instead, he was presented with the gaping butt of a man his age. At first the military man stared, then he dropped his sword, then he backed up a step and roared.

"Guards!! Guards!!! Come quickly!!!"

Before him the unfortunate Reynaldo lay tied on all fours, hind end prominent in the line of vision of his Master. He was gagged and could not speak save for grunting sounds.

"Guards!!!" the military man screamed.

Some bastard was laughing in some other part of the mansion.

Panama City
May 29, 1987
4 o'clock p.m.

16

"Holy . . . Santa Maria . . . look what's coming."

Eva looked up from the letter she was writing and glanced over at Roberto. He was at his usual post on the balcony scanning the avenue below. Eva let the pen rest on the small table and watched as Roberto edged out farther. She wore the look of a woman with great but finite patience on the verge of expiring.

"A motorcade, maybe eight cars with motorcycle escorts, it looks like the 'Estado Mayor' is making a move, there's Quevedo's car in the lead. . . ."

Behind him Eva picked up the pen again and dashed off a few final lines to her letter. When she had finished, she read it over briefly, then folded it up. Then she stuffed it in an envelope and sealed it with a long lick of the tongue.

"Looks like a hit squad!" Roberto marveled from the balcony.

Eva stood up.

"I'm leaving you, Roberto," she said quietly, placing the letter in her purse.

"They're moving fast, listen! Sirens!"

Eva stared at her long-time friend and lover and felt the tears begin to come.

"I said I'm leaving, Roberto," she repeated, this time a little louder.

And this time he heard her. Lowering the binoculars just a bit, he rolled his eyes back in the direction of Eva.

"My bags are packed," she said, "and I'm on my way. I won't be back until you stop this madness, get a job, and return to the real world. Then you can look me up again. For now, though, it's all over. If you want to get in touch with me, leave a message with my mother. Good-bye, Roberto, I still love you."

Roberto turned around but said nothing. He watched Eva walk over to the other side of the bed, pick up her bags, and make for the kitchen. She stopped by the door and began to say something else. Her voice broke, though, and she didn't attempt to continue. Eva dropped her head, brushed at the tears, and turned to open the door.

"Don't leave me," Roberto said softly from across the apartment. Eva stopped again, now with her hand on the doorknob. She turned around and looked at him.

"My moment is coming," he said, slowly walking toward her from the balcony. "My moment is coming. Just wait, just a few short days. To all tyranny there is an end. To all problems, great and small, a final solution."

"You're mad, Roberto," Eva said. She was shaking her head and trying to control her voice.

"No, I'm not mad," Roberto replied, "I have a plan now, it's a good plan, it will work, it will save our country."

Eva gazed out in his direction and leaned her back on the door. Roberto stopped at the entrance to the kitchen and smiled.

"Don't you see, Eva, it's the Americans who are responsible for our problems. They got us into this mess, and they can get us out. Nobody in this country can kick these military bastards out, not me, not nobody. Only the gringos can, because they have the strength to do it. That's why it made so much sense, what they suggested at the meeting, my friends."

Eva looked puzzled and listened closer.

"We get the Americans involved, then they come in here and give our strutting little masters a boot in the ass. You'll see, Eva, I, Roberto, I will be the one. The new republic will be born out of a single, brilliant act. I will be the father of a new Panama."

"What are you talking about, Roberto?" Eva asked, taking a small step forward. "Who are these friends, and what are you going to do?" Roberto's eyes flashed.

"My comrades," he continued, "my comrades at the University, we are brothers in the struggle, we are the three founders of the new. . . ."

"Just a minute," Eva interrupted, "Beto, what are you going to do, and where did you meet these people?"

Roberto placed the binoculars on a kitchen ledge and wiped his mouth with the back of his hand.

"You'll see," he said, "just stick with me, I promise you it will turn out o.k. We will forge the new order, you and I. My act will be remembered as the catalyst of national salvation."

He stood staring, eyes wide and face twitching. Eva reached for the doorknob again and turned it. Her tears were gone. In their place was the frightened look of a bewildered friend.

"You're sick, Roberto," she murmured, opening the door and reaching down for her bags, "you're sick and you need help. Dear God, please get it."

With that she picked up her bags and backed out the door. Eva was in the elevator with the doors closing when she heard his last words from the apartment door.

"Eva, don't go. I need you."

The young woman began to sob uncontrollably as the elevator descended.

* * * *

"So," Bob Friedan began, hand over mouth in a thoughtful pose, "I guess that does it. The good Senator makes a stop at the monument to Balboa on his way up Avenida Balboa to the Marriott, he lays down a wreath, says a few words, and continues on. Simple enough. We can certainly fit it into the itinerary, and it would look so . . . so nice. Such a 'neutral' thing to do. Balboa is a national hero here and it's sure to please the people: and Balboa doesn't rub anybody the wrong way. No problems with the General, no problems with the businessmen. Everybody comes out on top. Any reservations, Phil?"

The young American paced back and forth by Bob's study door. He had his hands in his hip pockets.

"No, no reservations, Bob," he said, "it's just that I don't see the point in saluting Balboa at such a critical time. A . . . salute to Balboa, stuff like that usually happens during smooth times. It's a maintenance type move. Why now?

He stopped pacing and looked over at Bob. Bob was coming back from the window where he had been standing and heading in the direction of his desk chair. When he arrived at the chair, Bob paused for a moment, then sat down.

"That *is* the point," Bob said, picking up a shot glass and examining it. Your Senator Dodge will be here to bolster that sense of "smoothness" you refer to. He wants an easy transition. No bloodshed, no disturbances, no. . . ."

He looked up at Phil.

"No embarrassing problems. Business as usual. The smoother the better. Stop and see Balboa, say a few words of friendship. Slip away and dine with business at the Marriott. It's an American tradition, it's our way. You've got a lot to learn, son."

Phil frowned and walked over in front of Bob's desk.

"Sure, I'm not objecting to Balboa. It's just that the arrangements for this trip have got me nervous. I'm in charge of the damn thing, remember. I don't want anything to go wrong."

"What's to go wrong?" Bob laughed. "These trips come and go, they're a dime a dozen. But get a good translator. You don't want anything happening like what happened to that silly-ass Carter in Poland. His translator had him "carnally embracing" the crowd he was addressing. What a botch-job. Good thing I was over here at the time."

Bob's younger partner smiled and shook his head.

"I've got good translators, Bob, don't worry about that."

"I know you do," Bob replied, now no longer smiling.

Phil watched him as he gazed up at the window and disappeared into some inner thoughts.

"Take it easy, Bob," Phil said, picking up his attache and turning for the door. "See you this evening for the staff briefing."

"I'll be there," Bob answered from some place quite distant.

In a moment, Phil was gone.

Out in the street, in line with but not the object of Bob's revery, a man pushed a cart and rang a bell. Occasionally children would run up and cajole the man with gestures and pleas. To each such child the man gestured back. He would hold his palm outstretched and look into it, then look back at the child. Slowly he would shake his head and smile. Once a mother strolled up with two children and the man's expression changed. Reaching into his cart he produced three cups. He filled them with shaved ice and scooped flavors on them from wide-mouthed bottles he kept on top of the cart. The woman paid for them and walked off with the children. A car roared by and Bob suddenly came to. He blinked a couple times, then looked down beside him at his top desk drawer. With a limp hand he opened it.

Children in that other room were reciting their Spanish lesson again, filling the long corridor with soft recitations. Bob lifted a photo out of the drawer and looked at it a long while. His eyes were blank and watery, his skin too white and soft for the lines drawn down from his brow through his cheeks. "An American Hero" was the caption of the photograph, old gold letters trimmed in black over a serious looking young football player . . . and his beaming father in the background with his arm around his shoulder. The phone began to ring, but Bob kept staring at the photo. It rang a few furious times, then went silent.

Nata

"I am Mr. Santos, Father, and these are my associates. We are detectives from the Capital. We'd like to ask you a few questions if you don't mind. Would you come along with us to headquarters? It won't take long."

Miguel stood in the middle of the church at Nata and looked at the three men standing before him. He didn't recognize any of them and quietly motioned at the breast pocket of the one who had addressed him.

"If you are police, I am sure you have credentials, Sir," he said.

The man who had spoken smiled and showed his teeth.

"Of course, Holy Father, I have credentials."

Santos pulled a leather, fold-open badge from an inner jacket pocket. He held it up to the priest's face and let the man look. Father Miguel studied it for a brief moment, then looked back at Santos.

"What in the world do you wish to ask me about?"

"It would be easier," Santos replied, "if you just came with us. The longer we stay here, the longer this unfortunate matter will last."

"I am not in charge, here," Miguel protested as one of Santos's men slipped a hand under the priest's arm, "I am only the assistant, you must speak with Father Sandoval first, I cannot leave here without asking his permission."

"I'll phone him from headquarters," Santos said, lighting up a cigarette and watching as his other man moved in to help the first. He blew out a large cloud of smoke.

"Gentlemen," Father Miguel stuttered as they began to lead him away, "this is not right, this is a church and you are on sacred ground, this is a sanctity, you are violating this sanctity, please listen to what I'm saying."

"This is a routine police matter." Santos said. He extinguished the match with a wave of his hand and tossed the still smoking stick out onto a nearby pew. Standing still for a moment, he lifted his eyes to take in the inner design of the church around him. He looked up at the rafters, down at the windows, then straight ahead at the altar up the aisle before him.

"Let me go, I have done nothing," he heard from the entrance of the church.

"Come on, you'll be back before supper," one of the men was saying. Santos looked down at his feet, then back up at the altar. The flowers that adorned it were motionless, their perfume was heavy throughout the church. He coughed and wiped at his mouth. Turning to leave, he hawked and spit on the floor.

"Fuck you and shut your mouth," they were saying out by the car.

* * * *

"So?"

The corpulent Major Villalobos looked up expectantly from his examination of a sleek new Jaguar and studied the face of a pensive Angel Mendez. The latter was running his fingertips over the smoothly painted red surface of the magnificent car and contemplating its lines.

"So . . . what?" Angel asked in reply, stooping down for a better look at some details of trim.

"So we want to know what the hell's going on!" Villalobos retorted angrily but in a controlled voice.

The Major was looking around to make sure no one was listening. No one was.

"All you have to know . . .," Angel began before pausing to inspect the tire.

He flicked at a speck of dust, then went on.

" . . . All you have to know is that the matter is in good hands, not to worry."

Villalobos suffered a hot flash down the back of his neck.

"Oh yeah? Not to worry? Well I'll tell you something, bush boy, we're plenty worried. I guess you don't get the picture."

The Major glanced around again and squatted down beside Mendez.

"This is it," he whispered, "this is the whole kettle of corn, this is my, your, and everybody else's future. This is it or else, botch this and I don't give us much beyond Christmas, if that. I don't have a crystal ball, Angel, but that's what it looks like to me."

Villalobos watched a salesman saunter by, then produced his handkerchief and mopped his brow. Angel Mendez slowly stood up. The Major stood up with him.

"Don't think I don't know that," Angel said, running his fingers over the car's finish one final time. "Everything's taken care of, not to worry. I've got my two best boys on it, they'll be there when it happens, one to talk, the other to make *sure* it happens. They're pro's. It's taken care of."

Another salesman suddenly approached them from behind. The man smiled and began to speak, but Villalobos waved him away with a furious gesture. The man bowed slightly and discreetly melted into the showroom between two cars.

"There are a couple minor problems to resolve before the light turns green," Angel continued, eyes now gazing out into empty space.

"You know when the light turns green," Villalobos said.

The Major took a long look at Angel, then turned his back and walked briskly over to the showroom door.

"What did he want?"

"He's nervous, let's go."

"But what the hell did he. . . ."

"I said he's nervous! Now let's go!"

"O.k., o.k.," Matos replied, putting the car into gear, "don't get touchy, Angel, my boy. Remember, we've got a date with you-know-who tomorrow, and he's nervous, too."

"Just drive the car," Angel mumbled, watching the store fronts blur by.

Panama City
Later that Evening

17

It hadn't been raining when she left, and it hadn't rained the whole trip there on two different buses, but as it often happened, the skies opened up just minutes after she'd gotten off the second bus. She was too far away from the bus stop shelter to return, and still two full city blocks from her destination. So Eva Icaza grimly lowered her head and marched through sheet after sheet of driving rainstorm. A car sideswiped her as she rounded the first block of her short but miserable journey, drenching her with waters from the first puddles of the downpour, and a sudden surge from a high eaves trough completed her soaking. Eva felt the rainwater churning in her shoes and trickling down her back. At one point it rained so hard that it almost drove her from the sidewalk. She had to recoup near the gate entrance of a single dwelling about thirty meters from her destination. At least, she noted from behind the drizzle falling streaming from her brow, at least the bags were keeping dry. She saw the water beading up on their shiny surfaces and knew they were safe. With a determined stare Eva forged out from the doorway and made it to her highrise destination. She dropped her bags as soon as she had arrived and searched the marquee directory for the name of her friend. Unable to locate it at first glance, she looked up into the main glass doorway and searched for help. She saw a calm, uniformed doorman there watching her.

"Open up!" Eva shouted, tapping on the glass. The door was locked. The doorman remained standing there with an impassive expression. Eva squinted through the rain and tapped on the glass again.

"Please, open the door!"

The man shook his head.

"Ring the buzzer of the occupant you are visiting," he called out, hand cupped at his lips to amplify the message.

Eva put on an astonished look.

"What?!?" she asked in a loud voice. "Let me in, for God's sake, I'm soaking wet."

"The buzzer," the doorman repeated, pointing to the marquee directory.

As soon as he had spoken, he resumed his original erect, professional position. Eva slammed the door with her fist and turned around, eyes searching in all directions. Pushing her hair back out of her face, she went over the directory and looked desperately for her friend's name. No use. It wasn't there. Her friend must have been listed under her roommate's name, and Eva had no idea. She turned to the doorman again, but the man had his eyes closed. He was wetting his lips with his tongue and rocking back and forth on his heels. Eva pushed her hair back again and turned around. Only this time there was a whole different picture.

"Eva, you're soaked," she heard a tall man say.

She looked up and saw the face of Angel Mendez, he was in full uniform and as always, impressive. Before she could answer, he did.

"But of course you are, here, let me help you with those things. Men, over here, get these things into the car!"

Two soldiers came running from a car, each one swooping up a different bag.

"Angel," Eva protested, "I'm fine, I'm waiting for a friend. Really, don't worry."

"Nonsense," Angel said, sweeping her away with a powerful arm. "You can come with me and get dry. Open the door, boys!"

As the two arrived at the staff car the rear door swung open and Angel helped Eva in. Then he jumped in himself. Eva heard the trunk slam shut and the engine rev up. The front door opened and closed and the car roared off. Eva brushed the water off her blouse and looked over at Angel. He, too was brushing at the raindrops on his formal coat.

"Damn'dest storm," he smiled, looking at Eva.

Eva smiled back and watched the Captain closely. He began to brush drops off his pantlegs and looked down at his shoes. The car speeded up and swung violently to the right.

Angel was quiet during most of the trip. He looked preoccupied with something or other and only occasionally addressed Eva with his famous smile, making only light conversation when he did. They drove on through the rainy streets with Eva wondering how this all could be happening to her. She was nervous and not a little frightened. In spite of the fact that she thought she knew Angel, she had never ever been comfortable around him. To her questions regarding their destination, Angel would only answer that they were going to a nice place to relax and dry out, that she'd like it, that he'd have her driven home whenever she wanted. She kept wanting to say that the whenever was now, but she let it go as the car cruised on. Soon, however, she noticed that they were heading through the Canal Zone, and when they had reached the Puente de las Americas, she became alarmed. She looked over at Angel as they crossed the long, high bridge for some type of signal as to where they were going. But the Captain sat there lost in thought, gazing out his window at the soggy terrain. Something in his calm quieted Eva's tensions, too. She closed her eyes and leaned back in the seat, now conscious only of an overwhelming weariness and a dull itching brought on by the wet clothes. The evening was coming on and she was a long way from Roberto. She was beginning to miss that.

With a start she woke up and it was nighttime. Eva sat straight up and looked at Angel. The car swerved sharply off the road and rocked her into her corner by the window. Angel was holding up a hand and saying something to the driver.

"Angel, where are we?" Eva asked.

"Shhh," he replied, "we're there. Stay put and I'll come around for the door."

Eva watched as the car came to a halt. Angel opened his door and leaped out. In a moment he was opening her door and motioning her to get out, too. Eva felt a slight chill in the still drizzling air and swung her legs out. Angel helped her stand up.

"Where are we, Angel . . . tell me," Eva said. There as anger in her voice.

"Trust me, we're some place safe and wonderful," the Captain answered.

Eva heard music in the background and looked up to see a very attractive chalet not far from where they stood. She hesitated for a moment, then let Angel lead her on.

"Hurry, you don't want to get any wetter."

From everywhere Eva smelled the familiar smells of the country, wood smoke and animals, the wet earth and smells she could not identify but knew belonged to rural life. She pulled her arm away from Angel's grasp and walked quickly along beside him at a distance more comfortable than he had established. Angel laughed and held his hands high.

"Don't worry, Eva," he smiled in the faint night light, "I am a protector of the people."

Eva didn't answer. Instead, she kept pace with him and examined the chalet they were approaching. Inside she could see people in silhouette in the windows and there was abundant laughter. By all appearances it was a party, some festive occasion in the middle of the country. The chalet was a beautiful affair. It had a large, airy porch and sleek, modern arches, some architect's baby. And it was large, very large. It had an expensive look of the type Eva recognized so well. Angel put his arm around her waist and began to help her up the porch steps. Once again, Eva pulled away. Stopping on the first step, Eva looked up at her military friend.

"Angel," she said, "for the last time, where are you taking me?" He looked down at her and stepped back to ground level to where his eyes more nearly met hers.

"This is my house," he said quietly, and you are my guest of honor, old friends take care of one another, don't insult me by questioning my motives."

Eva watched him for a moment, then nodded.

"O.k.," she agreed, "just show me to where I can shower and change, I'll need my bags."

"They're on their way," Angel said, looking back at the car. "They're on their way, come on in."

Eva climbed the steps in front of him and headed for the front door. Angel skipped up behind her and, reaching over her shoulder, opened it wide.

"Welcome," he said as they entered.

The light was brilliant as they entered. A general cheer went up as Angel walked in behind Eva. As she looked around she saw mostly military people and attractive young women around them. The women, she noticed, were very well-dressed. There were a few older officers, but in general, it looked like the new set. The foyer and the large living room it led into were exquisitely furnished and decorated. Eva looked down at her ruined street clothes and edged off into a foyer shadow. Angel caught her by the arm.

"This is my lovely Eva," he said, strutting out into the company, I want you to know that she is the dream of my childhood, my princess and my closest friend."

A second cheer went up, mostly from the men. Several clapped. The women looked on with different degrees of curiosity and reserve, and only one came up to greet Eva. She was a bleached blond with a nice figure, about the same age as Eva. In her own way, she was pretty. Eva frowned and pressed at her clothes.

"Let me take you to where you can change, Eva," the woman smiled, replacing Angel's hand with her own. "There's a room upstairs we can use."

Eva glanced up at Angel . . . half angry, half exhausted, very completely ashamed at the way she looked and the way she had been introduced.

Angel waved good-bye as the two women walked up the staircase to the upper level. As Eva ascended, she looked down at Angel. He was now surrounded by a group of officers. She noticed a number of women watching her as she walked up the stairs.

"Come on, Eva," the woman leading her urged, "you'll feel brand new." Eva reached the top of the stairwell and followed the woman along a winding passageway to the left. In a moment they disappeared behind a fresh stucco wall and left the party crowd behind. Eva brushed her hair back and walked in silence. The party sounds faded as they arrived at a back room half hidden in deep shadows. Eva hesitated at the doorway but the woman with her smiled and held out her hand.

"This is your room, Eva, there are many clothes in the closet and they are yours, all of them. If you don't find something you like, pick up the phone on the dresser and dial 0. Tell the man who answers you want to speak with Marissa, I will come and help you. This is your house, and everything in it is yours."

Eva looked at the woman for a brief instant, then walked into her new room. She heard the door close behind her and she was alone.

The place was air conditioned but Eva soon found the window and threw it open. Outside, mixed with sounds of merriment from below, there was a sound of soft falling rain and the same smells of the country she had sensed when she arrived. A gentle wind lifted up out of some nearby field or forest and caressed her face as she stood looking out into the night. At length she sat down in a nearby chair and laid her head back on a cushion. First he shuddered. Then she sobbed. Then she buried her face in her hands and wept for the better part of a half hour.

Near Nata
Evening, May 29, 1987

18

"I don't have much time," Santos began, walking slowly across the room toward the bound, helpless priest, "so I'll be brief."

"You don't like violence, neither do I. Or do my associates," he said with a suddenly serious expression, sweeping his hand in the direction of the two other men. One of them bit into a cigar and spit a soggy, chewed up portion on the floor. The other sat there calmly watching.

"They came with me on a moment's notice this morning. They're gentle folks from Penonome, old acquaintances, family men. I haven't seen them in years, have I gentlemen?"

Santos winked and the two of them acknowledged his remarks, the man with the cigar lighting up and nodding, and the quiet man muttering a soft "that's right."

"So you see," Santos went on, gesturing like a college professor with his hands, "you see, a lot of good people have come here just to make you feel at home . . . and," he said, pausing for a moment, "and, to discover the truth."

The priest squirmed and closed his eyes in anguish. He was standing up against a pole, unable to move a limb two inches.

"So help us," Santos said, "help us."

He walked over to the man, looked him in the eyes, then pulled a switchblade knife from his pocket. Smiling again, Santos flicked the knife open and raised it to the priest's eyes.

"But how stupid of me," he said, "how clumsy and impolite. Of course, you cannot speak. Here, let me help you with that problem." Santos carefully slid the sharp blade of the knife down into the gag and paused. Then, with a savage jerk of the hand, he sliced the gag off the man, slashing into his cheek and lips in the process. The priest grimaced and closed his eyes down hard. Blood began to trickle from his chin.

"Careless!" Santos said with mock surprise, "how careless of me, dear God. Now look what I've done."

One of the men behind him chuckled. The other just looked on, expressionless as always. Santos walked completely around the tied up man and whistled.

"Just tell me one thing, my penguin friend, just one thing and you will live. Where is the gold kept in Nata, at your church. I know you have it hidden."

The priest looked out with terrified eyes. As Santos came the full turn he stopped and toyed with the knife.

"I know of no gold," the priest stammered.

Santos shook his head and looked down at the floor.

"A pity," he mumbled, looking up to smile at his friends. "A pity. That means it's invention time. What do you suggest, Humberto?"

The quiet man rolled his head over on an exaggerated angle and smacked his lips.

"Put out his eyes," he said in matter-of-fact tones.

"Too direct," Santos replied, shaking his head again. "Once they're out, what's the point in talking. No. Not that. How about you, Horacio?"

The other man, the one with the cigar, stood up and put his hands on his hips.

"Let's give his the 'Spade' treatment, that was pretty effective. Start by crushing his balls."

"This is a priest," Santos warned with little "no no" gestures of the finger. "I doubt if his genitals are that important. Let's think of something even more creative, what do you say?"

"Electric shock?" the quiet man said.

"Wooling," the man with the cigar said, stepping forward and spitting on the floor again.

Santos grinned from ear to ear.

"Now there's an idea, wooling."

He glanced back at the priest and approached him slowly.

"Do you know what these bastards are going to do with you?" he asked.

The priest again closed his eyes. He began to pray softly. Santos slapped him hard across the face.

"Quiet!!" he screamed, lips trembling.

The priest looked back in panic and squirmed again in the rope bindings. Santos stared him in the eye.

"They're going to wrap a leather cord around your pitiful skull and tighten it until your eyes pop out, then you can watch your nose and feet for a while. Then I will begin with what will hurt you so bad you'll . . . you'll. . . ."

Santos quivered with rage and seized the priest by the throat.

"You'll tell me!!!" he screamed again.

As the priest began to turn blue and choke, Santos released his grip. Slowly, as the priest gasped for breath, Santos regained his composure. In a minute or so, the smile had returned to his lips.

"So tell me now . . . my Catholic friend . . . and I will save you all this pain . . . this mutilation and horror . . . tell me and. . . ."

Santos stroked his chin with his hand and shrugged.

"I'll let you go."

The priest's eyes wandered around the dirty cement room and located a window in a far corner. Still gasping, he swallowed and looked at Santos.

"I have a map," Santos said to him, "but I don't understand it. The instructions are in . . . English . . . or German . . . I think. You'll have to help me."

"Don't go to Nata de los Caballeros," the priest whispered hoarsely, "don't go there again."

Santos dropped his hands to his sides and leaned closer to his captive.

"What, you insolent pig?" he said, raising the knife to the priest's face again.

He placed the knife blade tip in the priest's nostril and slowly pushed it up. He stopped at he mid point and listened as the poor man spoke.

"I am a Christian, and I have compassion for all souls, yours included. There is still time for you to redeem yourself, to ask for forgiveness from the Father Almighty. So I beseech you, brother, do not return to Nata de los Caballeros. There awaits you a death more hideous than any agony you may have in mind for this wretched soul. Now do as you wish, I am a dead man, and I now expect the peace that has been promised to me for my devotion and my service. This is the moment of truth I have striven to attain for so long, may there be the Promising One at the end of this path. May these struggles of mine be rewarded." Santos skewed up his face and scratched his head. The men behind him stood there staring.

The Embassy, Panama City

"Any words of wisdom you wish to share with Congress before I go?" The Congressman sat looking over Bob Friedan with a sarcastic smile.

Bob scratched his side and picked up a mitful of peanuts.

"Nothing special," he replied, popping a few into his mouth.

The Congressman glanced over at one of his aides and gave him a knowing look.

"Bob's got his finger on the pulse of things down here," he said.

Bob munched on the peanuts and nodded, looking the aide in the eye and watching the Princeton creature look away.

"That's right," Bob smiled, "always on top of things."

Junior officials were crowded around a doorway beyond the small group. They were in the midst of some animated discussion. Bob saw Phil in the middle pitching. A young man with thick, round glasses was contending his every point.

"I'm going to recommend that we do everything in our power to ensure that these monsters are overthrown," the Congressman remarked, also eyeing the discussion. "I am going to introduce a resolution to that effect in the House next week. They'll see we mean business. Ten to one the resolution will be unanimous."

"But nonbinding," Bob said casually, dipping his hand into the peanut bowl again.

The Congressman looked back at him.

"Short of military intervention, what else can be done?"

"Nothing," Bob replied.

Bob sorted out the peanuts in the palm of his hand and pushed two or three aside. Rejects. He tipped them off into an ashtray while holding the rest with the fingers of his other hand.

"Excuse me," the aide said abruptly, looking over at the Congressman, "excuse me, but I get the distinct impression that you favor this bunch of animals. Why am I left with that feeling?"

"I don't know," Bob answered, now chewing on the selected few, "I never liked these clowns either. I said that twenty years ago when I was a rookie, and this place was a democracy. That was the first time I came here. It was my first assignment. I said . . . I. . . ."

The Congressman and his aide looked on as Bob swallowed slowly and put his hand to his throat. He looked off to the side and quietly sat back in his chair.

"Are you all right?" the Congressman asked.

Bob raised a hand and waved it in an affirmative gesture.

"I'm fine," he said.

The other men continued to look at him but Bob seemed to recover.

"I said," he went on, "that we should have prevented the coup from ever taking place. Our government had different ideas."

The Congressman looked puzzled. He watched Bob rub his throat and noticed that he was sweating. Bob's brow looked damp. The room was amply cool.

"Are you all right?" he asked again.

"Just fine," Bob repeated. "A lot of us thought we should never have allowed this place to become . . . a dictatorship. But we were young punks, what the hell, the senior staffers had the inside line to the policy-makers. Nobody listened to us."

Bob coughed and lowered his head for a moment.

"You are suggesting," the aide carried on, "that the United States government sanctioned the coup?"

The Congressman raised a hand in the direction of his aide and sat forward on the edge of his seat.

"Bob, tell me, are you all right?"

"I'm fine, Sir . . . don't trouble yourself, just a peanut down the wrong pipe, I always do that."

Bob's eyes were watery and his color was off. Still, he smiled and began to motion with his hands in lively fashion.

"No one sanctioned anything, the whole mess was spontaneous. It was a case of a civilian government," Bob coughed again, "with insufficient control over the military. It's a world-wide thing. But we knew it was going to happen."

"Where was . . . our conscience?" the aide insisted dramatically, "did no one react? Where was Congress?"

"They were neck-deep in the Viet Nam thing," Bob said, now much more in control, "nobody had time for this little corner of the globe."

"Still, didn't you feel morally obligated to take your feelings to the top? I mean, was the press informed? Were the people made aware of this situation?"

Bob held his hand over his mouth and stared at the aide. He smiled weakly.

"Most presses didn't cover the coup, Sir, they fed the public a few wire service scraps and moved on to the real news, riots on campus, riots in cities, free love . . . but you're kind of young. Ask yourself this, though. If sensibilities have become elevated, how many folks in the USA could locate this burg on the map? How many of them could tell you who's in charge down here? One in five hundred? One in a thousand? What the hell does your sodbuster on the back forty care about who's in charge here? All he knows is the truth." The aide had grown a touch angry. He was gazing at Bob and tapping his foot.

"And what's that?"

Bob picked up a stale drink and washed down what was left of the peanuts.

"That it doesn't matter to him, that one fucker's no worse than another. Unless you do this thing intellectually, that's just what you'll get. Just another fucker out to one-up the last one."

The Congressman had relaxed back into his chair and was watching the exchange calmly. The aide took a deep breath and clapped his hands together.

"And . . . what do you suggest, Mr. Friedan?"

Bob closed his eyes and adjusted his wristwatch.

"I suggest, that before you rush off half-cocked to Congress to pass non-binding resolutions, you take the time to think out a workable scenario for the peaceful passing of power from the military bunch to your darling civilians. It can be done, you know, but it will take a lot of planning."

"Nonsense," the Congressman said, breaking his silence, "we'll have these cracker jacks out before the summer's through, and we'll have a democracy here."

"For how long, Sir?," Bob asked. "You keep saying 'we' when you should be saying 'they.' 'They' will have to maintain the democracy, and 'they' probably won't want anything to do with us, and I don't blame 'em. Play this thing stupid and you'll get Russians in here."

"This is just a bull session, Bob, you're saying nothing, nothing at all."

"Yes, I am," Bob replied, bending over to examine his shoe laces. "I'm saying that the United States used to kick ass when it wanted change. Why not here, and why not now. You don't like the pompous little sausage-stuffed uniforms you see strutting around? If you see any difference between them and the goose-steppers that rallied to the swastika, let me know. Otherwise, your farmers back home have a more sensible solution. Let 'em be. You either do, or you don't, there's not a lot in between."

The aide stood up suddenly and marched toward the door. The Congressman looked on as Bob untied, then retied a shoe.

"The change will be spontaneous and permanent, Bob," he said. Then he too rose and headed for the door. Bob sat back up and pulled out a cigarette.

* * * *

"Father Sandoval, they came and took Father Miguel away. We saw them from the field."

Father Sandoval walked forward in the soft light of the church to meet the small group of townsfolk who had entered. He was wiping his hands on a soiled cloth. His face was dirty and he was sweating profusely. He looked like he had just been engaged in heavy exercise.

"What's that?" he asked his parishioners, now standing before them.

"Father Miguel, he was led away in a car, three men came here and took him away in your absence. We say them."

In the background, from somewhere behind the church, came the sounds of horses. They were the sounds of the animals catching their breath. Father Sandoval closed his eyes and let his chin drop against his chest. He let the hand with the cloth fall to his side. He stood that way for a long moment, then looked up at the people who had brought him the news.

"Thank you," he said. " I hadn't expected them so early. Everything will be fine. Go back to your homes and rest. God be with you. Go home now, bless you."

The people filed away, some looking back at him as they left. A man walked out of the shadows behind Father Sandoval and stood watching as they disappeared into the night.

"What is happening?" he asked.

Father Sandoval turned around to see a young, athletic-looking man who, like himself, was streaked with sweat and the signs of strenuous work.

"It is beginning," the Catholic Father said, turning to walk away. "We must be ready sooner than I thought. Come."

January 18, 1671
Panama City

19

"They're coming, Lord President, San Lorenzo has fallen and Morgan is advancing up the Chagres with a strong army. They're advancing on Panama!"

"Hah!" the military man exulted from a large sea window, "so the churl has opted for folly and now marches to his doom. So be it! We are ready!"

The President of the Audiencia stood up from his table on unsteady knees and stared at the messenger standing in the doorway. It was a moment before he could speak.

"San Lorenzo has fallen . . ." he said numbly, "good God. . . ."

"Pay no attention to the fate of that outpost," the military man continued, "the real test lies ahead, here, in Panama!"

"It was an extraordinary seige and battle," the messenger added, "the fortress held out until a conflagration forced the defenders to divide their attention. A corsair, shot clean through with an arrow, pulled the shaft from his chest, dipped it in incendiary oils, lit it, and sent it flying back up and over the castle walls. The place caught fire. The corsairs carried the day. They have murdered most of the defenders, and they have taken the rest prisoner."

The President sat down again. His face was ashen and his lips trembled.

"My God, San Lorenzo fallen. . . ."

The Corregidor, now a familiar sight in the President's entourage, stepped out of a corner by the outer patio and put a finger to his nose, discreetly eyeing the President as he advanced. The military man was busy chasing the messenger from the room and shouting bold predictions.

"The moment we have been waiting for," he was saying as the messenger hurried off, "the planets are in line, and the stars hold us in their sway, this is the end of corsair mischief on the Spanish Main. We are ready." The Corregidor stared at the man.

"They were 'ready' at Portobelo, too, my dear Alferez, quite ready. Most of them are in their graves now, or impoverished, I don't know which is worse."

The military man walked back to the center of the room and struck a polished pose in front of the Corregidor.

"This is not Portobelo, my dear Corregidor, and we are not the drunkards who defended it. This is Panama, and we are the grand forces of his Majesty, King Charles. How dare you compare that backwoods port with the splendor of His Grace's Audiencia?"

The Corregidor stepped evenly to the table and bent over to sniff at a glowing red flower. Rising, he carefully pulled out his handkerchief and gently patted his cheek.

"That 'backwoods' port was, as the President so correctly described it. . . ." The Corregidor smiled and performed an impeccable sweeping bow in the President's direction. "Portobelo was designed by the finest military engineer of his time. But I do not think, do you, that Panama has even a mirage of a fortification resembling those, your 'puny' lad Morgan howled in laughter at, as he crushed them in a single evening's work. It's time we considered fact, not fantasy."

"Fortifications?" the military man said, walking in a wide arc behind the Corregidor, "We have cavalry! We have fine trained horsemen by the score. We have cannons and all manner of field artillery. We have musketeers and European war veterans, all trained and honed into a marvelous fighting force . . . by me. We are the pride of His Majesty's Viceroyal Guard."

"All the better," the Corregidor smiled, waving his handkerchief across his brow, "providing they can shoot straight. Why have I missed all of your target practices?"

The courtier glanced up at the ceiling with a puzzled look.

"No," he resumed, "I haven't heard much shooting."

"My men are trained marksmen," the military man objected, "they are experts who need no practice."

"The corsairs practice," the Corregidor went on. He was now walking toward the same sea window the military man had occupied earlier when the reports had arrived. "I watched them practice every day they were in Portobelo. Nasty savages, but they would sit beneath the trees and pick off birds at incredible distances. They had fine French rifles, the new type of guns I haven't seen around here, all well-oiled and tuned to their major purpose . . . killing men."

"So you're saying," the President interrupted him from his seat by the table, "you're saying that we're finished, is that it?"

The Corregidor looked startled.

"Oh, no, My Lord, I am not saying that at all." He stopped and returned his handkerchief to his pocket.

"I am only saying that we must be truly ready. We must have a plan. I see nothing like that now, but I am convinced that we could come up with something splendid. You see, Morgan is coming up the Chagres. That means he will have to cross a jungle hell at the wrong time of the year for his purposes. The waters are low and he will have to hoof it. The place is scorched and barren to boot. He'll get here, all right, half dead from the hunger and the heat. And we have plenty of time. Two weeks at least. Let us prepare a surprise party. I have plenty of ideas for dirty tricks. Let us have a hundred first class kegs of wine ready for the thirsty bastards as they emerge with parched throats from the jungle, each keg sufficiently doctored with just a touch of poison. Let the famished cutthroats gorge themselves on a herd of fat beef left out to graze in the plain before them. Then, while they stuff their filthy faces and drink themselves blind, let us wait until nightfall when they sleep the orgy off. I doubt they would even notice as we slit their throats. For God's sake let us have a plan, there must be a dozen ways, but let us *not* fight them tired musket against rifle, dull sword against cutlass, gentry fold against swarthy hood. We have brains. That is our advantage. And we have time. We need strategy."

"We need," the military man interjected loudly, strutting across the floor again, "we need to meet Morgan on the plain with a host of brave horsemen and true. It will be our finest hour, the English banners flying in the breeze, standards dancing above this Spanish Majesty's finest knights. For Santiago and Spain, the glory of our Lord Charles' illustrious ancestor relived!"

The Corregidor stared at the prancing Alferez for a while, then turned his eyes to the heavens beyond the ceiling. He lowered his face and shook his head.

"Tell me," the President was asking, "how many men can we mount up?"

"At least a thousand," the military man bellowed in a deep, resonant voice, "strong hearts, manly men, all battle tested and severe."

"How could Morgan resist that?" the President went on, following the military man with his eyes.

"Hah!" the latter shouted, finger poised in the air, smile growing across his mustachioed upper lip. 'He can not!"

The Corregidor walked quietly back to the outer patio where he had been before the news arrived. He was surprised, however, by the appearance of the Bishop in the doorway leading out. The Bishop looked at him and motioned for him to keep quiet. The Corregidor stopped, then followed the Bishop's beckoning fingers. The two exited out into the patio. Behind them, in the inner chamber, the President and the military man were engaged in a lively discussion.

A cool breeze rushed in from the sea and refreshed the Corregidor as he followed the Bishop to the center of the patio. The Bishop turned to face him as they arrived, then looked around to make sure that they were alone. Satisfied, he turned his intelligent eyes on the official standing before him. The Corregidor cocked his head on an interested but reserved angle and placed his handkerchief to his lips. He lowered his nose slightly to breathe in its perfume.

"We'll let these fools work out the details of the city's defense," the Bishop began, "but in the meantime, I need to ask you a favor."

"The Corregidor's eyes grew studiously wide as the word "fools" passed his ears, though not too wide, and not too shocked looking. He, too, glanced around on the outside chance that someone less than discreet could be listening. Now one was.

"In the short time I have known you," the Bishop went on, "I have come to like you. You are a veteran of survival in a nasty world, and you have a keen, sharp mind. You have experience and an extraordinary sense of timing. You understand, in a word, and those who understand, need not be counseled in the proper treatment of human endeavor. Those who do not understand . . ." the Bishop gestured with his head in the direction of the inner room, "will never comprehend."

The two gentlemen listened as the President and the military man parried point after point of applied conventional strategy. They were engaged in a discussion on modern theories of harquebus placement in open plain warfare. The Bishop nodded and sighed.

"You see what I mean."

The Corregidor watched as the Catholic magistrate turned and walked over to a high wall with bougainvillaea.

"So listen closely," the Bishop said.

The sun was partially hidden behind some waving trees and aerial vines above the patio. Its light quivered and sprayed over the two men as they stood there. The sound of the ocean was audible from so very close by.

"I need you for a mission," the Bishop continued at length, now turning back to face the Corregidor from a distance. "We are loading a fleet of small ships for a short journey up the coast. The ships stand by close at hand. We are loading them at night, so as not to raise suspicions."

The Corregidor expressed interested surprise at the Bishop's words. He went on listening.

"When Morgan marches into this place, I hope to have my . . . possessions at a safe distance . . . the Church's possessions, that is. When the loading is accomplished, the ships will sail . . . they need a hand to guide them."

The Bishop now looked the Corregidor in the eyes. The Corregidor looked away and coughed, placing his handkerchief to his mouth.

"Just what are you suggesting," he asked of the Bishop.

"I am suggesting," the Bishop said, stepping closer to the Corregidor, "that you guide my little fleet to its destination. It will sail in a fortnight or less from Panama to the Bay of Parita. There the goods shipped will be transferred to a mule train on the mainland for a short but treacherous journey to Nata de los Caballeros. I need a man in charge who can deal with whatever nosy official gets in the way. You're just the man. I will give you letters of authority signed and sealed by the Archbishop of Seville, you will bluster and feign indignation that any petty peon of His Demented Majesty Charles would dare to question the Holy Sacred Roman Catholic Church. That's where you're unequaled and vital to our success. By Holy Seal I will make you an emissary of the Viceroy himself. The goods get to Nata de los Caballeros, do you understand?"

The Corregidor raised his eyebrows and gently nodded, discreetly enough, however, to dispel any ideas of disloyalty or intrigue. Under questioning he could always defer to the role of spy. The Bishop drew close to him and let his face come no more than a few inches from the man he confided in. Again the President and the military man were arguing some inane point or other in the now very distant inner chambers.

"You will be handsomely rewarded," the Bishop continued, "so well so that you may choose to retire forever on your income from this petty assignment, live the hidalgo's life in Spain, your well-deserved rest." The Bishop slowly withdrew a scrap of parchment from his breast pocket. It had a figure written on it. The Bishop showed it to the Corregidor. The Corregidor's eyes opened wide, then narrowed. He studied the figure carefully.

"Yes," he said, nodding his head, "I am always at the disposition of the Holy Roman Catholic Church, I am a servant of God, nothing more, nothing less . . . I. . . ." The Corregidor paused for a second or two. The Bishop looked on.

"Yes?"

"When do we sail?"

The Bishop returned the scrap of parchment to his breast pocket and smiled.

"Best of all," he said, turning away, "you will not be here when Henry makes his appearance, you will be far away. And you will be far away when Henry leaves."

His Catholic Reverence stopped and looked up at the thin, high clouds.

"You will be far away from this madness. I will give you several packing lists, one to suit any occasion. Do you understand?"

The Corregidor nodded.

"Those who understand, My Grace. . . ."

"Need not be counseled," the Bishop smiled. "I will call upon you in the next two to three days. Await my calling."

"I am at your entire disposition," the Corregidor murmured with a deep, reverent bow, "a humble servant of the Church."

Coronado, Panama
Saturday, May 30, 1987

20

Eva looked up as a very primly dressed maid in her late forties approached the table with coffee and fruit. Behind her on the patio the morning sunshine played off stainless steel and polished glass and chairs. The house was silent and refreshing, clean and new throughout. Outside a man was quietly raking in the garden. Angel, across from Eva at the breakfast table, sat watching her as breakfast was served. He saw her lower her head to take in the aroma of the steaming coffee in her cup. The graceful maid bowed gently and moved off when she was done with her serving.

"When I woke up this morning," Eva said, studying her cup and its contents, "my first thought was that I was home."

She slowly turned the cup in its saucer, then picked it up and had her first sip. She smiled.

"I was not startled at all, it was as if I had just woken up on another morning . . . in Paitilla . . . it seems like a long time ago."

She lowered the cup a bit and took another sip.

"Then I remembered. My first thought was where I was, my second. . . ." She stared at the middle of the table while placing the cup back onto the saucer.

"My second was what the literature professor told us one day when we were reading Manrique's 'coplas,' that poem about his father's death. In medieval Spanish, the work 'awaken' was the same word as for 'remember' . . . 'recordar.' . . . When one awakens, one certainly remembers, for better or for worse."

Angel followed Eva's lead and also raised his cup of coffee, in his case, for a single, longer sip. He withdrew the cup, though, and made a face. Licking his lips, he put the coffee cup down and reached for a glass of ice water. He took a drink and continued watching Eva.

"And for you," he said, "was it for better, or for worse?"

"I was frightened last night, Angel, I had a bad day and I was frightened by what happened. And now I wonder how you found me in the rain yesterday. I would like to know that."

Angel placed his forearms on the table and leaned out toward her.

"By accident," he said, "we were coming up the main avenue when I saw you duck off onto that sidestreet. I said, 'that looks a lot like Eva Icaza out there in the rain.' I had my driver double back and we found you, soaked, standing there by that building. That's all there is to the story."

He sat straight up, eyed an orange, and picked it up out of the fruit basket the maid had served them. Examining it closely, he began to peel it, carefully placing each strip of peel into a small porcelain dish.

"I see," Eva said softly, lifting the coffee cup again.

Angel finished his small project and held the peeled orange up to the light.

"They are bitter at this time of year," he said.

He separated two sections and popped them into his mouth. Eva watched him chew and discreetly remove the pips from his mouth.

There was no one there, Eva noticed, no one at all. She had woken at around eight thirty, and the house had been silent then. Eva barely remembered the shower she had taken the night before. What lingered in her mind was the magnificent bathroom and the luxury of the bath. Angel had become a wealthy man in his own right, perhaps even wealthier than his father.

"Where are the people who were here last night?" she asked.

Angel helped himself to more orange.

"A house rule," he said, "no overnights . . . except for special guests."

He looked at Eva.

"I do not savor ghosts. But Eva, perhaps you would like something more substantial, eggs, toast, ham . . . Aida!" he called out in a loud voice, turning his chair to look back at the hall entrance. "Aida, ven aqui!"

"No, Angel," Eva replied, raising a hand to cancel the request. "This is fine, I'm happy, thank you."

Angel paused, turned to meet her eyes, then raised his hands above the table.

"Nothing else?" he asked with almost childlike innocence.

"Nothing else, Angel, thank you," she repeated.

In a moment the maid appeared in the hallway walking their way.

"It's all right," Angel said, motioning to her without turning around.

The maid stopped, did another slight bow, and returned to where she had come from. For a prolonged instant the two breakfasters sat looking at one another.

"You're a liar, Angel," Eva said, lifting a napkin to her lips. "You followed me from Roberto's, that is what happened."

Angel sat up straight and looked uncomfortable, a little irritated.

"It happened as I said it happened." he replied, "I saw you walking in the rain. But no matter. You were walking out on that loser and he deserved it. You made the right decision, you should stick with it. Don't be a fool. Roberto is going nowhere in life . . . this could be for you . . . look around . . . what you had before."

Angel gestured with a sweeping hand at the interior of his splendid villa. Eva kept her eyes on the man, though, not the villa.

"You are the most beautiful woman in Panama," he continued, "the classiest woman I have ever known. I said to myself a long time ago, on the beach that night when we were finally together and all alone, I said I would have you for my own one day. That day has come."

Eva smiled.

"You have money, and beautiful things all around you, Angel," she said, "precious things, I, too, knew a long time ago that you would have all of that. But why me? I know you have no lack of lovely ladies to help you pass your time . . . so why me . . . why now?"

"Why you?" he asked, picking up his orange again. "You called me, don't you remember? I knew what you wanted. I knew that time had come. Yes, you, now. Eva I love you, I'll make no apologies for that. And I sense you are falling in love with me, too. What could be better? I can give you everything you grew up with, and so much more. I can bring you back to where you were. This house, your house, and three more like it. Two more here in Panama, and another in Florida. You tell me where. We'll build there, too."

He was incredibly handsome, Eva marveled. She smiled again. Just incredibly handsome. Yet the looks were misplaced somehow. They were too sculptured, too sharp.

"We would be two good candidates for goodness," she remarked. "The literature professor said that in medieval times, beauty was a characteristic of goodness."

Angel sat back and looked puzzled. He placed what was left of the orange on his plate.

"What?"

Eva looked down at the table and laughed.

"Nothing, Angel," she replied, "it was nothing. You make interesting offers. How many young ladies have taken you up on these bargains?" Eyes set in an unamused stare, Angel looked on as Eva took another sip of coffee.

"Perhaps you take lightly what I say," he said, "perhaps you do not know Angel Mendez. I do not ask or cajole any woman for favors, that is not my circumstance in life. But when it comes to *the* woman and *the* moment, I do not approach any woman. Listen. You will be royalty. Next week after the . . . next week when I am not so busy, we'll start by flying to Paris for a wardrobe, I see Roberto keeps you in sackcloth. Or Rome, your father used to take you to Rome. Or anywhere . . . Hong Kong, Madrid, New York, you name it."

The man outside had finished raking and was walking slowly away, large bag of grasses, leaves, and roots slung over his shoulder. In a distant corner of the house some type of generator switched on and the coolness of the air conditioning rose around them more pleasantly with every passing minute. There would be a pool, Eva knew, someplace quite near. Angel had been a champion swimmer. Just another refreshing thought.

The maid appeared again and walked over to the table with her usual professional bearing. She was still a handsome woman, Eva noticed as she stopped beside Angel, about a foot behind him, and held up some kind of note. Angel glanced over, took the note, and nodded. The maid backed away and vanished once more down the hallway. Mendez briefly read what someone had written, frowned, then stuffed the note in his guayabera pocket. He looked up at Eva and maintained his serious expression for a moment. The smile reappeared, however, and Angel was back to the matter at hand.

"What happened to your career in social work?" he asked.

Eva raised her eyes to a point above his head.

"It was interesting while it lasted," she replied, "but funding for the Canal Zone seemed to dry up. That's where I worked."

"Hard times," Angel said.

He pushed the last few sections of orange off onto a placemat and stared at them.

"The monies for our work were, shall I say, diverted, Angel? It was in all the newspapers, if you remember. Something about a Social Security scandal."

Angel flicked a finger at the orange and mumbled something. Then he looked up at Eva and shifted position in his chair.

"Some bureaucratic incompetence," Angel said, "it's pretty common."

Eva smiled.

"Sure, yes. Tell me, Angel, why the military? Why did you choose the military?"

"It had been a good life for me," he replied. "I rose fast in the ranks, I made a favorable impression on the High Command . . . and here I am."

He gestured again at his house and rolled his eyes around. Eva continued.

"Some terrible things have been going on in the military, Angel, I hope you're not a part of them."

Angel stopped rolling his eyes and looked back at Eva. He sat up slowly and stiffened his shoulders.

"I am a . . . paper pusher, Eva. I push papers. They have me in charge of the engineering brigade. I just work on official projects. I am not involved in any kind of dirty business . . . but you know me, how could you think that?"

Eva wore a thoughtful expression. She studied Angel and shook her head.

"Yes I do know you, Angel. You like to be in charge. That could be a wonderful gift. You are a born leader. I like these things you have, who wouldn't?"

She looked around and smiled again.

"But I have a commitment or two back in Panama City, and I'll have to attend to business. It was very nice seeing you, Angel, I thank you for this unexpected trip and your kind hospitality. Now I must go back. Can you arrange that?"

Angel's eyes grew narrower as he considered what was being said.

"Back?" he asked, "back? To what? We just talked about that. You walked out on that bum. Before that you were calling me on the phone. O.K., here I am, there he is. He's gone. I'm sitting across the table from you and offering you a life a princess in Europe would envy. You can't go back, Eva, any more than I can go back. We're big kids now, not teenagers. The politics we left behind in high school and college, the social work was for kicks. This, what you see around you, is adult living. As they often say, you can be young and poor, but you had better not be old and poor. What you had in Paitilla can never be again unless you tie up with a man like Angel Mendez, and in Panama, the Angel Mendez's are not easy to find."

Gaining steam, he stood up from his chair and stretched. Then he leaned out over the table and stared at Eva.

"I'll ask you one more time. Do you like what you see? Have you seen it before? And will you see it again?"

"I like what I see, Angel," Eva replied, "and I even like you, in my own way. You were a friend back then, and you are again. But I didn't ask to come here. I want to back to the city. Now respect my wishes."

Angel stood straight up and began to take small steps around the table in Eva's direction. He was about to say something when the maid appeared again, this time in the company of a small, officious man in neatly pressed white tropical garb. They were carrying a telephone on a long cable.

"For you, Captain," the small man called out as he and the maid walked up to Angel. "It's Major Villalobos."

"Damn you!" Angel shouted, seizing the phone and hurling it out across the floor. "Get that thing out of here and tell him I'll call him back!"

The small man and the maid scurried around picking up the phone and cracked receiver as Angel watched them. He was seething. Eva watched him follow his house staff with his eyes until they had disappeared. She made a move to get up. He turned quickly and stared at her.

"Where are you going?" he asked angrily.

"Home, Angel, with or without your help."

"To rot with the trash and the heat," he said, advancing toward her, "to cook and scrub and sit around reading magazines about clothes and gringos and places and things you'll never see or have. To *live*," he almost shouted, now standing less than a meter in front of her, "with a scumbag little radical out peeping from a balcony! That's living?"

Eva went blank as Angel finished. She looked up into his eyes and raised her fingers to her cheek.

"How do you? . . ." she began, but her voice trailed off and she continued to stare.

Angel dropped his head and looked behind him. He threw up his arms and shook his head.

"I won't let you do it, Eva," he said, looking back at her. "You'll stay here."

Eva held her fingers at her throat now. She swallowed and slowly sat down in her breakfast chair. Angel stood watching.

"Yes, I'll stay, Angel," she said quietly, "but I'll need a little time to think this over."

Eva reached for her coffee, lifted the cup, and wet her lips. The liquid was now quite cool. Angel kept watching her, not really sure of what he was seeing. His anger was beginning to subside.

"That's good, Eva Icaza, that's good. It'll be just like the old days, you'll learn to be happy again, I promise you."

He suddenly glanced down at his watch.

"Call Marissa if you need anything. I must leave. Relax, you need rest."

Eva looked up and smiled weakly.

"Yes, of course," she smiled.

Angel bent down to kiss her but Eva turned her head. His lips fell on her neck.

21

About thirty meters from the highway there began a stretch of woods and low hills that rolled off into the hazy distance without a trace of disquiet. A large bird soared and winged its peaceful way above the tree and savannah shrubtops on its way to somewhere under the morning sun, perhaps an early meal. A "lazy bear" sloth looked out at creation from its perch on a leafy tree in a shaded glen and a ground animal scurried along in the grasses, stopping every so often to glance around in the fear of a nearby predator's presence. Above the sun slipped in and out of hurrying low clouds. The day was warm to begin with, and promised to grow steamy and heavy. An old woman scolded a child at a roadside fruit stand. The child replied with shrill accusations.

"I have fresh information," a young officer said to a tall lieutenant standing on the front seat of a jeep alongside the road. The young officer had come trotting up from quite a distance and he was slightly out of breath. He waited for an answer, but the lieutenant seemed to ignore him. He was scanning the road with a pair of binoculars. The young officer stood there watching, quietly catching his breath and looking out in the general direction of the lieutenant's scan. In a moment he continued.

"We have information regarding Santos," he said, tugging at his throat with his fingers. "It seems an old guardsman saw him late yesterday afternoon down by the old armory. Lieutenant Cruz, the guardsman swears it was Santos."

The lieutenant lowered the binoculars but kept watching the road with his eyes.

"Go on," he said.

The young officer pointed in the direction of Penonome.

"He was in the company of a man named Horacio Rodriguez, the guardsman recognized him. There was another man, too, but the guardsman wasn't sure."

"Old friends from the Paredes area," Cruz said, raising the binoculars back up to his eyes. "Keep talking."

"The guardsman said they took off in a black Mercedes, they took a road that could have taken them to the west side of the city, or back to the Pan American Highway. Or, I was thinking, maybe off to the boondocks. The route the guardsman described could lead you to Rio Hato and the coast, or even. . . ."

"Forget the west side of the city, and forget the boondocks. Santos hit the highway, and he headed west. He hasn't been by here."

Cruz let the binoculars hand down on their cord to his chest. He appeared to be studying something on the horizon. The young officer looked on with an interested expression. Behind him three soldiers were forming a circle to light up smokes. Cruz slowly stretched out his arm and pointed at points west.

"We've had no reports from Aguadulce, right?" he asked the young officer. The officer shook his head.

"None, Sir. And none from Divisa, on the outside chance he slipped through Aguadulce last night. He's somewhere between here and there."

Cruz tapped his fingers on the top edge of the jeep windshield.

"What's between here and Aguadulce," he asked.

"Not much," the young officer replied, "not much at all . . . except for . . . nah, nothing."

"Except for what?" Cruz asked, finally looking down at the man.

"Nata," the officer answered, "a little burg called Nata, just a wide spot on the road."

Cruz returned to scanning the road. He raised the binoculars again and stared.

"What the hell is in Nata?" he asked.

The officer made a "who knows" gesture.

"Some old damn church, horses, not much else. Like I said, just a hamlet."

The wind came up and swept across the tops of the grasses, bending thin bows in its passing. A car sped by on the highway.

"Called . . . 'Nata de los Caballeros', or something like that. Somebody told me it was the first church in the Americas, old damn thing."

"Let's roll," Cruz growled, "get the boys out of the city and let's get this show on the road."

"Yes, Sir," the young officer saluted, backing off and signaling to the soldiers behind him. They followed the officer over to another group of vehicles on the other side of the road. Cruz's driver was walking up to the jeep from the field. He was zipping up.

"Let's go!" Cruz roared, lowering the binoculars and taking a seat. The driver skipped around to the driver's side and hopped in. He turned on the ignition and revved up to go.

"Lieutenant Roma, they're moving, the entire squadron. Look!" Roma snatched the binoculars from his sergeant's hand and scanned the distant column down in the long valley before him.

"Wait just a minute . . . then we'll follow . . . just where the hell can this be going?"

The sergeant looked out over the valley and slowly shook his head. Behind him no fewer than forty men in the detachment watched with renewed interest from their vehicles in their blinds. Two engines turned over, and in a moment, the entire force was ready to go.

"Steady," Roma whispered to his aide.

* * * *

"This must be it. Stop here."

Santos stood in a dark passageway holding a flashlight up to an old, wooden door. With his free hand he brushed away dust and gritty sand from the massive old frame, attempting to see how it opened.

"Light a flare," he snarled to one of two nearby men who had followed into the ancient tunnel.

The man fumbled with a bundle he was carrying and eventually pulled out the flare Santos had ordered. He struck a match to light it just as Santos discovered the way in. Down to his right his flashlight shined on what looked like a brand new hasp and latch. He reached down and fingered a large padlock hanging on the recently installed assembly.

"Here it is," he mumbled as his associate lit the flare. The flare caught on with a brilliant flash and evidently burned the hand of the man who lit it. The man muttered an angry oath and let it fall on the ground. Santos turned around and looked at it, then motioned to the two of them.

"Here, let's bust this fucker off, what can we use?"

"Mr. Santos," the man who had burned his hand said, "I thought you had a key. . . ."

Santos looked at him, then at the latch. Then he smiled.

"Of course, I'm an idiot. Stand back."

The two men stepped back in the darkness and leaned against the far wall of the passageway. They watched in the red light of the flare as Santos produced a heavy pistol and inspected it. Placing the barrel a few inches from the padlock, he aimed, then fired. The sound of the pistol was deafening in the tunnel. Small clods of dirt fell from the ceiling and the noise echoed for a full quarter of a minute. Santos lowered his face to look at the padlock and saw that it was still intact. He stood up straight again and took aim. This time he fired two shots. The concussion started a minor landslide. When the smoke and noise had cleared, though, he looked down to see a cleanly severed lock.

"Let's go in and took a look," Santos coughed.

Pulling the broken padlock from the hasp and latch, Santos attempted to open the door. It was a moment before he could pry it open, however, and the other two had to pitch in and help. The door suddenly shot open as they worked at it. A small pin inserted at the top had been responsible for the delay. They had popped it off with their efforts.

"Take it easy," Santos said as his two partners pushed from behind. He held the flashlight up and carefully advanced into the inner chamber. After going about three meters, he stopped and shined the light around. He saw strange shapes and dusty forms, some stacked on shelves, some piled on the floor covered with eons of passing time.

"Get another flare!" Santos menaced, flashing his light even deeper into the chamber.

Santos turned to one of the racks and ran his finger along one of the objects. To his surprise, it was smooth and heavy underneath, unyielding as he pushed against it. He brought his flashlight up and examined it a little closer. Rubbing the object with the side of his hand, Santos cleared away a patch of dust about ten centimeters wide. His mouth dropped open as his light suddenly reflected off what was below the dust.

"Holy god," he muttered, standing back a ways.

Behind him his friend lit up the flare. A burst of red light illuminated the cave's depths. Catching a glimpse of something strange beside him, Santos wheeled back and pointed his flashlight straight ahead into the chamber. The light of the flare was more than sufficient, though. What had spooked Santos was standing there in plain view . . . smiling.

"It's gold, my friend," Father Sandoval said. "Isn't it lovely?"

Santos stared at him and let the flashlight drop to the floor. His two friends had started to bolt from the chamber, but they stopped by the entrance just inside.

"Who the fuck are you, asshole?" Santos demanded, recovering from his start.

Father Sandoval laughed and took a step toward him.

"What difference does it make?" he asked.

He stopped, crossed his arms, and kept smiling.

"You have come here for the gold, now you shall have it, for all time. look around you, treasures such as you have never dreamed of. The last dream of our former Spanish majesties. To think you now stand as an equal of his last Hapsburg Excellency, Charles the Second."

Santos followed the priest's gaze around the eerily lit vault and began to realize the meaning of what he had said. The place was teeming with dust-concealed objects, from floor to ceiling, from wall to wall. Santos' mind ran wild.

"I . . . don't have much time, you faggot," he menaced, "others will be here soon, so you will help me now. Where can I get a truck near here?"

"A truck?" the priest asked with a concerned expression, taking a step closer to Santos. "A truck?"

"Yes, a truck, mother fucker, get wise with me and I'll hang you up by your dick."

Santos pulled out his pistol again and his friends, growing bolder,advanced to stand behind him. The flare's light flickered and glowed at Santos' feet, sometimes brilliant, sometimes dim. The priest looked worried.

"Yes a truck," he said quietly, putting a finger to his chin, "a truck."

"Now you cocksucker or I'll shove a red hot rod up your ass! A truck! Don't stand there! Get the fuck moving!"

"Right away!" Father Sandoval said, easing off to the side in the face of the pistol. "I know where there is a truck."

"Move, fuckface!!" Santos screamed.

"I'm moving!" the priest replied.

By the door the quieter of the two men looked around. There was no shadow of an outside light. The vault was sealed. He looked back at the door behind him, then at the priest. Then he looked at Santos, then at his 'associate'.

"I . . . ," he began.

His voice was extinguished in a damburst of renewed Santos bellowing.

"Now!!" he was threatening.

The quiet man began to shudder.

22

"So, Bob, just what have you been able to set up? I mean, Monday's coming up and we're in the dark. What's on your mind?

Bob Friedan flicked the ash from his cigarette and looked up at the tropical invention before him . . . sunglasses and a big, wide smile, a brightly colored silk shortsleeve shirt and baggy white cotton trousers. Bob took another drag. Matos. Ugly bastard.

"My end's all taken care of, now I guess it depends on you."

"*We've* got a perfect arrangement, Bob," the tropical man said, drawing closer, "something you dream about. But how about you, pal, it's not that we don't trust you, it's just that what's coming down is more important than your average shenanigan. What about the goddam Senator?"

"I said, taken care of," Bob replied. "He'll leave the Embassy in a motorcade about a quarter to ten . . . give him a half an hour to forty five minutes leeway . . . and head up Balboa Avenue. At about ten, more or less, he'll stop at the Balboa monument and lay a wreath at Balboa's feet. There'll be a moment of silence, or a brief speech, or who knows what, then they'll be off to the Marriott for brunch with business, I'm sure you've heard about the affair."

"Yes, we have, Bob, and we correctly figured you were behind it. But go on, give us the details."

Bob looked at him and crushed out the butt.

"What? There are no details. What the hell details could there be? He'll be at the monument to Balboa at ten or roundabouts. I thought that was what you wanted? What's the problem, Matos?"

"The link, Bob, the link. So far, so good. Now what about the damn link?"

A hood peeped in the door to check on the situation. Bob watched the man and sighed.

"Yes, the link. It's a good one. The Drug Enforcement people have already picked up rumblings of a Cuban-Sandino plot out there hatching. The information they have is too vague to figure out. It won't make sense until it happens. That's the cute part. They'll put two and two together . . . but they'll have to divide it by three, then find the square root . . . in the end there'll be wild speculation, but nothing concrete . . . except for the notes they'll intercept. You're looking at an international incident, boy, with widespread repercussions. Get this, though, down the line, when the wise men finally get a word in edgewise, there'll be a lot of questions asked. I'm just buying you a little time. I hope you can handle it." The tropical man turned abruptly to the window and covered his mouth with his hand.

"God, Bob," he murmured, "that's real good, you did a good job. So Monday at ten-ish, right where we said . . . good work."

The man walked over to a window with the shade drawn down and turned back to look at Bob.

"You'll get your money at 11 on Monday, then you can catch that little plane."

Bob closed his eyes.

"I'd better have it on Monday morning at 8," he said quietly, "or I call some shots to kill the deal."

The tropical man smiled and nodded slowly.

"O.k., Bob, o.k., you drive a hard bargain."

Now three hoods stood in the doorway, all mutely gazing at the gringo and his friend. Bob pulled another smoke out of his pack.

"Got a beer?" he asked the tropical man over his shoulder.

"So it's all set?" a short, pudgy man in a fresh, blue guayabera asked the tropical man as Bob sped away down a country lane.

"It's a go," the tropical man said.

Bob's car raised a cloud of dust behind it as it disappeared in the distance. The two men stood watching. Behind them in the small villa maybe ten civilian-dressed men milled around. Twenty or more uniformed guards manned posts along the lane. The short man frowned.

"These meetings have been risky. I've got a feeling they may be watching him."

"Bob?" the tropical man asked with a surprised look. "No, I kind of doubt it. Besides, he's the only one in Panama outside of us who knows you're here. Or was, I should say. What do you think?"

The short man shook his head.

"That man could rise from the dead, and probably would. He can outthink our best boys while he's asleep. So let sleeping dogs lie. What's going down outweighs Bob. And besides, I'm hearing strange things. What's this about Quevedo and Arias involved in some secret struggle. That could fuck everything up."

The tropical man kicked at the dust and cursed.

"Who knows, some stupid romp out to the west. Arias is impatient and Quevedo's getting senile, I swear. But at least it'll get 'em out of the city for a while. I know for a fact that American intelligence is on to it. A good diversion."

The short man turned to go back inside, then stopped and rubbed his chin.

"Yeah, that's right," he said, "especially in the case of our pal Quevedo. It'll keep his mind occupied. But get me information on the damn thing. In the meantime . . . who's in command?" The tropical man chuckled and threw up his arms as if in jest.

"Never more than now, My General, you are in command. This is going to be a day we'll long remember."

The small man smiled and ran his fingers back through his greasy black hair. Suddenly in the sun, his pockmarked face gleamed.

"See to it that it is, my friend," he said, turning to enter the villa, "see to it that it is. I'm holding you responsible."

The tropical man's grin slowly faded from his face as the small man vanished into the inner darkness of the country place. Looking down at his watch, he snapped his fingers and pointed at a civilian saluted crisply and hurried off to a near-by car.

Panama City
January 27, 1671

23

"Don Juan, you will hold the right flank, you must be unyielding in your defense. If the corsairs get by you, we are lost. Is that clear?"

Don Juan Portando Bargueño, the Governor of Veraguas posed silently in the early morning sun, head erect, sword drawn and resting point down into the earth. He sniffed arrogantly and closed his eyes. Behind him several hundred head of cattle moved nervously in tight quarters, cowherds driving them together with heavy sticks.

"Don Alonso, you will take up the left flank, to you will be entrusted the crushing of our foe once they have fallen into the trap. You have many stout hearts and true at your command. What say you?"

"Steadfastly in your service, Lord President," Don Alonso Alcandete replied with a slightly affected bow.

The President of the Audiencia stared at him for a moment, then moved on.

"And to you, Don Francisco," he said to the military man, "to you will be entrusted the glory of the day, the cavalry charge and our resounding victory."

"The sounds of a thousand hoofs will thunder across the plain, Your Grace," he said, also bowing. Yet his was an even more studied bow than Alonso Alcandete's. He removed his hat and bent low enough to let its brim sweep across the tops of the grasses, legs crossed underneath him. Francisco de Haro, the main bastion of the city's defense, presented a striking figure.

"Then for Santiago and Spain," Don Juan Perez de Guzman concluded, "for our Majesty Charles and the Holy Roman Empire, let us drive this English scum from the face of the earth, and let us rejoice and give thanks to Santa Maria Purisima and the host of saints. This is our hour."

"The Sisters of Rosario, Mercedes, and Santo Domingo stand by with all manner of comfort and succor for our men should the battle grow fierce," the President's confessor said from a few feet behind him.

"We thank you, Juan de Dios," the President replied, surveying the plain.

A tropical storm had broken just the day before and white wisps of clouds were rolling in off the Southern Sea on the fresh, cool airs of the morning. Sunshine fell everywhere and its light sparkled on the deep green foliage.

Near the military contingent the cattle continued to stamp and move restlessly in a large, flowing circle. At times their aborted stampedes were cut short by the crack of whips and poles well brandished and applied by the attending cowherds. The Spanish armies were ablaze with relucent colors and banners in hues unfurled by the gusting sea winds. There was no sign, as of yet, of the enemy.

The Coastal Road to Nata

"Highly irregular," a local military official chirped, holding out a hand to lift up the cloth covering one of the drawn wagons. Without warning, the Corregidor slapped his hand away and stood up stiffly with an indignant air.

"I'll thank you to keep your hands off the Archbishop of Seville's personal possessions," the Corregidor said sharply, advancing a step in the direction of the official. "These are holy relics and belongings of His Holy Catholic Majesty's Church, ritual urns and altar embellishments destined to the greater glory of Gawd! How dare you!!"

A group of ruffians vaguely distinguishable as militia stood behind their leader looking on. One or two had stepped forward when the Corregidor roughed him up, but all were dully in awe of the courtly-mannered spectacle standing before them.

"But I must inspect this shipment!" the official insisted, "it is the law and my obligation as the 'Regidor' of this municipality, His Royal Highness has decreed. . . ."

"His Royal Highness has *sent* us!" the Corregidor interrupted, "I am the envoy of the Viceroy of Peru, here, look!!"

The 'regidor' leaned forward to view the papers held out before him. Slowly, he nodded his head.

"Yes, I see that is true," he said, "yes, the papers seem to be in order. But what on earth are you doing in this outland? And why in heavens name are you going to Nata by this route?"

"That," the Corregidor muttered, now walking slowly back toward the front of the caravan, "is a matter of concern to no one but His Royal Highness and my leige the Viceroy . . . unless . . ." he said, turning to face the 'regidor', "unless you feel you must contramand their expressed written orders . . . ?"

"Of course not, My Lord," the official said with a bow and an expression of misunderstood intentions, "of course not. I am only obeying the orders of my commission, you must understand. The caravan goes on!I will see to it that you receive full military protection while you are passing through these parts. I personally will see to your safe passage!"

The Corregidor looked at the man and sniffed loudly.

"I am much obliged," he said, "I am proud to see that His Majesty interests are so well served . . . by gallant men such as you. What might your name be, so that I may mention it to the Viceroy?"

"Sanchez, My Lord, Pedro Aurelio Sanchez de Carrillo Sotomayor, at your service."

The man did a half bow and looked back at his men.

"No doubt a knight," the Corregidor added, now returning to his mount.

He stopped half way there and turned back to face the regidor.

"We will be off again, we fear the shadow of certain folk we took to be corsairs a while back during our ascent from the seashore. I have a dreadful fear of the nasty fellows, so crude, so uncivilized, so . . . so . . . impossible to control. . . ."

"Where, might I ask, My Lord, were these wretched beggars?" the regidor asked.

The Corregidor waved his hand up into the air in a gesture of frustration.

"About a half a league back, we counted five or six of the devils, there couldn't have been many."

He carefully eyed the 'militia' with the regidor as he spoke. There were more than twenty of the unruly bastards, each one of them anxiously attuned to the mule train and its cargo.

"Just five or six?" the regidor asked.

"Yes, I believe so," the Corregidor answered, pointing off toward the Bay of Parita to the south, "five or six. But you can never trust these English sons of whores. Five or six . . . why, it might take at least thirty Spaniards to chase the foul bunch. It's dirty business and risky."

"Have no fear," the regidor pronounced solemnly, "we shall go now and dispatch this filth without delay."

The Corregidor looked shocked.

"You . . . would go back there and give battle to the Englishmen alone? But . . . what courage! What manly resolve! This shall go straight to the ears of His Majesty Himself!!"

'We depart immediately, Your Excellency. I shall personally attend to the devastation of the ungodly invaders."

The regidor signaled his men and walked briskly toward his lean, savannah steed. Some of the men hesitated a long moment, alternately glancing at their leader and the mysterious large bundles and shapes on the backs of the mules and burros.

"I said, let's go!" the regidor ordered.

The less sullen of the lot began to follow the regidor to their mounts, a few lingered to contemplate the load.

"For Santiago, and . . . Spain . . . ," the regidor began boldly. But his voice trailed off as he spotted the stragglers by the caravan. "Let's go!!" he shouted.

The 'militia' was moving now, to a man. The Corregidor cheered a mighty battle salute as the party began to depart, then looked back at his charge. When the hoofs had faded sufficiently in the morning sun, the Corregidor leaned against a mule and yanked out his perfumed handkerchief.

"Let us proceed with all possible haste," he said to a driver of the cloth on a nearby horse. "To Nata, I pray, before that bunch returns."

The muleteers were already applying their whips.

In a Woods Near Old Panama

A graying, but still enormously powerful man sat chewing on his breakfast in a wooded thicket. Cold, half-cooked beef and a small ration of fruit lay on his cloth dish on the ground. He winced sharply as his now less than sturdy teeth bit into something like gristle or a soft bone. He was eyeing a scrawny, eagerly intense youth a few feet in front of him on the other side of a low, burnt out fire. A few faint wisps of smoke rose up between them in the morning air.

"The Spaniard is near!" they heard a distant sentry cry. "Ho! Many Spaniards, all in battle array!"

The graying man spit out the cause of his discomfort and carefully inspected what remained. Just a few hours before he had been gnawing at the leather soles of his shoes in the isthmus jungle on the way to this battle. Then they had discovered the South Sea as had Balboa. To their great surprise, they were greeted by cows and tender calves. So began the feast that had lasted the night and was now resumed before the inevitable battle that lay ahead.

"Spaniards boasting of our imminent death!" the sentry shouted.

Suddenly, the scrawny lad leaned across the fire and snatched the graying man's fruit right off his plate. The graying man stared at him for a moment and watched as the young man consumed his food. When the fruit was gone, when it was devoured and deeply ingested,the scrawny man laughed and slobbered at the mouth.

"Fooled ye!" the scrawny man said, wiping his lips of foul froth and filth," 'tis I who ate your pretty pear!"

He made a face at the graying man and gestured at him with his hand,leaning out over the fire to bring the gesture home. But in a flash that hand was caught by the wrist and held tight. The graying man squeezed hard, then lowered the scrawny man's hand down forcefully to where he pressed it onto the surface of a hot rock by the fireside. As the scrawny man screamed in pain, the graying man withdrew his razor cutlass. With an air of nonchalance he raised the weapon and let it slash with an expressionless face. In an instant the scrawny man sat there staring at a stump of an arm, hand and wrist neatly lopped off.

"Ay . . . ay-yai-yai-yai-yai!!!" he screamed as the English lads scooted here and there around him to form up the ranks.

"Ay-yai-yai-yai!!!!!"

The scrawny man danced around in wild circles gazing at the gushing blood and hopeless future of it all, eyes in a living horror. He saw his hand lying on the ground and half-stooped to collect it. Then, understanding in a second's grace, the youth skipped off into the brush with a blood-curdling scream and a mindful of anguish.

"Lively there, boys, this ain't no day in a skiff on a river," an officer barked, watching the scrawny man depart, "there's work to be done!"

The graying man quietly wiped off his cutlass and returned it to its scabbard. Bending down, he grabbed a last piece of meat and stuffed it in his mouth. Then he picked up his beautifully polished long rifle and slung it over his back. In a minute he was up trotting after the others.

"Good God, what was that?" a Spanish officer asked, staring off in the direction of the wooded plain below his position. "Did you hear that?"

A mounted officer beside him squinted in the same direction and nodded.

"Yes, I did," he whispered, "it was awful, they're coming . . . they're really coming."

"Steady men!" the military man shouted from somewhere behind them, "steady, this is our hour! Glory is nigh!"

They looked out over the descending plain at the dense cover at the lower end and saw only movement behind the tree line, but they knew. The Englishmen were there in full force after a hot and angry march through the jungle, and they were readying to bring forth the fight. A Spanish gentleman with a ceremonial jeweled sword brandished it above his head on horseback, pausing occasionally to hitch up a silk stocking improperly gartered. Two blacks pressed into service cautiously eyed the distant woods whence they knew the enemy would come. One of the blacks nervously stroked the barrel of his musket with an oiled cloth, the other rubbed a large, smooth stone in the palm of his hand. To their side three Genoese mercenaries stood pointing and commenting on the movement below. And in the open plain, not too far before them, the Spanish cattle flowed in the same raging circle they had maintained for half the morning. Their sounds filled the silence left by the waiting defenders.

"There they are!" the military men squealed loudly, suddenly spotting the first plainly visible corsair contingent exiting the brush. He watched them closely, mouth half open in amazement. They were puny enough and damn few.

"But I see . . . ," he began.

His voice trailed off and he raised a glass to his eyes, trying to focus from atop an anxious horse.

"Damn, I see white crosses on a field azure, the Knights of St.John, I do believe . . . that means there are God fearing Catholics among them."

An officer at his side raised his own glass to look, but after a lengthy appraisal, he frowned.

"My Lord, I see no white crosses . . . I see only cutthroats . . . besides, if memory serves me, the Knights of St. John have no white crosses, their emblem is. . . ."

"Silence!" the military man shouted, holding up his free hand. "The time has come! Loose the infernal herd on the heathen bastards! Ho!! For Santiago and Spain!!!"

The military man pulled out a pistol and shot it into the air. At a distance, the cowherds looked back for a moment, then furiously whipped at their cattle. A wild stampede began in the general direction of the corsairs and the Spanish ranks cheered loudly.

'Your death and destruction!" the military man now roared. "Die, you dogs!!"

The entire Spanish force looked on as the cattle ran off down the plain. Soon, however, it became evident that the stampede was losing force. The main body of cattle began to splinter into smaller groups. The pace slowed.

"Look, Sir, the Spanish are sending cows at us. I swear it." The commanding officer looked up from loading his pistol and puzzled at the strange sight.

"What do you mean, they're sending cows at us?"

His adjutant shaded his eyes with his hand to get a better look.

"Yes . . . cows, Sir. It must be some kind of Spanish trick."

Indeed, cattle were bearing down on the from the upper plain. The Commander smiled.

"God must have told them to do it" he muttered, "it must have been a vision."

"Sir?" the adjutant asked, looking at his leader.

"Nothing," the Commander answered, "it's nothing. Keep our men moving and pass the word, nothing has changed."

On the plain the cattle rush had petered out into a mushy, casual trot, and the Spaniards' cheer had died down to an echo.

"More beef, that's good" the Commander said.

He had reached the rendezvous point and smiled to see the other principals of his contingent standing ready.

"Good work, men, gather 'round'."

Three men came together and watched as the Commander surveyed the plain from the thicket and finalized his plan.

"Lawrence Prince, you will command the van. Take your men and lead them up to the top of that hill . . . over there. . . ."

He pointed to a location not too far away and looked back out over the plain.

"That will render their notion of a fixed defense useless, and I believe they have no contingency, listen up, then go quickly."

The Lieutenant Colonel nodded in approval and the Commander looked to another man.

"You, Edward Collier, will head the left flank. The main brunt of the Spanish attack will fall on you initially. Set up your sharp-shooters and devastate them. If you can make them fall back, their day is lost. Clear?"

"Yes, Sir, quite clear."

"Thank you, Colonel," the Commander said, moving on. "Bledry Morgan, you will take charge of the rearguard, you will be our anchor, our hope, and our salvation if things go wrong. By all means, be on the lookout. If you feel your presence could turn the tide, come forth. If we are charging ahead, or falling back, close ranks and take up a rock solid position. Do you understand, Colonel?"

"I do, Lord Morgan, but Sir Henry, we are outnunmbered two to one. That is an army I perceive on the plain, a full-blown Spanish army. What makes you think we can succeed."

Henry Morgan stared at the man and advanced a step or two, curly long hair blowing in the freshening sea breeze.

"You have always been a brave man, Bledry," he remarked, almost to himself. "But you have never been a confident man. How many times have you routed Spaniards?"

Colonel Bledry Morgan looked around and nodded.

"Let's get on with it," he sighed.

"Don Francisco, the Englishmen, they are avoiding our lines! They're circling off to the flank!"

The military man stood staring at the scattered herd of splendid cattle off grazing on the plain before him.

"An omen," he said in a low voice.

The young officer looked around and studied his Commander for a moment.

"Sir?" he said with a quizzical gaze.

"Let the cavalry charge!!!" the military man said suddenly, "for Santiago and Spain!!"

Plunging his spurs into his mount, the military man surged ahead and was quickly flying along at a full gallop. In an instant the rest of his gallant men followed. They headed toward what had emerged from the woods as the main force of the invaders, and the cavalry was a sight to see. The plain glowed for a minute with brilliant scarlet, blues in a full spectrum, emeralds and sparkling golds. These were the colors of the Spanish ceremonial uniforms and standards rippling in the winds, as impressive a sight as the city had or ever would see. Then came the popping of long rifles from the closing ranks of the distant, kneeling invaders. At first, nothing seemed to stem the fury of the Spanish cavalry charge. Perhaps at the pinnacle moment of a long and tedious career, the military man, Don Francisco de Haro, heard in his very ears the sounds he had so vividly evoked in the longing imagination of his Lord, the President of the Audiencia; the thundering of hoofs of a charging brigade on a fateful plain. But then a few of the lead men flew off their horses and pitched to the ground as the cavalry reached the midpoint, and not much farther on the entire vanguard was decimated by hot, accurate fire. By the time the cavalry had reached the final quarter of its charge, a full third of the company had been annihilated. There hadn't been a thousand, as the military man had promised, but fewer than three hundred now stood face to face with the cheering lads blasting away with rifles, and those who made it were spent and fightless at the end of the road. The cavalry turned and retreated, corsairs hurling insults after them as they galloped half way up the hill to regroup.

"Gather around, men!" a young officer shouted, frantically searching for the military man. He could not locate him.

"Again, for Santiago and Charles!" he cried out hoarsely. Sweat streaming down from his brow into his eyes, the officer wheeled and charged off again, strangely enough, at the head of the entire remaining cavalry. This time the buccaneer army's fire was less effective. Perhaps due to the thinned out nature of the charge, perhaps because they were less excited, the corsair fire caused fewer casualties the second time around. But no matter. As the Spaniards approached their lines, quick, swarthy sons of bitches ran out from the invaders' positions to leap up and wrench the horsemen from their saddles. When the horses came to a halt at the corsair line, the fighting was hand to hand, cutlass to dull saber. Those who could peeled off from the massacre and fled back to the main Spanish force above. Not many survived.

From above the Spanish army watched and waited. Not a few men had already bolted. Troops toward the rear, hearing strange and terrifying rumors, grew edgy and eyed possible routes of escape. Officers at the fore shouted instructions and the mercenaries shook their heads and muttered comments. The blacks, those who remained, chattered in dialect. They were engaged in unintelligible but lively dialogue.

"There! On the hill! There on the flank! Look!! The dogs have scaled the hill!!!"

The Spaniards and allies looked over at a nearby hill and saw parties from the invading army taking up positions on the slopes. Their intent was now obvious. They would advance from the hill to support the full attack on the plain leading up from the valley. Some idiot discharged a musket in their direction.

'Hold, there!" an officer shouted.

The President of the Audiencia looked on limply as the pirates closed the vise.

Nata
January 27, 1671

24

The Corregidor watched as the mule train crossed the plaza in Nata. The weary beasts hung their heads in the midday sun and mournfully looked around for a cool drink. They would have to wait. Several Spanish clergymen approached the newly arrived party and spoke with the attending brothers. There were 'abrazos' and back slapping greetings as the two groups came together. The Corregidor looked around at the small village and stoicly kept his chin erect, his eyes bright and darting. It was, after all, the worst place he had ended up in in the many years of his service. A dusty backroads nothing a far cry from the viceregal court he had expected . . . some day. The Catholic brothers before him saluted one another with fond hello's and smiles. The Corregidor for the first time felt truly old and past the magic line. He looked down and patted at a small dust mound with the tip of his shoe. Holding the toe there for an instant, he wondered at what had finally occurred.

Without warning he felt a presence behind him, and a hand on his shoulder. The Corregidor stiffened and turned to face the soul who had approached him. To his surprise, it was the Bishop from Panama City. Before he could speak, the Bishop motioned him to be silent.

"Discretion is your breeding," the Bishop said softly, finger to his lips, "let us talk in private."

The Corregidor, recovering from his initial shock, followed the beckoning finger of the church magistrate. In a moment, the two were walking together under a splendid shaded covering of high trees and boughs at the edge of the plaza. Behind them, the brotherhood was guiding the mule train into the main churchyard.

The two walked without exchanging a word until they had arrived at a fresh, shaded patio beside the large, lovely church. The bishop motioned to the Corregidor and the latter discovered a comfortable palm-wicker chair on the stone patio. He waited a moment, protested with his own gesture to the bishop, then reluctantly seated himself before the Catholic officer. Drawing up his tails, the Corregidor was the proper picture of a Spanish official in waiting, in conference. The Bishop remained standing by a small garden of flowers. He looked at the stones, then back at the Corregidor.

"You have done a splendid job," he said, brushing his hand back at his temple in response to an insect's landing. "You are what I knew you would be . . . an excellent man."

"Why, thank you, Lord Bishop," the Corregidor replied, modestly addressing a crease on his lapel. "You are too kind."

The Bishop looked at him with an indifferent expression.

"This is not flattery," he said, "this is an honest opinion. You handled yourself exemplarily, marvelously well."

"I thank you," the Corregidor repeated.

Nata was a dusty place, the Corregidor noted, dry and silent under the eleven o'clock sun. He had not slept the night before on the journey and the weariness and tension of so trying and dangerous an adventure were taking their toll as he relaxed in the peaceful church gardens. He watched the Bishop gazing up at the treetop canopy and wondered at the mystery of it all; but not for long. A fresh breeze rose in the patio and circled up across the flowers to touch the Spanish gentleman in its passing. This jewel of a garden, he thought, some kind of oasis the church could always impose upon an unwilling climate. The Corregidor appreciated that.

"If I may ask, Lord Bishop," he said in curious but respectful tones, "and of course, if the issue is not too sensitive . . . how might you have come to Nata?"

The Bishop looked back from his quiet revery amidst the flowers and smiled.

"I rode," he replied, "on horseback, we are accomplished riders here, that is a tradition. And the trip is much faster that way. I obviously had only myself to bring. There were details to attend to before I left . . . after the ships had departed. But let's talk about your journey. I understand you were detained by the local militia."

"Twice," the Corregidor said, rubbing his eyes, "once just after we landed, and once half-way up from the coast. This is truly the far fringe of civilization."

"The very end of the world," the Bishop agreed. "Yet in its own way, Nata is refreshing. There is so little formality, so little pretension, so few problems to deal with."

He looked closely at the Corregidor and grew serious.

"But you are past that now. You needn't bother yourself with senseless triviality anymore."

The Corregidor looked back at him and raised an eyebrow.

"I beg your pardon, Sir?"

Instead of answering him, the Bishop went on.

"You have served his Majesty long and well," he said, "in many parts of the world. Where were you before Portobelo?"

"Portobelo, my lord? Why. . . ."

He paused for a moment, then continued.

"Before Portobelo, I served in the Villa Rica de Veracruz, in New Spain . . . before that, Puerto Principe, Hispaniola, Cartagena, in Lima, briefly in La Plata . . . I held posts in Italy and France . . . once in Flanders. My first official post was a station in Cadiz, but I was raised, you know, in Madrid."

The Bishop nodded.

"I can tell. Where were you born?"

"In Oviedo," the Corregidor said, "Asturias, the north country . . . perhaps you've been there?"

A faint smile crossed his lips as he prepared to elaborate. The Bishop cut him short.

"Yes, I have," he said, looking away.

The Corregidor grew silent and watched his host's mind wander away to thoughts unknown.

There were distant hoots of laughter in the background in the direction of the churchyard as the brothers unloaded the mule train. No doubt there would be a celebration. The Corregidor turned his head that way and listened to their sounds of amusement. His feeling of sadness returned.

"And where would you go if you were to retire today?" the Bishop asked suddenly. "To Oviedo?"

The Corregidor turned to find the man staring at him.

"Retire, Lord Bishop?"

"Yes, retire," the Bishop said, "your days of service have . . . almost ended, and successfully, I may add. Now soon you will be free to go anywhere you want, do anything you wish to do. Will you go back to Oviedo?"

"I may only retire, Lord Bishop," he said, "when I am notified of the Viceroy's intentions regarding the matter. Retirement is not something I will decide."

"So I have decided for you, and for the Viceroy," the Bishop responded. "It is quite official. I have the papers here."

The Catholic prelate reached inside his black robe and produced a thin leather folder of documents. Untying the cord around the folder, he opened it up and pulled out what appeared to be letters. He held the first one up to the light of the day, then handed it to the Corregidor.

"This," he said, "is your official notice of retirement and honorable discharge from His Majesty Charles's loyal service. It speaks of a sizeable pension and certain other privileges to which you are entitled." The Corregidor glanced over the document, then looked back at the Bishop. The latter was already scrutinizing a second document.

"This communication," he said, handing it over as well, "is a letter for the Archbishop of Seville. Hand deliver it to the Sacristan at the cathedral and he will arrange for an audience with His Grace the Archbishop. The Archbishop himself will award you the second portion of your reward for your service to the Church . . . it will be considerably more than I will give you in a moment. As for the remaining letters. . . ."

The Bishop paused, looked at them closely, then returned them to the folder.

"The remaining letters you will give personally to the Archbishop. They will be sealed and confidential. I shall entrust this confidentiality to your proven qualities of discretion and diplomacy. To you shall I commend their safe delivery . . . unread by *any* living soul. . . ."

He looked up at the Corregidor for a long moment, but the latter had opportunely taken an interest in a speck of dust on his breeches. The Bishop continued.

"A Dutch ship will take you back to Spain. What say you?"

The Corregidor sat still and listened. He raised his hand to stroke his chin, then closed his eyes and took a deep breath.

"Were it as you say, my Lord, I would be the most thankful, grateful soul in the world. God help me, I had resigned myself to living out my life in these tropics. How can I thank you enough. . . ."

The Corregidor leaned back in contentment.

"Thank me?" the Bishop asked, rising to his feet. "Oh, that won't be necessary. By the way, here is the first part of your reward. I believe it will be satisfactory."

Reaching in his robe again, this time on the other side, he pulled out a soft leather pouch. It was tied to his belt and it was a moment before he had it free.

"There," he said, handing the pouch to the Corregidor, "gold, enough to tide you over until you make it back to Seville."

It was heavy and it jingled. The Corregidor sat forward and accepted it with both hands. He stared first at the bag, then at the Bishop.

"My Lord . . . I. . . ."

"Enough for now, I trust?" the Bishop smiled.

"Why, quite enough, my Lord, quite enough."

The Corregidor marveled at his new possession.

"Good, the Bishop said, turning his back and lifting his eyes to the trees again. "So that settles it. You take care of one small, final mission, and it's off to Spain." He turned again to face his liege.

"Mission?" the Corregidor asked, looking up from the pouch.

"Didn't I tell you?" the Bishop said with a surprised expression. "Why, how thoughtless of me. There is but one last chore to your residency, a detail that requires your attention."

The Corregidor mustered his strength and rose too. Facing the Bishop, he slowly pulled his perfumed handkerchief from his coat pocket.

"My Lord?" he asked cautiously. "What is this mission, if I may be so bold."

"You will rest tonight, then return at dawn to Panama City."

The Corregidor's jaw dropped.

"My Lord?"

"To talk Henry Morgan into leaving."

". . . Surely you jest. . . ."

"I do not jest. You are just the man, Don Francisco, you and Henry go way back. You talked him into leaving Portobelo, why not Panama?"

The Corregidor had already turned pale. He twitched nervously and fingered his buttons.

"In Portobelo," he said, "the corsairs walked off with a king's ransom, literally, I speak, they held the entire city hostage until Panama payed them to leave. It was all I could do to prevent them from turning the entire female population into a personal harem. My Lord, I beg you, reconsider. Morgan will leave when he is ready. I can do nothing to speed up the process."

"Good!" the Bishop smiled, raising a finger, "then you will do it. I knew we could count on you."

"But my Lord, I. . . ."

"Tomorrow at dawn . . ." the Bishop insisted, this time pointing the finger out in the Corregidor's direction, "you will be well compensated."

The Corregidor closed his eyes and opened them again. Faint, he back-stepped a pace and sat down.

"As you wish, my Lord."

The Bishop advanced toward him and lowered his voice a notch.

"You will be safe, you needn't fear, I know. Go first to Father Boniface at the ancient Church of St. Augustine. It may already be in ruins, but he will be there, or thereabouts. He will give you precise information. Godspeed, my son. All I have said about your retirement is true. The Dutch ship will lay anchor off Panama, it is the ship you will depart on. Fear not. Henry has not found gold in the churches. He will have to content himself with what the lay sector has to offer . . . not much, I suppose, most private treasures were shipped out to the islands well in advance of his coming."

The Corregidor looked puzzled.

"But my Lord, what we have transferred here to Nata is but a small portion of the . . . Church valuables . . . in Panama City. I know for a fact that much gold remains. Once discovered, Henry will. . . ."

"Once discovered," the Bishop interrupted, "ah, there's the catch. . . ."

The Corregidor stared blankly at the man and wondered.

In Panama City Henry Morgan departed with his trusted inner circle and was now walking down a cobblestone street toward the ocean, leaving an old church behind. The place had been ransacked, turned upside down. Everywhere the holy articles were scattered across the wooden floor and smashed and broken. Pews had been hacked to pieces and the walls decimated in the coming of the corsair fury. The doors were hanging loose on their hinges and the windows were uniformly shattered.Nothing remained. Nothing save a last, curious Englishman poking around at the altar. The beefy lad of twenty eight or nine had his sword drawn and was sticking it into wood, tapestry, choir stall, anything he happened to encounter. Including the altar itself. Having run out of other things to slice, the lad stabbed the altar itself. His sword thrust met with a sharp twang on the black,opaque surface. But then something happened to capture his immediate interest. As the sword slid along the length of the altar, unable to penetrate, it peeled off a long, thin line of black paint. The pirate's eyes bulged out of their sockets.

"General Morgan," the man whispered. Stepping back a pace or two, he repeated the name, this time in a shout. "General Morgan!!!" the man cried out, wiping his mouth with his shirtsleeve and advancing back toward the altar.

He quickly looked around at the entrance of the church but realized that the party was at least three or four minutes away, now out of earshot.

"General Morgan!!!" he shouted regardless, edging up toward the large, substantial structure.

For a long moment he stared at his discovery. He touched it and even wet a finger to rub it and taste its flavor. Yes, black paint on a solid gold surface. The corsair grew rigid and was about to bolt. But he did not.

A noose dropped over his head from above and tightened with someone's skillful handling of the line. The Englishman clutched instinctively at his throat, tossing his sword away in the panic of the moment. Then it was too late. The line went completely taught and he began to rise in the dim light of the church. Struggling, kicking with the strength of a wildman, but mute, he rose up toward the high ceiling on the end of a rope. He staved off suffocation by hanging on with his hands above his neck. His efforts were cut short, however, at the top of the line. A bludgeon flashed to cave in his skull and the once devil-may-care dashing soul found peace at the dangling end of the unyielding cord.

"In nomine Pater, Filius, et Spiritus Sanctus, amen," a uninterested voice mumbled from above, "pax vobiscum, brother."

The Englishman then disappeared into the darkness at the top of the high dome.

25

"I've been waiting for you. Hard day?"

In the late afternoon Angel Mendez saw something he had not expected on the patio as he was hurrying by. Now returning to his house, as the voice had understood, after a long, hard day, he stopped to get a closer look at what awaited him. For a long moment he stood there and stared.

"Eva Icaza," he whispered, taken wholly by surprise.

While in the back of his busy mind he had known she would be there, he had not expected what he was now seeing. Angel took a step closer and surveyed the inviting scene. She sat in a metal lounge chair in an evening gown, one he vaguely remembered, but very much welcomed seeing again. Eva was stunning. Her hair, let down around her shoulders, sparkling chestnut and full, framed her beautiful face and lovely neck. Angel's eyes wandered the full length of Eva, from top to bottom, pausing for a sustained glimpse of what was revealed in the slow cut of her gown. This was the Eva that had haunted him for so long. The Eva of old, indescribable. She held a wine glass and lifted it to take a sip.

"Do you like how I look, Angel . . . ?" she asked.

The Captain didn't answer. He simply drew nearer to survey the woman from closer range. Eva smiled.

"Maybe you have time for a glass of wine, Angel . . . it's a splendid evening."

Angel eased his tall frame into a chair across the table from Eva and gazed at her without speaking. He was excited and suddenly felt nervous. The Captain looked down at the table for a glass. One was there; neatly placed beside the bottle. He reached out and picked it up.

26

"They're entering . . . Nata, Lieutenant Roma. Must be some kind of stopover."

The Lieutenant stood tall in his jeep, binoculars in hand. He looked down on Nata and saw Lieutenant Cruz's contingent enter the town. Several of the armored cars had stopped just inside the entrance to the village. A few others, including Cruz's jeep, pushed ahead into the center of the town. Roma saw some of the soldiers walking over to shops and milling around. His own column, now stopped along the sides of the highway behind him, awaited his orders. Roma lowered the binoculars and pulled out a smoke.

"Yeah," he grumbled, "some kind of damn stopover."

"Just what do you think they are after?" a sergeant standing beside him asked. "Why does Quevedo have us out here following these clowns?"

"Because he, and I figure something's up . . . that good enough for you?"

The sergeant nodded his head and wisely backed off.

"Sure, I understand," he said.

In the distance clouds bunched up on the horizon, high, thick white cumulus. There was almost no wind.

"Get a call in back to base," Roma said, "report our position, tell them we're on hold."

"Yes, Sir."

* * * *

"Everything's all set, Bob. The motorcade, the visit to the statue, they're even forming a 'clean up Balboa' committee, group of locals . . . they plan on meeting Senator Dodge down by the monument . . . children, photographers, you know, the works."

"Children?" Bob Friedman asked, turning around suddenly to face young Phil.

Phil looked blank.

"Yes, children . . . what's the problem, Bob?"

Bob walked over to his desk and sat down.

"I don't like it, that's what. These are state affairs, not picnics."

". . . A speech at Balboa's monument, Bob? A state affair . . . ?"

Bob pulled open a drawer and searched for a bottle. Finding nothing, he slammed it shut.

"There are too many people getting involved in this damn thing. This was supposed to be a small thing, a gesture, something for the papers back home and here in the capital. It was supposed to be a stop on the way to lunch with business. Looks like it's getting out of hand."

Phil shook his head.

"I'm sorry, Bob, if it seems that way to you. Maybe we can cancel some of the arrangements. Still, I. . . ."

"When does he arrive?" Bob interrupted.

"I . . . uh . . . tomorrow evening, Bob. Everything's on schedule. Did you see the itinerary I left you?"

Bob was drumming his fingers on the desk.

"Yes, of course I did. What needs to be done now?"

"Nothing, Bob, nothing at all."

Phil watched his boss closely.

"Say, why don't you rest? I'll handle the details. Looks like you need to take it easy. You've been working hard, Bob."

Bob Frieden rubbed his forehead with his fingers and loosened his tie.

"I'm fine, Phil," he said softly, "but you're right, I need to catch some shut-eye. See to it that no kids show up for this stupid Balboa thing, right?"

He looked up at Phil in a way Phil hadn't known his boss to look in the two years he'd known him.

"Sure, Bob, I'll take care of that. You get some rest."

* * * *

"They're just standing around smoking cigarettes, Sir. It has to be a stop-over. I'll bet they're headed to Aguadulce."

"Just keep a sharp eye on them, and get our column back off the road more. Hide the damn vehicles. Look! We've got tourists coming up to take photos."

Lieutenant Roma pointed at a middle aged American couple who had stopped their car by the military vehicles to gawk. They had gotten out and the husband was taking a snapshot of his wife beside a group of privates.

"Jesus Christ," the sergeant said, beginning to walk over in that direction, "Jesus Christ. . . ."

He broke into a run and began waving frantically at his men. The Americans smiled at him and stood to one side as he shouted orders to the troops. Truck engines began to rev up and jeeps lurched farther back off the road. With his best smile, the Sergeant walked up to the American couple and explained in not so bad English that they were photographing state secrets. The two threw up their hands apologetically and assured the sergeant that they were just sightseers from Muskegon, Michigan. The husband pulled out a business card and a 'Muskegon Booster' pin and handed them to the sergeant. His wife was saying something about the heat. The sergeant thanked them painfully and shooed them back toward their car. Lieutenant Roma frowned and continued spying on the Cruz detachment down the road. He was muttering something under his breath.

In the afternoon's fading sun Lieutenant Cruz stood by as his officers went door to door with questions regarding the whereabouts of his onetime companion Santos. The "no I haven't seen hims" ticked off methodically at the town's periphery and proceeded with the same monotonous blank looks as the group worked closer to the town plaza. The curious came up to sneak a look, and more than one local dignitary offered his services before the acid question was asked.

"You've seen this man?" Cruz's people asked, flashing a photo. None had, and the important men of Nata faded back into the forgotten quarters of the village as quickly as they came forward. Santos, it seemed, had disappeared.

"Get the men together and let's make a final sweep in the plaza area," Cruz ordered, boarding his jeep. "We'll stay here tonight and split back to the Captain's place in the morning. I've just about had it."

"Yes, Sir."

* * * *

"Long distance? Yeah, right. Get me Washington D.C. I've got a number here . . . yeah . . . ready? Here goes. . . ."

27

"It's not your fault, Angel . . . don't worry about it. We can try again later."

The Captain lay back on the satin sheets of his enormous round bed, covers up around his waist, and stared angrily at the ceiling. Eva lay covered to her shoulders about three feet away. An unusual smile crossed her lips. Not sympathetic, not really a smile of any type of mirth or . . . Eva watched Angel Mendez fume all by himself at her side.

"I think," he mumbled, "that you were a little aggressive, I wasn't ready for that."

"You're right," Eva replied, "I sometimes am . . . it's just that you excite me."

Angel closed his eyes and bit his upper lip.

"I'll be leaving tonight. I won't be back until Tuesday. I want you here on Tuesday, just like you were earlier. Then I'll be ready. I have important things on my mind."

"I'm sure you do, darling," Eva agreed, nodding her head, "I'm sure you do."

Angel looked at her suddenly, then threw the covers off. He swung out of bed and marched across to where he'd left his clothes.

"Where are you going?" Eva asked from the bed.

The Captain was picking up his shirt and eyeing it for wrinkles. Finding it inadequate, he walked over to a closet and threw the door open. He impatiently flipped through a rack of shirts and eventually found one that he liked. Angel turned back toward Eva to say something, then noticed that she was staring at him. Looking at her eyes, he followed her line of sight to his private parts.

"I'm going back to the city!" he snapped, pulling the shirt in front of him. "What are you laughing about?"

Eva shook her head, closed her eyes, and leaned back on the pillow. Her expression grew serious.

"I see," she said.

"I saw you!" Mendez bellowed, taking a step in Eva's direction.

"Just what the hell is funny."

Eva didn't answer. The Captain was furious. He walked stiffly over to a dresser and pulled open the second drawer. In a moment he was wearing underwear and fishing through socks.

"Nothing is funny," Eva said, lying motionless on the bed. Then she opened her eyes.

"Darling," she added, "please take me with you. . . . I'd like to go with you, keep you company. . . . I'm beginning to fall for you. . . ."

Angel stood straight up and hurled a shoe at her. Eva saw it fly over her face and heard it crash against the headboard.

"You bitch!" the Captain shouted, "you lying bitch! You'll wait here for me to return! And return I will!"

He quickly finished dressing, bending and stooping for this or another piece of clothing, delving into drawers, all the while in an obvious rage. Eva lay shielding herself with the covers, peeking out over the top at her very dangerous ex-friend. When he finished dressing, Angel strapped a .38 caliber pistol in its holster under his left armpit. He watched Eva as he threw on a light jacket and sneered.

"Tuesday, bitch, look for me then. Until that time you are to stay here, you are to say nothing to anyone, and it will be forbidden for you to make any calls. Understand?"

The captain stared at her for a moment, then walked briskly over to the door. After a final, icy look, he exited and began a walk to the head of the stairs. Eva suddenly threw off the covers and jumped out of bed. Naked, for all the world to see, she ran across the bedroom to the door and followed him out into the hall. By the time she caught up he was half way down the stairs. Three servants, two men and a woman, stood at the base of the stairs watching.

"Good-bye, chiquito," she laughed with mocking tones, "que te vaya bien."

Mendez stopped on the stairwell and whirled around. He saw Ana up there laughing, exposed to all spectators below.

"You bitch, you bastard," he said between his teeth. As if in reflex, Angel went for his gun, then paused, hand on the grip.

'That's right, you maricon," Eva taunted, eyes in a fury, "shoot me, pull it out and shoot me, do with the gun what you could not with your little useless thing, what a man you are, maricon!"

The captain fairly trembled with anger, one hand on the pistol, the other on the banister. Control carried the day. He straightened up and removed his hand from his jacket.

"Get me Barrios," he seethed, staring at Eva but speaking to the group of domestics below. "Tell him to come here right away. This woman is not to leave here, and she is not to leave my room. You will pay for this, bitch," he said to the women at the top of the stairs, "when I return . . . oh God will you pay!"

Eva stood straight up and stared back at the military man as he turned to leave. For a full minute after his departure she stood there watching. Then slowly she walked back to darling's room.

Eva sat on the bed for the better part of five minutes looking out at the window across the room. All at the same time she was frightened, angry, anxious, and terribly unsure what to do about it. Still undressed, she rubbed her knees with the palms of her hands and attempted to come up with some kind of plan. Then suddenly she spied something that caught her instant attention. Angel Mendez had left his attache behind. It was leaning up against the dresser on the far side of the room. Quickly she sprang to her feet and trotted over to the black leather case. With fumbling fingers she seized the latch button . . . and it unsnapped. The damn thing wasn't locked. Eva opened the case and sat down beside it. One by one she withdrew the papers and briefs that formed its contents. She had almost emptied it when at last her eyes come across the shred of information she sought. Eyes wide open, she devoured every detail.

"Oh God help me," she whispered, hand cupped over her mouth. "Dear God in heaven help me."

Then she heard footsteps climbing the stairwell outside. Hurriedly she placed the papers back in the attache and sealed it shut. She had just returned it to its original position when the door flew open. Eva stood and faced the intruder, a guardia of the usual type. The man stopped just inside the door and stared at the naked woman.

"What do you want?" she asked.

The Guardia was speechless. His eyes wandered up and down without pausing for rest.

"I said, what do you want?" Eva persisted.

"I have been sent . . . ," the man began, ". . . I am Barrios, Jose Barrios, Corporal Barrios, I. . . ."

"Tell me what you want, then leave, fast!" Eva menaced.

"My Captain sent me for his . . . attache . . . and to tell you that you are under . . . house arrest."

"So get the attache and beat it," Eva replied, turning to walk toward the bed and her clothes. But then she was forced to turn around. She sensed Barrios approaching from behind. Eva turned back to face him. He was just a few feet away, hands outstretched in her direction. He stopped when she confronted him.

"You want something?" Eva asked. "I hope it's not me. The Captain would be most displeased if you were to touch me."

. . . Barrios hesitated for a moment, then began to slink off in search of the attache. Locating it, he turned for one last look. Eva was dressing now and the guardia turned and ran for the door.

* * * *

"I'll take it in the study," Bob said casually to the maid. She stood there holding the phone and watching as he ambled down the hall in the direction of his hideaway. In a moment she heard the door close.

"Un momentito," she said to the party on the other end of the line, waiting for Bob to pick it up. When he did, the woman quietly replaced the receiver. Bob heard it click.

"It's me," Bob said, easing back into his chair. A search of the drawers revealed nothing to drink, as usual.

"So it's you," the voice on the other end remarked arrogantly, "it's really you."

Bob's expression changed and he sat straight up.

"What the hell is this?" he challenged, "this is my private line!"

"I'll chance it, Bob," the voice continued, "we're pretty nervous."

"Listen, this is crazy, I'll meet you at the 'casa', hang up."

'You'll meet me in hell unless we talk right now," the voice threatened, "how are the arrangements?"

Bob stood up and loosened his tie.

"They're fine . . . no problems . . . get it?"

"Let's hope so, Bob, for your sake, no fuck-ups, not a single one, or I'll personally see to your sex change. . . . I hear they're all the rage. It's now or never, Bob, you know who is sitting right here with me, and he'd be awfully pissed off if you screwed things up."

The line went dead before Bob had a chance to answer. He stared at the phone for a while, then calmly placed it down. Bob paced for half an hour or so, pausing occasionally to glance at his watch. Then he opened the study door and stormed out.

"You stupid fucker, Matos," Bob complained.

The maid watched him leave . . . and worried about Bob. Not in many years had she seen him that way.

* * * *

"Guards! Guards! The woman is gone! She has escaped!"

Barrios, inside the room again, hoping to catch another look, saw only an open window and a curtain flapping in the night breeze.

"Gone! Sound the alarm!"

H ran over to the window, looked out in all directions, then slammed it shut. Barrios turned and ran back to the bedroom door and exited on the fly. Throughout the house there were cries of fright and anger. The guardias posted outside turned on their searchlights and flooded the approaches to

Captain Mendez's mansiok. Several dogs were loosed from a nearby kennel and two men took off in a jeep.

Off on the nearby highway a woman sat on the weathered porch of her dwelling and examined two quarters given to her by a tourist in exchange for a mamey cluster just an hour before sundown. The woman smiled and clutched the coins, looking up occasionally to watch the headlights of speeding cars pass by in the night. Behind her in the dwelling several children played with an assortment of homemade toys while a man in his early thirties, her husband, lay back sleeping in the home's only easy chair. The light of a single 40 watt bulb illuminated the children's games. The woman looked around and began to get up from her chair when, to her surprise, she spotted a vehicle not far off coming up the highway with its lights off. The woman sat down again, stuffed the two quarters in an apron pocket, and watched. Guardias, she knew as soon as the vehicle's silhouette came into view against a light, open field across the road. She nervously glanced back at her husband, then back at the vehicle as it rolled past. It's occupants came to a stop directly in front of her, shined a spotlight on her porch and all around the surrounding area, then moved on. When they were gone she stood up quickly and rushed back into the house.

A clock chimed softly somewhere in a distant corner of Colonel Quevedo's mansion in the Altos del Golf. The weary officer leaned back in his favorite chair, unable to sleep, and closed his eyes in the darkness of the living room. Before him through the window lay the now sleeping city and its resting souls. Quevedo let a paper slip through his fingers to the floor. It took its place beside a thin book that had come anonymously in the morning's mail. "Japanese The Easy Way" was its title. "A million thanks!" had been the message penned inside the front cover. Quevedo wet his lips.

"Disappeared," a guardia said as he leaped from the returning jeep onto Mendez's driveway.

"So we let the Captain know?" Barrios asked the driver.

"It's your ass," the man replied with a laugh.

Nata
Sunday, May 31, 1987
Near Dawn

28

"I have the morning report, Sir, they didn't leave this village last night. Just as we thought. They're still there." Lieutenant Roma scanned the morning gray town before him from behind his binoculars and saw little that aroused his interest. Just a few people out of bed at that hour, the streets looked empty.

"Intelligence has it, Sir," his aide went on, "that Aria's men went door to door looking for Santos. Word is that they came up empty handed. That shouting we heard last night was an orgy. Booze, women, seems some of the men called in camp followers from Penonome and Aguadulce on the sly. Big party in the 'centro'."

"What 'centro'?" Roma snarled, "this burg's dead, dried up and blown away. What the hell can these guys be doing in Nata? I've missed my fucking weekend!"

"Me too," the aide sighed, shaking his head, "whoever ordered up this caper must have a hole in his head."

Roma continued to scan for a while longer, then slowly lowered the glasses. Traffic was picking up on the highway off beside them and one of his men was coughing loudly from behind the ambush. The day was already getting sticky and it couldn't have been seven o'clock yet.

"But where are they now?" Roma whispered to himself. "I see people, but no Arias' army. Where's that bastard Cruz?"

The aide overheard him.

"Sleeping it off," he remarked, "bunked down on the streets in the 'centro' . . . get their morning piece of ass maybe. Do you feel like going in? Enough of the goddamn hide and seek."

"We'll follow orders, soldier," Roma answered, now rubbing his weary eyes, "we'll follow our orders."

"Sir, begging you pardon, but I have been aware, these last two days, that we are been followed and watched. I have mentioned this three times to my sergeant, but he hasn't told me if you had been informed. I. . . ."

"I am aware of this information, private, you may go," Lieutenant Cruz interrupted. "I do not like anyone going over anyone's head in the chain of command. Get back to your position."

"Yes, Sir," the man replied, slinking off.

Cruz stood in the middle of the plaza in Nata facing the ancient church. Beside him were a sergeant and two lance corporals, the latter holding on to a miserable wretch writhing to free himself from their grip. He was a commoner, an elderly peasant farmer wearing a horrified look. In the background three jeeps, two armored cars, and a number of motorcycles were strung out across the plaza, men in and standing beside the vehicles. Cruz motioned to the rest and began a slow walk up to the church. In the early morning light he could make out wisps of smoke over the rooftops of the humble dwellings near the plaza . . . but no people. The only inhabitant of the town he could see was being dragged along by his men, feet scraping across the flat rocks. As he approached the church he was aware of a silence unheard of in a town like Nata. Cruz looked around suspiciously but continued to see nothing. Then as he had almost arrived to the church, he was surprised to see the priest walk out the front door, wide smile on his lips, hands clasped together at the red waist cord of his long, flowing black robe. The priest's smile turned to a frown for an instant when he saw the villager being dragged along. Then, however, the smile returned, albeit slightly more forced.

"Coming to mass on this fine Sunday morning?" the priest asked."What a wonderful idea."

"Go inside and search the place, Sergeant," Cruz snapped, eyeing the priest. "Take two men and be careful."

Watching the men go, he addressed the priest.

"I am looking for a man called Santos, I was told he was here."

Father Sandoval stared at the lieutenant. His countenance became serious.

"Who told you a man called Santos was here?"

"This pig!" Cruz replied.

Lieutenant Cruz signaled to the two corporals and they pitched the local through the air in the direction of the priest. The poor man landed in the dust at Father Sandoval's feet and came to his knees. Father Sandoval looked at the man, then looked at Cruz.

"Why do you harm an innocent old man?" he asked. Cruz stepped a few feet forward and laughed.

"What's it to you, 'Padre'? The bottom line is a scumbag by the name of Santos. Where is he?"

Father Sandoval helped the old man up, brushing him off as he came to his feet. The old man trembled and looked behind him at the terror in uniform.

"There are many 'Santos' here, my good man," Father Sandoval said, eyes trained on Cruz. "But none of them are scumbags."

Cruz bristled.

"Don't get wise with me, prayer-boy," he said, taking another step forward. "Just tell me where the fat pig is . . . and what he's hiding . . . and whether you know anything about what he's hiding. Come clean or I get tough!"

Father Sandoval gently pushed the old man away and pointed to him with a finger.

"Go home, my son, go home and rest."

The old man looked at Father Sandoval, then at Lieutenant Cruz, then crossed himself and walked, then ran away across the plaza. Cruz and Sandoval stood only a few feet apart.

In the church the search party of three walked through empty aisles and chambers. The place was dark, cool, and entirely vacant. The light filtering down from stained glass and windows spread eerily in all directions. Each one of the soldiers felt a growing uneasiness in the desolate place, the feeling of trespass on sacred ground, of Angst and unpleasant memory. By the time they had reached the vaults and the catacombs, they were ready to call off the search. The sergeant, bolder than the others, advanced a little farther and struck a match to see his way through one final door. Pushing it open, he gazed inside at a darkness and an inner silence so characteristic of such old, colonial structures. Nothing. Nothing at all.

"What the hell would Santos be doing in this place," he mumbled, throwing away the match.

The sergeant turned to exit, but bumped his head on some unseen, unremembered obstacle.

"Damn!" he cursed, backing off and lighting up another match.His two companions stepped closer to him as he regained his bearings. Then suddenly he was startled by the appearance of an old, cadaverous face shining out from a black hood . . . directly in his way. The three militaries jumped back, two gasping and the other letting out a frightened cry. Together, they stood still and watched the ghastly apparition before them.

"Epiphany, gentlemen," they heard the smiling skin-covered skull say, "we've been expecting you. We've even added a few new gargoyles in your honor . . . three to be exact: look!!"

Pointing a bony finger up into the air, he called their attention to three grotesque, absolutely horrible looking heads protruding from the entrance to the inner vault. In the last light of the match they saw a familiar face contorted to agonizing, almost unrecognizable heights of pain and anguish . . . cast in lovely gold for all eternity. The sergeant dropped the match and staggered backward toward the exit. His mouth was wide open, but he was too frightened to scream. The other two were off and running. The sergeant's legs had gone numb. The old man had disappeared into the darkness as the sergeant backstepped out, mouth forming a word in silence again and again.

"Santos!!!!" he screamed without making a sound. Beyond Santos were the castings of a dozen more skulls and twisted heads. In the corner a few dozen more guarded the entrance to the catacombs and the wine cellar.

In the plaza in front of the church Lieutenant Cruz came face to face with the Catholic Father. There was no disguising the anger in the face of the former.

"We've come a long way on a short supply of patience, you holy bastard. We know Santos was here. Now where is he, and what was he after?"

"He came . . . " Father Sandoval replied, eyeing the surrounding streets, "to confess. That would be a good idea in your case, too, for believe me, the Resurrection is at hand. But not for you. Yours is a journey to Terra Repromissionis Sanctorum, cui est honor et gloria in secula seculorum, of course . . . the Promised Land. In Nomine Pater, Filius, et Spiritus Sanctus. . . ."

"Ayyyy Christ!!!!! Jesus God!!!!!!!"

Cruz's attention was drawn momentarily away from Father Sandoval to the startling sight of one of his men fleeing desperately from the church. The man was literally sprinting away screaming some unintelligible gibberish about hellfire and damnation. Such was the impact of the spectacle that at least a dozen of Cruz's men experienced chill tinglings down the spine. Cruz stared at the running man, then looked blankly back at Father Sandoval.

"Hold your breath, Lieutenant," Father Sandoval smiled, "please be calm, Salvation is at hand!"

An instant later a gasp went up from the military contingent. Cruz looked up . . . and saw. . . ."

". . . Sergeant Rollo, what . . . ????"

Like a bowling ball, the sergeant's head was rolling down the church steps toward him. It slowly came to rest at his feet. Cruz had just enough time to look it over before feeling a crossbow shaft enter his right ear, and partially exit through the left. He staggered and stared stupidly into Father Sandoval's eyes. The latter continued smiling.

"Have a pleasant journey," he said, lightly rubbing his index finger in the sign of the cross on the now teetering lieutenant's forehead.

A pair of lance corporals began to look around in all directions beside their falling chief. One pulled out his pistol and screamed.

"We're surrounded!!! Take cover!!!"

He was about to fire his weapon when he took a red hot musket ball in the guts.The man vomited twice. First a mulch of half-digested food, then a torrent of dark, black blood. Holding his abdomen, he trotted around in small circles, then did a curious little skip, then a hop, then keeled over in a heap in the dust.

"Pax vobiscum," Father Sandoval pronounced from a distance, "pax vobiscum, brother."

He looked back just in time to see a dozen red and black robed hooded horsemen descending on the army in the plaza, some with rifles, some armed with swords. Behind them came a host of villagers wielding every imaginable type of weapon. Before the soldiers could get off more than a few startled shots, they were overwhelmed by a deluge of wild Cristeros. Father Sandoval watched his horsemen sweep across the courtyard, cutting down Cruz's fleeing men in their tracks as they ran. Robes flowing in the winds, they were the spectacle he had worked long and hard to maintain. The Catholic Father slowly turned his back to the slaughter and walked back into his church. With the screams fading behind him, he walked up the central aisleway of the nave and ascended the steps leading to the altar. There he paused for a long moment, then he knelt down to pray. His eyes wandered up to the remarkable Caravacan Cross overshadowing him from the high altar and he smiled with the centuries.

"Shooting!!! Lieutenant Roma! I hear shooting down there! And screams! Listen to that!"

Roma suddenly went pale.

"Crank 'em up!!!" he screamed in turn, "let's rock!!!"

In less than a minute the entire armored column was on the road, and speeding toward the village.

"Move, you sons of bitches!!!" Roma exhorted from atop his jeep, "into Nataaaaaaa!!!"

Panama City
Noon
Sunday, May 31, 1987

"Colonel Quevedo! Nothing more! I swear to you, we have tried every means of communication!!"

"What have the locals reported?"

"That there is no sign of Roma, or his men, or any of the Arias' Cruz group. They are all gone, or so it would appear." Anastasio Quevedo slumped into his chair, deep in thought.

"What the hell was the last message again?"

His aide shrugged his shoulders in exasperation.

"That there was some kind of conflict in Nata, some tiny four corners just outside of Aguadulce. Roma said he was going in to look. Then about fifteen minutes later he came on the air screaming for assistance, some nonsense about an old church and a priest, some Father Sandoval . . . then the transmission went dead. That was the end of it."

Quevedo looked up.

"And we've searched the area?"

"We had men in there by helicopter about an hour and a half later. Nothing. No Roma, no Cruz, no vehicles . . . nothing. They checked the whole towns, and the church, too."

"What did they find in the church?" Quevedo suddenly demanded.

The aide looked at him and cleared his throat.

"Just a church service, my Colonel, a mass in progress. There was no Father, uh, Sandoval. The priests had other names. I tell you this thing is absolutely nuts! Nobody had even heard of a Sandoval!"

Colonel Quevedo leaned back farther into his chair and closed his eyes.

"No," he murmured, "no one would have heard of Father Sandoval. He hasn't been here for quite some time. . . ."

"Sir?" the aide inquired.

Quevedo reached for his glass of water, but discovered it was empty. He let the glass slip out of his hand and fall to the floor. It shattered with a crisp smash.

Panama City
Monday, June 1, 1987
10:00 a.m.

29

High above the tropical city a man dressed entirely in loose fitting, comfortable white scanned the length of Avenida Balboa from as far as he could see toward the city to the nearby monument by the sea. He was a young man in his early to mid-twenties, a lean man with an intensive look. Beside him stood an older, more relaxed looking type about ten years his senior. He also scanned the Avenida with binoculars. Their features presented a sharp contrast, the man in white still showing evidence of the kid in the lines of his expression, an earnest sincerity; the older man beside him looked hardened and tough. Behind them stood a third man smoking a cigarette. Like the man beside the quiet youth, he was in his thirties. Arms crossed, he eyed a gleaming rifle leaning up against the high-rise balcony in front of them. He raised his wrist for a moment, glanced at his watch, then lifted a hand to pull the cigarette out of his mouth.

"What do you see?" he asked calmly.

The man in white lowered his binoculars and shook his head slowly.

"Nothing," he said, "nothing at all. The people are waiting,but no sign of a motorcade."

"Hang in there, Roberto," he said, flicking the still lit butt out over the balcony into the breeze. "It won't be long."

Somebody had a barking dog a couple of floors up. It would intermittently break into a short burst of yaps, then whine once or twice, as if someone had it tied up in a pen or something, or someone was teasing it. But then it wouldn't be whining, Roberto thought, looking back out on the city. The palms along the ocean were particularly active that morning. Their leaves whipped up and around in the winds all along a line curving off from the monument to the distant structures where Roberto lost them. His stomach was knotted and queasy, his legs a little uncertain. He had noticed earlier that his fingers were trembling slightly. Too much coffee.

"In a moment, triumph! . . . comrade," the man standing beside him said casually. "The revolution will begin, and you will be the hero. Your name will someday be on the lips of revolutionaries around the world."

"That is correct," Roberto agreed, "there are not many revolutions, there is only one."

"The people united . . . ," the man behind him said, stuffing a stick of chewing gum into his mouth and glancing at his watch.

"Will never be defeated!" Roberto whispered loudly.

"Today we'll show those pigs a thing or two," the man beside him said.

Roberto smiled weakly and focused his glasses.

"Are the arrangements complete?" he asked.

The man beside him coughed and looked back at the third man.

"Very," he said. "I have seen to every detail."

"A blow struck on behalf of the people," the third man said, turning to walk back toward the kitchen. "Say, any more of those sandwiches in the refrigerator?"

Roberto was busy watching the streets. It was not a large crowd at the monument. In fact, it was a little disappointing.

"Nice, small crowd, good for such a celebration," Captain Angel Mendez said, eyes on a high rise not far from where he was standing.

Two cars sped by and he was wondering when the barricades would go up to control excess traffic. But it wasn't a state matter, he understood. It was a private affair. The gringos and a few lower echelon dignitaries. Bob had taken care of the arrangements. No big-wigs from the government. They would be conspicuously absent and prominently in view elsewhere. Bob was so good at that. Mendez looked down and fingered the buttons of his tastefully conservative tropical suit. He adjusted his sunglasses and took a peek at the time. Ten on the nose. But Bob had told them to give or take a few. Angel smiled and glanced over in the direction of the high rise again. Perfect.

"When's the gringo coming?" the tropical man beside him asked.

"When he's ready, Mr. Matos," Angel answered, smiling at a pretty woman beside him. She saw the handsome sight, smiled shyly, and turned away.

"A ripe plum," Angel chirped.

"Yeah? Well I'm worried," Matos remarked.

The tropical man was peering up the Avenida from the monument and tapping a foot.

"Bob's been acting strange lately. I'd hate to think he'd fucked up on us."

"Relax," Angel said. The Captain popped a fresh mint into his mouth and rubbed his hands. The tropical man leaned out again and searched for the motorcade with his shaded eyes.

"Where's the General?" Mendez asked him out of the side of his mouth.

"Home 'conjuring'," Matos said sarcastically. "Who's keeping an eye on the chump?"

"I said, relax, brother, here comes your motorcade, and my best men are watching the chump. Get ready."

Matos looked out anxiously at the passing cars and noticed, as had Mendez, that the official American delegation was arriving. But it was small. Just three cars. The first one, though, had the typical flags flying and the dignified look of an important component of a diplomatic entourage. Amidst the polite applause of the sparsely represented well-wishers, the three American vehicles pulled up and stopped beside the monument. For a long moment they sat there.

"Get out, god-dammit!" Matos whispered loudly, "get the fuck out, gringo!"

Mendez rocked heel to toe uneasily. The first signs of anxiety were crossing his hitherto merry brow. Slowly, without the slightest indication of urgency, the lead diplomatic car doors cracked open. Matos fidgeted with his belly button and watched. Then the passenger door opened.

"Steady, lad, steady," the older man beside Roberto said, hand placed firmly on his shoulder.

Roberto had the car door squarely in his sights and was taking careful aim. The man behind them had tossed the remains of his sandwich on the bed and was furtively assembling his own weapon, a rifle similar to Roberto's, from parts he was extracting from a black leather case.

"Steady now, boy," the man beside Roberto continued to caution, just one, single shot, clean and true, right in the chest, just like we talked about."

The third man had completed the assembly and was edging up behind the pair in the balcony for a better look. Roberto concentrated, blinking once or twice from the perspiration running down his brow. Suddenly Roberto stiffened.

"The door's open . . . funny, no one opened it for him . . . he's getting out. . . ."

Then he looked up. Eyes puzzled, a maddened frown on his face, Roberto quickly looked back through the rifle's powerful scope.

"That's not Dodge . . . that's not the person in the pictures you showed me! That's . . . some other gringo!"

"What?!?" the man beside him demanded in a loud voice.Seizing his binoculars, he focused in on the scene below. To his great surprise, he saw. . . .

"Bob Friedan, everybody, buenos dias!"

Matos took a step backward and stared, eyes wide, lips twitching.

"Where the fuck is the Senator, Bob?" he asked in a voice loud enough for Friedan to hear.

"He couldn't make it, asshole," Bob smiled, straightening his tie.

Phil stepped out of the car behind him and cast a very worried look in the direction of a high-rise out across the way and a few other men followed behind him. The small crowd became uneasy and people began to make gestures and point.

"You . . . bastard . . . you . . . mother . . . ," Matos began, edging farther back beside Mendez. Angel was looking around quickly in all directions. Far above him in the apartment there was confusion.

"Jesus Christ, that's . . ." the man with binoculars beside Roberto sputtered, "that's Bob . . . Friedan. Damn! What the hell?"

"That's impossible," the man behind them said, advancing forward even farther, "Friedan's one of us, he's G-2 Intelligence."

"What?" Roberto asked quietly, unnoticed by the other two. He turned around and stared at the man behind him, then did a double take when he saw his rifle.

"God-dammit!!" the man beside Roberto continued to curse. "Where's the goddam Senator?"

Roberto turned back to the balcony and sighted up the scene below once again through his rifle scope. Several men had now exited the car, and a few of them were looking up . . . right at him!! One had binoculars.

"Shit, they know we're here!!" the man beside Roberto shouted."Something's gone wrong!!"

But then something suddenly went wrong down below as well. Roberto saw what looked like a furious brawl break out near the lead vehicle. Lowering his rifle and resting it on the balcony wall, he picked up his own set of binoculars and scanned the action. Once he had it in focus, he couldn't believe his eyes. There was Eva Icaza pulling a man's hair, wrenching it out by the fistful and scratching at his face.The poor wretch was busy trying to defend himself, hands in front of his face, bent over in defense. Then he stood up and Roberto saw his face. Unmistakably, it was. . . .

"Angel Mendez, you son of a bitch. . . ." Roberto muttered, eyes pressed tightly against the lens.

"There's been a fuck-up!" the man beside him said, now beginning to withdraw from the window. "Let's split."

"Mendez, you bastard," Roberto whispered.

He saw the tall military man slap Eva with such force that she flew back through the air and landed hard on the cement, obviously stunned. Roberto noticed with now furious eyes that she was wearing terribly torn and soiled clothes. She looked a mess. But Mendez was back after her in an instant, now kicking her violently as she lay there.

"Bastard," Roberto said, dropping the binoculars and raising his rifle. In no time at all he had him in his sights.

"Die!" he shouted, squeezing off a round.

There was a general scream when Angel Mendez lurched backward, hands clutching his chest, toward the center of the plaza. The people watched as he seized a much smaller man, a man dressed in bright tropical garb, in an effort to keep on his feet. The tropical man, though startled, was not at all anxious to be used as a leaning post for the mortally wounded. No one seemed to hear the shot, perhaps because a loud truck was passing at the moment, but after the initial shock, no one seemed to care. Spotting the blood rushing out of what had been a handsome man's back, everyone scrambled to get away, each and every one of them in their own direction. The men around the cars dived back in . . . all except for Bob Friedan. Bob stood there staring at the dying Mendez and his reluctant pal Matos. The woman had gotten up and was staggering away in the general direction of the high-rise.

"Let go of me!!" Matos screamed up into Angel's face.

Mendez gazed with almost sightless eyes on the man holding him up. Then a second shot tore through him, this time from the back. Mendez looked straight up at heaven, then began a long, slow spiraling slump to the ground.

"Jesus," Bob Friedan said, even more astonished when he saw Matos staring blankly in his direction. When Mendez finally collapsed in a pile, the tropical man took a crazy, swerving step forward, then collapsed himself. The shot had entered his open mouth after exiting Mendez, and had lodged somewhere in his brain behind it. He lay there making a gurgling sound.

"Get in the goddam car, Bob," Phil shouted from behind him, "Goddamn it!! What the hell is this?"

Phil grabbed Bob by the shoulder and jerked him back. In an instant the American cars were speeding away, people fleeing in all directions.

"Jesus Christ," the man who had been standing beside Roberto gasped, again gazing down through his binoculars. "He shot Captain Mendez!"

Roberto, now standing up and looking wildly out at the city, seemed to be gulping for air. The man beside him lowered his binoculars and stared, first at the scene below, then at Roberto.

"You stupid fucker," he snarled, backing off into the apartment.

"Let's waste him now!" the third man behind them said.

Raising his rifle, he took aim at Roberto's head. For an instant, he could not shoot. His partner, still coming back, was in the way. Then when he had a clear shot, he began to squeeze the trigger. Roberto, however, recovering his senses just in time, took notice and leaped. The third man's shot went slightly wide, grazing Roberto on the temple. When Roberto came down he was behind a large, overstuffed chair. The third man fired into it but the bullet ricochetted off something metallic in the inner works. By this time the other man was heading out the door. Roberto seized his own rifle and stole a glance around the chair. The third man was advancing, rifle pointing in his general direction. Roberto pulled up the barrel for a shot, but it got stuck on an adjacent chair leg. He was jerking at it when the third man spotted his position and maneuvered his rifle over for a shot. Roberto saw him sneer and zero in on his forehead, barrel-tip not two feet away. Roberto closed his eyes.

The sound of the gunshot came, but he felt nothing. Roberto reopened his eyes just in time to see the third man standing straight up, limbs rigid, rifle dropping at his side. His eyes bulged and he seemed to be wanting to say something. Then he fell like a load of dead lead on the floor, blood flowing from the back of his head. Roberto scrambled to his feet, again tugging at the damn rifle. There was a thin man standing in the doorway dressed in a black overcoat and loose fitting slacks. In his hand he held a large, smoking gun. The man looked at Roberto and his rifle, and Roberto wisely let his weapon drop to the floor. The man in the doorway broke open his pistol and shoved in another cartridge. Then he snapped it back together. Watching Roberto through narrow dark eyes, he cleared his throat and spoke.

"Get your ass out of here," he said in badly broken Spanish, but good enough for Roberto to catch on in a flash.

Roberto, watching the man, trotted over to the doorway. He slowed down as he passed the man, then broke into a run in the hallway. By the elevator he saw his other 'friend' sitting on the floor, resting up against the wall . . . dead eyes staring off into space. Roberto raced into the stairwell and took the steps two by two, three by three, falling down once or twice on his way to the bottom. When he got there he dashed out across the lobby into the street.

30

"So Friedan sets up this "bless Balboa" deal to be included in . . . Senator Dodge's visit, then panics and convinces Washington to call off his visit, hush hush, that's Bob . . . then he gets you guys to head out there . . . to the monument . . . at the appointed time, talking about some assassination plot . . . is this pretty much what you're telling me, Phil?"

Phil stood tugging nervously at his tie in front of a 'most' superior diplomat and nodded. He blinked several times.

"Yes, Sir, that's right."

The older, very well dressed man seated at his desk in front of him looked puzzled . . . and concerned.

"Good God, young man, two prominent national military figures are dead tonight and the High Command is in an uproar. Number Two is being forced to resign. That means trouble. The whole thing could blow up. What the hell was Friedan doing out there? And where is he now?"

Phil shook his head.

"I don't understand what happened today, and Bob asked to be dropped off near Calle 50, said he had to make a contact. Bob had been acting pretty . . . strange, lately. I think he needs some rest and relaxation, maybe a vacation."

The senior diplomat looked around the room at the men who had accompanied Phil and reached out to pour himself a glass of water.

"Dear me, this is serious. Has he reported back to anyone?"

Phil watched him take a long drink.

"He hasn't, Sir, not to my knowledge.

Phil looked around at his associates, but everyone was shaking their heads.

"No, Sir, not to anyone, it seems."

The diplomat leaned back in his chair and clasped his hands against his chest. For a long moment he sat there quietly, lost in thought. At length he spoke again.

"Bob's been a good man," he said softly, "so let's give him the benefit of the doubt. We'll give him twenty four hours to report . . . but if he doesn't. . . . You are temporarily in charge of your section, Phil, give the order for an all-points and Bob's immediate arrest on sight if we don't see him before then. Bob's got sources he's not sharing, and that's bad. We're looking at a national crisis here. Give Washington a full report within the hour."

"Yes, Sir," Phil replied.

The others began to shuffle out.

* * * *

An old, white foreign job sped up the highway in the darkness through a light mountain rain. The driver, a middle-aged man dressed in fashionable, loose fitting tropical clothes, glanced over at one of the two riders going with him. It was a young man dressed in white seated in the front passenger seat beside him. In the rearview mirror he saw an attractive young woman in absolutely disastrous clothing seated in the middle behind him. In the soft light of the dashboard instruments he could tell that she had been beaten on the face. One eye was swollen. He'd seen her before.

"So, where'd you say you were headed?" the middle-aged man asked them.

He'd picked them up about a kilometer or so back on the highway at a little restaurant. They'd fairly begged him for a ride. The young man looked back at the young woman and seemed to ask her the same question with his eyes. The woman answered from the back seat.

"As far away from here as you are good enough to take us, Sir. We've been through a lot."

The driver nodded and pulled a stick of gum out of his breast pocket. Peeling it, he popped it in his mouth and took another look at the young lady. In fact, she was lovely . . . save the getup. He'd seen her. . . .

"Trouble with mom and dad?" the man asked. The conversation was in Spanish but he seemed up to the task. The young couple had noticed his accent.

"I wish," the young woman laughed, "oh how I wish."

The driver smiled, then frowned, then it dawned on him. She'd been the one . . . at . . . the. . . . He let his foot off the gas for an instant, then resumed his acceleration.

"I'm going as far as Cerro Azul tonight," he said, checking on her again in the rearview mirror. Then he noticed the young man looking at him. The driver looked back at the road. "But you're welcome to stay there with me. I've got a little shack up on the highest part, I go there now and then. You won't . . . be noticed there."

The young man beside the driver looked back at the woman again and made the same inquiring gesture with his eyes. A long moment passed.

"Yes," the young woman said, "that would be fine . . . for how long?"

The driver chewed his gum and squinted through an increasingly stiffening rain.

"For as long as you'd like," he said. "I'll just stay there tonight, then I've got to beat it."

He looked back at the woman, then at the young man in the front seat with him. The two were down and out, no doubting that.

"There's plenty of food there . . . canned, mind you, most of it . . . and you can get a rest. Just take care of the place for me. I'd like to come back some day."

He looked back at the woman one final time and saw her eyes closing. She was struggling to keep them open, but she was losing the battle. The young man beside him was drumming his fingers softly on the glove box compartment.

"Thank you," he heard from the back seat and the front.

The driver checked the road in front of him and turned off to the left. In a moment he was beating down a country road toward the highlands. The rain continued to fall.

* * * *

The evening winds swept across the plaza in old Panama. In the nearby areas smoke rose from burning structures and a sullen Henry Morgan looked out across the wide Pacific. He was unapproachable and his trusted officers kept their distance. His old acquaintance the Corregidor from Portobelo was engaged in animated discussions with Edward Collier, Morgan's second in command, and the two of them walked in slow circles by an ancient, burning church. In the growing darkness the pirate armies were already bunking down. Five days of revelry had taken their toll. Morgan, their leader, closed his eyes and shook his head.

On a nearby patio in what was left of what had recently been a splendid colonial mansion, a young pirate held a dark woman close and ran his fingers through her hair. Their rapture would continue on through the night.

"Actually . . . ," a young officer ventured in a soft voice from behind his leader, ". . . actually, we have found very little gold and silver, General Morgan. Seems the Spanish hid most of it . . . I guess. . . ."

High above a falling star shed its light on the ruined city. It appeared to trail off and fall somewhere near the city itself. Morgan watched it disappear, then looked down at the ground by his feet. A rotten, smashed pineapple lay there smiling at him from a gash that looked like a grin. With his boot, Morgan kicked it and smashed it into smithereens.

"Then we'll have to come back," he snarled.

Henry Morgan turned to look out to sea.

". . . then we'll have to come back."